The Breaking Point

THE
Breaking
Point

MAXINE BILLINGS

THE BREAKING POINT

A New Spirit Novel

ISBN 1-58314-715-2

© 2006 by Maxine Billings

www.kimanipress.com

Printed in U.S.A.

This book is dedicated to my number one supporter:
my husband, Tony.

Thank you for your ongoing love, patience and
encouragement. Having you by my side helps
make my life complete.

ACKNOWLEDGMENTS

My heavenly Father Jehovah, the originator of the family arrangement: thank you for my family and for always being my guiding light.

My children, Natasha and Stefan: thank you for your love and support and for always being great sources of encouragement to me.

My editor, Glenda Howard: thank you for being such a joy to work with and for helping me to grow in my writing skill.

My agent, Pamela Harty: thank you for being approachable and for always making yourself available when I need you.

Other individuals who have helped me in different ways:

LaShaunda Hoffman (*Shades of Romance* Magazine)

Marilynn Griffith (*Word Praize*)

Michelle Roach (Department of Juvenile Justice)

Pat Conklin (Department of Juvenile Justice) & Renfroe Middle School of Decatur, GA

Bob Heaberlin, Gwen Church & Temple High School of Temple, GA

Yvonne Bell & Herschel Jones Middle School of Dallas, GA

Pat Johnson (Warren P. Sewell Memorial Library) & staff

Pam Merritt (my sister-in-law)

Chapter 1

Justine Mercer smiled as she glanced across the crowded room at her brother and his bride. The newlyweds looked fabulous in their wedding clothing. For the reception, they had chosen hues of lavender, pink and fuchsia. The colors went well with the bridesmaids' long flowing dresses in fuchsia, with flowered-print silk sashes draped elegantly over their shoulders.

Being in Savannah, Georgia, for her brother's special day made Justine think back to her and Evan's wedding. Five years ago, they had honeymooned here. Savannah was a beautiful, enchanting city of history, charm and grace. With spring just three weeks old, the surroundings were lush and green with life.

Justine prayed that Justin and Shayna would be happy in their new union. Justine loved being married, but marriage was hard. It required commitment, dedication and effort to make it successful. From the moment Justine and Evan had met, she'd known he was the one for her. He possessed all the qualities she'd wanted in the man she'd hoped to marry one day.

But people changed. So far Evan hadn't, but she imagined it would be just a matter of time before he did. She hated such pessimistic thinking, but she couldn't seem to control it. Justine's mind drifted to her parents, who'd been through a lot together. Still engrossed in her thoughts, she flinched when Evan tickled her left earlobe with his finger.

"Earth to Justine," her husband whispered in her ear.

Justine gazed fondly at his finely chiseled face. They made a charming couple, her with her reddish-brown hair cut in a neck-length bob with a bang, and Evan with his shiny bald head and neatly trimmed mustache and goatee. She loved to run her fingers over his slick scalp.

She placed the palm of her left hand on top of Evan's freshly shaved head. "What'd you say?" she asked.

Evan replied, "You looked like you were daydreaming."

"Did I?" Justine whispered softly.

"Yeah. Are you okay?" Evan was concerned. Sometimes she seemed to drift away from him and go off into her own private world.

"I'm fine. I was just thinking about our wedding day." At least that part was true. Justine decided to leave it at that.

Evan grinned as he looked at the newlyweds on the dance floor. "I hope they're as happy as we are."

"Me, too," Justine earnestly concurred.

Evan grabbed his wife's hand. "Let's dance."

"Okay." She promptly hopped out of her seat and allowed him to lead her onto the dance floor.

Estelle Brickman, Justine's mother, watched the happy couples from the table where she and her husband, Justin Roger Brickman, Sr., sat. They had celebrated their thirty-seventh wedding anniversary just last month. However, in her heart, she couldn't call it a celebration. They no longer wished each other a happy anniversary like they had years ago. The flames of love and passion that used to flicker between them had disintegrated. To them, a wedding anniversary was just another day, like any other. They didn't even buy each other gifts anymore. What had happened to them?

Weddings always put Estelle in a romantic mood. Existing in their loveless marriage in the privacy of their own home was hard enough. It was times like these, sharing the happiness of others, that sent her spiraling into added hopelessness, loneliness, and regret that she'd ever met the man she'd married.

Estelle loved to dance. When she and Roger were younger, they'd danced all the time. She would give anything for him to lead her onto the dance floor and hold her in his big, strong arms the way he used to, making her feel as though she was the only woman alive. Now he simply sat beside her, not saying a word. He used to talk more, too. If it wasn't their son's wedding, he wouldn't even be here. It was like pulling teeth to get him to go anywhere with her. However, he never had a problem going where he wanted to go or doing what he wanted to do.

At fifty-five, Estelle was an attractive plus-size woman. She was of average height and wore her soft black-and-gray hair in a really short fro. Roger was tall, very handsome, and of medium build. His black-and-gray hair, mustache and side-burns suited the fifty-six-year-old.

As she danced with her husband, Justine admired the attractive older pair seated at their honorary table. Appearances were so deceiving. Just to look at her parents sitting beside each other, one might think they were a happily married couple. While her mother was talkative, her father was more quiet and reserved.

Things were not good between her parents, but Justine felt confident that they would work out their differences. Every now and then, her mom would smile. She had the most beautiful smile in the world, even with a gap between her front teeth. Justine wished that she could see it more often.

Against her better judgment, Estelle reached over and gently grabbed her husband's hand as it rested on the table. "Roger, let's dance."

He politely withdrew his hand from his wife's. "Stelle, you know I don't like to dance."

"You used to," she said with a pout.

He failed to give her a response. She hated it when he ignored her. She waited a brief moment, expecting that he would utter some sentiment. When he didn't, she turned on him and whispered, "You're so selfish. You only think of yourself. You never wanna do anything with me."

Roger answered, "Will you stop? Do you have to do this here where everybody'll hear you?"

Estelle snapped, "I don't care. Let 'em hear. I can't talk to you at home, either. If you think I'm not gon' voice my feelings, you're sadly mistaken." Having vented her fury, she abruptly rose from the table and hurriedly made an exit.

Justine and Evan were still dancing when they caught sight of Estelle leaving. The older woman didn't look happy.

Justine whispered, "They're at it again."

Evan asked thoughtfully, "You wanna go check on her?"

Her sigh was tinged with sadness. "Yeah. I'll be back in a few minutes." She kissed her husband's cheek and left him on the dance floor to go in search of her mother.

She decided to check the ladies' room first. When she

pushed open the door, she saw her mom at the sink, washing her hands. Justine walked to her side. Placing her hand on her mother's back, she asked, "Mama, are you okay?"

Estelle shut off the water, grabbed a couple of paper towels from the dispenser and began wiping her hands as she blurted, "All I did was tell him I wanted to dance, and he wouldn't even do that one little thing for me. He acts like I don't exist, and I'm sick of it."

"Mama, calm down. You know how Daddy is."

"Yeah, I know, and I'm tired of it."

"I know, Mama." Justine didn't understand her father. His neglecting them was what had almost torn their family apart all those years ago. Now her parents had drifted apart, and her father acted as though he didn't even care. She loved him, but sometimes he made her so angry.

Estelle dropped the damp paper towels into the trash bin and turned to face her daughter. "I'll be fine. I don't want you worrying about me and your daddy. We'll work things out."

Justine hoped so. She was scared. She said a quick silent prayer for her parents.

The next morning, Justine arose early to bid her parents farewell. The Brickmans were heading back home today. Justine and Evan planned to stay in Savannah one more day so they could explore the city they had come to love. Evan felt they needed this mini-vacation from the everyday stresses of their busy lives. As a travel agent, Justine meticulously assisted her customers with planning business trips, dream vacations and getaways. Even with her employee travel benefits, she and Evan didn't do much traveling themselves. Evan's job as a short-haul truck driver for Coca-Cola kept him quite busy. However, they both loved their jobs.

Justine and Evan were deeply in love with each other, and enjoyed their time together. Evan felt there was only one thing missing. He yearned to bring some children into their union while they were still young. Justine was thirty; at twenty-nine, he was six months younger than her. He wanted to be a father before he got too old to do things with his kids and enjoy them.

When Justine got back to their hotel room, Evan was awake but still in bed. "How's Mom?" he asked, genuinely concerned.

His beautiful wife plopped down on top of the bedcovers beside him and rested her head on his arm. "She's still upset, but she'll be okay." Justine wasn't sure about that. Perhaps if she said it enough, though, it would happen.

Evan felt that his in-laws loved each other even though at times they didn't act like it. His own parents had divorced when he, his brother and his sister were very young. He had vowed that he would be a good husband and father if he ever got married and had children. He had a beautiful, wonderful wife. Now he was ready to extend his family.

Evan snuggled closer and caressed Justine's cheek. "I was thinking," he said, "wouldn't it be nice if you got pregnant while we're here in Savannah? It's where we honeymooned, and we've been trying for a year now. Maybe this is where it'll happen."

Evan was such a romantic. Yet his mere suggestion of her becoming pregnant sent a chilling current through Justine, despite his warm breath on her neck.

After his parents' divorce when he was sixteen, Evan had tried to take over his father's role as caretaker and provider for the family.

Then, a year ago, he and his brother had lost their sister, Miranda Mercer, to colon cancer. She was only twenty-five. That was when Evan had started fantasizing about starting a family.

Not long after, his mother had died, from what Evan termed "a broken heart" from losing her only daughter. His brother, emotionally fragile and constantly battling a drug addiction, had overdosed and died six months after their mom.

To this day, Evan had no idea where his father was, or if he was still alive. After their parents' divorce, the Mercers had lost all contact with the man who had fathered them.

Not until the day his sister died had Justine ever once seen Evan take a drink of alcohol. And although he only drank occasionally, she was unhappy that he drank at all. The memory of how her father's heavy drinking after his mother's death fifteen years ago had nearly torn her family apart was enough to keep her on edge.

Evan didn't know about her father's dark past. It was a family secret. No one openly discussed alcoholism not even among family members. You just dealt with it the best you could. It became a way of life. During that time, her father had turned from a loving husband and father to someone they no longer knew. He'd stopped caring for the family's spiritual, emotional and financial needs. It was as though they no longer existed. He seemed to give up on life. Because he was too drunk to go to work most of the time, he lost his job. As a result, the family suffered financial hardships. Finally, his neglect had forced her mother to pack up their two children and take off.

Justine realized that Evan was not a heavy drinker like her father had been, but she was scared to death that eventually he would be. She grew tense whenever he mentioned them starting a family. She had determined in her mind and heart that she would not have children with Evan until he stopped drinking altogether. She would not take any chances with the lives of the children they might have.

However, she couldn't voice such feelings to her husband. Justine didn't want him to think she felt he wouldn't make a good father. She had no desire to hurt him. That's why she simply kept her mouth shut about the matter and went through her private routine of taking her birth control pill every night before going to bed, in order to prevent the conception from happening.

To conceal her thoughts, Justine slowly closed her eyes and leaned against Evan, hoping it would give her another moment of reprieve.

Chapter 2

As Estelle watered her flowers on the front lawn of their cedar home in Bessemer, Alabama, she grew angrier at Roger. She had been busy at the flower shop all day on Wednesday. They had planned to leave Thursday for the wedding on Saturday. She had asked—no, practically begged—him to water the flowers Wednesday evening. Again, he had failed her. The poor little things were dying of thirst.

She was still upset, too, for the way he'd treated her at the reception. Sometimes she felt as though he didn't love her anymore. Sure, she'd gained weight since they'd gotten married, but she'd delivered two kids, too. She used to wear a size ten. Now she wore a twenty-four, but kept herself up and considered herself a fairly attractive woman. He'd put on some weight himself. What was his excuse? She still loved him and yearned for the closeness they'd once shared. That was why she got so enraged at him at times—because she seemed to care too much about their marriage and he not enough. Now they were like two strangers living in the same house.

After quenching her flowers' thirst, Estelle stormed into the house in search of Roger. She found him in the den, lying back in his favorite black leather La-Z-Boy. She practically threw herself down on the matching sofa opposite him. She knew she was about to strike a nerve, but she felt the need to vent.

"We have to talk," she announced.

Roger asked himself, *What now?* He knew she was still upset about him not dancing with her at the reception. She'd given him nothing but grief about it, plus a million other things she said he was doing wrong, on and off during the long ride from Savannah. Her bickering and complaining had made the eight-hour drive home seem like double the time.

He didn't understand why she made an issue of everything and always got angry at him when he didn't see things her way. And of all the times for her to want to talk, she had to pick now, while he was watching football? She talked too much. It was all she wanted to do, and most of the time, it was about nothing.

Roger rolled his eyes as he moaned begrudgingly, "Stelle, you see I'm watching TV. Can't it wait?"

Estelle rolled her eyes at him as she breathed out a heavy sigh. "No, it can't wait. We need to talk now."

"Well, what is it?" Roger asked, his eyes never wavering from the television. Whatever she had to say, he wished she'd hurry up, say it and leave him alone.

"We can't talk with the TV going," Estelle complained. "Will you turn it off for a few minutes?"

The sooner we talk, the sooner she'll leave me alone. Roger lifted the remote from the arm of his chair, aimed it at the television and pressed the power button.

Estelle began, "We need to talk about our marriage."

Before she could go any further, Roger demanded, "How many times do we have to do this? We've been over it before. We don't have any more problems than anybody else."

She was tired of him telling her that. "I'm not talking about anybody else. I'm talking about us, and I'm unhappy."

It was obvious from the scowl on his face that Roger was not pleased with what she was saying. It was the same look of disapproval he gave her every time she attempted to express her feelings to him.

She challenged him. "Why do you have to look like that every time I try to talk to you?"

Roger's frown broadened. "How many times do we have to have this conversation?"

Estelle retorted, "Till you hear what I'm saying and start putting forth some effort to improve our marriage. You never spend any time with me. You wouldn't even dance with me at Justin and Shayna's wedding."

Roger was tired of hearing her complain about something as trivial as him not wanting to dance. She could take the smallest thing and blow it all out of proportion. He was tired of arguing with her. "Are you gonna start that again?"

Estelle knew he wanted her to shut up, but the thought made her rattle on. She was mad, and she wanted to wrangle with him. He needed to hear what she had to say. "Yeah, I'm gonna start it again, and I'm not gon' stop till I'm finished."

Roger grabbed the remote and turned the television back on. "Well, talk to yourself, 'cause I'm through listening."

Estelle couldn't believe he'd flipped on the television in the middle of their exchange. She yelled over the noise of the set, "I'm tired of you ignoring me."

Roger didn't say a word, but kept his eyes glued to the television. He never liked arguing with her. She just didn't know when to hush. Usually, if he just ignored her, she'd walk away.

Estelle sat silent for a moment, staring at the man she no longer knew. When no response was forthcoming, she hauled herself up and went to the bathroom to cry.

A week ago, when they'd had one of their last disagreements, she'd been too angry to shed tears. Yet this time she was deeply hurt by her husband's insensitivity toward her feelings. She locked the door. She was a strong black woman. She refused to let Roger see how much he had hurt her. There'd been a period years ago when, if he thought she was the least bit upset, he'd run to her side to comfort her, but not now.

Estelle seldom prayed anymore, since it seemed as though all her petitions went unanswered. Once upon a time, she and her entire family had been very active in their church. She didn't remember the last time she and Roger had attended services. She often wondered what she had done to deserve such an ungrateful, uncaring husband.

As she sat on the side of the tub with her head laid back against the tile, she again asked God that question as the tears spilled down her face.

"Stop and Smell the Flowers." Estelle pasted a fake smile on her face as she spoke into the telephone, greeting her caller with the name of her floral shop. She was still hurt and fuming from her argument with Roger the day before.

The two of them had started the floral business together twenty years ago. Although Roger was employed as an electrician with Alabama Power, he helped out on weekends and his days off. After his mother died, though, he'd lost interest in it, his family and everything else. It was difficult at first, but Estelle had taken over the business and somehow managed to keep it thriving. However, Roger never returned. Fortunately, after he'd sobered up, the power company had rehired him. Estelle ran the business herself, with the aid of an assistant and Justine, who would help out occasionally during the peak seasons.

"Yes," Estelle politely uttered into the receiver, "the flowers will be delivered to the funeral home today. Thank you, Ms. Adams." She returned the cordless phone to its stand and turned to her assistant.

"Lidia, before you make those deliveries to the hospital, will you go by Wheeler's Funeral Home and deliver Ms. Adams's flowers for the Sykes funeral tomorrow?"

Young, attractive and very personable, Lidia answered, "Sure thing, Mrs. Brickman."

"Thank you."

Lidia smiled. "You're welcome."

Estelle headed for the supply room. When she returned to the front of the shop, Lidia held out the phone to her.

"It's Mrs. Edmonds."

Estelle took the telephone. She really wanted to talk to her best friend. She needed a sympathetic ear so she could vent. However, she didn't have time for it now. She'd already been away from the store three days, and she had a lot to do.

With her friend, Estelle didn't have to pretend, although she'd noticed that Gloria wasn't as empathetic as she once was with her situation. When she spoke into the receiver, her pretend voice faded, replaced by the one that sounded the way she felt. "Hey."

On the other end, Gloria replied, "Hey. What's wrong with you?"

Estelle's eyes roamed the store in search of her assistant. She liked Lidia, but she didn't want everybody knowing her business. She spotted her in a corner gathering up some plants.

Estelle whispered, "I can't talk now. Didn't you say you're on spring break this week?"

"Yeah," her friend answered.

"Can you stop by around lunchtime today?"

"Yeah," Gloria answered. "You sound like you're half-dead."

Estelle didn't respond.

Gloria asked, "Is twelve o'clock okay?"

"Yeah."

"Want me to order a pizza or something and bring it? We can eat in."

"Sure. That's fine."

"Okay. I'll see you at twelve. Bye."

"Bye."

After Lidia had all her deliveries in the van, she said, "Okay, Mrs. Brickman, I'm off."

Estelle conjured up another bogus smile. "Okay, Lidia. Be careful."

"Yes, ma'am. I will."

After she'd gone, Estelle's thoughts involuntarily drifted to her husband. How could two people who were once so head over heels in love grow so far apart?

It was almost four o'clock in the afternoon when Justine and Evan pulled into the driveway of their ranch-style home in Bessemer, which was only about ten minutes from Justine's parents' home.

"Home sweet home," she happily uttered.

"Yeah," Evan agreed, "but I wish we could have stayed longer."

They exited the vehicle and grabbed their suitcases from the trunk.

"Maybe next time," Justine stated.

Grinning, Evan winked at her. "I'm gonna hold you to it."

As they made their way to the front door, she said teasingly, "Yeah, I'm sure you're not gonna let me forget it."

Evan snickered as he unlocked the door and pushed it open. They took their bags to the bedroom and dropped them in the middle of the floor. They were exhausted. Justine decided to call her parents before taking a short nap to revitalize herself.

When she got off the phone, she informed her husband, "Mama said she cooked enough supper for us, too, because she knew we'd be tired. You feel like going over there later to eat?"

Evan plopped down onto the king-size cherry-oak sleigh bed and began removing his tennis shoes. "I don't know. What time?"

"Six o'clock okay?"

"Yeah, I guess. That'll give us a little time to get some rest. Man, I'm tired. I had a good time, but that trip wore me out. The way I'm feeling now, when we do have kids, I'm gonna be too tired to enjoy them."

Justine wished he wouldn't start talking about having children again. "That was a sixteen-hour drive round-trip. You should be tired. I am, too. Lie down and take a nap. You'll feel better when you wake up."

"I am. What about you?"

"I want to call Catina first and tell her about the wedding. I'll lie down in a few minutes."

"Can't you tell her about it at work tomorrow?"

Justine sat down on the bed and leaned over to kiss her husband's cheek. Smiling, she said, "Yes, but I don't think I can wait that long."

"Okay," Evan whispered as he closed his eyes, falling asleep almost instantly.

During dinner, Justine sensed that things were still tense between her parents. Afterward, Evan and Roger talked in the den while mother and daughter cleaned up the kitchen.

Evan felt that it wouldn't hurt either of his in-laws to be a little more loving toward one another. All they did was bicker. His own parents had divorced. At least Estelle and Roger were still together. That had to mean they still loved each other.

Evan felt the need to share some scriptural encouragement from the Bible. But the Brickmans didn't attend church anymore, and Evan didn't want Roger to feel that he was being preachy. However, he couldn't just sit idly by and not say anything. Roger was older than him, but Evan felt confident that he could find something to share with his father-in-law in a respectful manner.

"Dad, I really admire you and Mom."

Confused, Roger stared at his son-in-law. "What d'you mean?"

Maintaining steady eye contact, Evan answered, "Despite your differences, you're still together. My parents divorced when my brother, sister and I were young. Marriage is a lifelong commitment. It takes a lot of hard work and effort to make it work. I just appreciate the fact that you and Mom have hung in there all these years."

Roger felt slightly offended. He knew that usually when people commended you for something, it meant they were about to say something derogatory. Was Evan about to try to chastise him regarding his and Estelle's marriage? If so, he'd have to set the young man straight. He liked his son-in-law. Evan was a good man, and it was obvious that he loved Justine. However, Roger wasn't going to have some kid who had been married only a few years try to tell him about the bonds of matrimony when he'd been married for more than half his life. Let Evan wait until he'd been married as long as him and see just how tough it could be.

Roger agreed, "Yeah, it's hard. Every marriage has its problems." To stop Evan from saying anything that might make him have to argue, he added, "Stelle and I are okay. You and Justine don't have to worry about us."

Evan begged to differ, but decided against saying anything further. All the signs he was seeing were telling him that the Brickmans' marriage was definitely in trouble. However, there was nothing anyone could do if his father-in-law refused to acknowledge it.

Chapter 3

Justine cast a friendly smile at the elderly couple seated across from her as she leaned forward to hand the gentleman the brochures. "Mr. and Mrs. Johnson, I think you'll love Hawaii. The islands are simply breathtaking. Take these home, look them over and let me know what you decide."

The Johnsons cheerfully thanked her before departing.

As soon as the couple were out the door, Catina James popped her head inside Justine's cubicle. "Hey, it's almost lunchtime. Where do you want to eat today?"

Justine looked at her friend and coworker. "Oh, I don't care. You know me. I love everything." She glanced back down at the form on her desk.

Catina grinned as she responded, "Yeah, I know."

Justine did a quick double take as she peered back at Catina and facetiously replied, "You didn't have to agree."

Catina giggled. "Hurry up. Grab your pocketbook so we can go. I'll drive."

As she pulled open her bottom desk drawer and grabbed her purse, Justine replied, "'Kay, I'm coming. Give me time."

They informed the receptionist that they were going to lunch and would be back in time to cover the telephone for her one o'clock lunch break.

At the restaurant, Justine filled Catina in some more on her brother's wedding and the trip to Savannah.

"Sunday evening, Evan and I went for a carriage ride. It was so romantic." Suddenly recalling that Catina and her boyfriend of three years had broken up a few weeks ago, Justine quickly added, "I'm sorry, Cat. I keep going on about Evan's and my weekend. It's very inconsiderate of me. Are you okay?"

Catina was one year younger than Justine. An attractive woman of biracial heritage, she possessed very fair skin. Her thick black, curly hair, which was tapered at her neck, complimented her round face.

Justine was very protective of her. Whenever she called her "Cat," Catina knew Justine's role had gone from friendly to serious. Catina appreciated it but quickly asserted, "How many times do I have to tell you I'm okay? Stop acting like you have to walk on eggshells around me."

Justine admired her friend's strength but knew the breakup of a relationship was devastating and emotionally draining.

She apologized again. "I'm sorry. I know you keep telling me that. It's just that I can imagine how I'd feel if it were me. I definitely wouldn't be handling it as well as you are."

Catina grinned. "Well, it's not the first breakup. Probably won't be the last."

Justine cocked her head as she kindly countered, "Don't say that. You have to think positive." However, in the back of her mind, she was thinking, *I'm the wrong one to be telling somebody to think positive*. Although she didn't voice her pessimism much verbally, she certainly did mentally.

"You're right," Catina said. "When we think positive, we surround ourselves with great energy."

Justine came up with a brilliant idea and cheerily proposed, "Hey, Evan can introduce you to one of his friends. His buddy Darryl is a great guy. I think you'd like him. Ray and Jarrod are married, but even if they weren't, I wouldn't want you to get involved with them. They're too fast."

Catina listened to the mother hen who was her dearest friend, and grinned inwardly at Justine's description of Evan's friends. She'd never before heard men called "fast." In her younger days, it was a term aimed at girls who had bad reputations. Quickly holding up her hand to silence her friend, Catina firmly stated, "I don't want to meet anyone."

The excitement in Justine's voice dissipated. "But…"

"No buts," Catina said. "I'm fine. I'm happy and content with my life as it is right now. Maybe I'll want to meet someone one day, but not now. Okay?" She looked her friend square in the face.

Justine released a shallow sigh and lifted her hands in surrender. Catina had won this round. "Okay. Whatever you say."

She knew her friend wasn't happy being alone. No one wanted to be lonely. Justine needed that special someone in her life. If she didn't have Evan, she wouldn't feel whole. Now if she could only convince him that they didn't need children in order to be happy….

Estelle removed the last piece of fried chicken from the black iron skillet and set it on the paper towels with the other three pieces. She placed the baking sheet containing the crispy golden meat into the oven to keep warm until Roger got home. She was in a better mood today. During lunch the day before, Gloria had told her to try to make the atmosphere more pleasant by preparing a nice dinner for her and Roger, and perhaps eating by candlelight to make it more romantic.

She already had the dining room table set. The squash casserole was staying warm in the oven with the chicken. The green beans with slivered almonds, one of Roger's favorite dishes, was on low heat on top of the stove. Surprisingly, Estelle was excited about the evening she had planned. She couldn't wait for Roger to walk through the door. She knew he'd be exhausted, and a nice quiet, romantic dinner would do them both good. As soon as he had showered, she would brown the dinner rolls and have everything on the table before he got dressed.

She was stirring a pitcher of tea when Roger walked through the door. Estelle turned around quickly, greeting her husband with one of her dazzling smiles. "Hey. How was your day?"

Roger placed his lunch box on the counter. "Rough."

As she took the tea to the refrigerator, Estelle offered her regrets. "I'm sorry. What happened?"

He wearily responded, "I can't go into it right now. I just want to shower, put on some clean clothes and relax."

Estelle replied cheerily, "Okay. Well, dinner's all ready except for the rolls. As soon as you finish your shower, I'll put 'em in the oven, and we can eat."

"Stelle, I'm not hungry. I picked up a burger on the way home. I didn't know you were planning to cook. I thought you'd be at the shop late like you usually are."

Estelle felt like screaming. Here she'd gone to all this trouble to rush home and make him a home-cooked meal, and he'd already eaten a stinking hamburger. It took all the strength she could muster not to go off on him. "Well, I guess I'll be eating all this food by myself tonight and over the next few days. Lord knows I don't need it. I'm big enough as it is."

Roger eyed her guiltily before scanning the stove and kitchen counter. He blandly apologized. "I lost my appetite. Okay, Stelle?" He hesitated as he was leaving the kitchen. "But, um, if I get hungry later, I'll eat some."

The tears in her eyes stung like bees as Estelle fought to hold them back. "Never mind," she said, as she began removing the food from the oven.

It was obvious she was upset. But it wasn't his fault she'd come home and prepared a meal unexpectedly. He was tired and had no intention of remaining to argue with her about it. As he walked away, he could hear her slamming the cabinet doors and banging dishes.

While Roger showered, Estelle sat alone at the dining room table and attempted to eat. She was so mad that she'd lost her own appetite. What would be the next thing to go in their marriage? Was anything left? The love, happiness, communication and respect they'd once shared were nonexistent.

Up until a few weeks ago, they had eaten nearly all their meals together, at her pleading, of course. Estelle mentally admitted that she sometimes stayed at the shop several minutes past closing. When she did, however, she'd call Roger's cell phone and leave him a message. He would either pick something up to eat on his way home from work or cook when he got there. Though she could hardly get him to talk to her while they ate, they at least sat down at the table together.

This time, he hadn't even thought of her, and had only

gotten something to eat for himself. She should have known that one day things would come to this. She grew half-angry at herself for the times she'd worked late, even though she'd long felt there was nothing to rush home to anymore.

Estelle could only pick at her food while she contemplated all the things that were wrong with her marriage. As thoughts of Roger's total disregard for her feelings resurfaced, she stopped blaming herself for their problems. All her planning and hard work this evening with dinner had been for nothing. She was always thinking of Roger, and he only thought of himself. This was the last time she'd ever do anything special for him.

Later that night, as they lay in bed with their backs towards each other, Estelle's lips trembled as she continued to fight down her tears. As usual, he hadn't asked about her day. And when she'd made the comment about how big she was, he hadn't even attempted to reassure her that he still found her attractive.

What hurt more was that he knew how upset she was, yet hadn't bothered to try to talk to her and console her. He was so uncaring. At the moment, she longed for him to turn over, pull her into his arms and just hold her.

What was she thinking? He hadn't done anything of the sort in a long time. Why would he do it now?

The next morning, Gloria called Estelle to see how her and Roger's evening had gone. If it hadn't been for Lidia being close by, Estelle would have yelled into the phone.

Instead she attempted to whisper. "You and your bright ideas. I went home and slaved in the kitchen over a hot stove, and guess what he tells me when he walks through the door?"

Estelle's tone had Gloria too scared to ask, but she did anyway. "What?"

"He ate a hamburger on the way home!" Estelle declared into the phone.

Gloria quickly put up her defenses. "Well, now I did tell you to plan a nice dinner for the two of you, but how was I supposed to know he'd stop and get something to eat on the way home? He's *your* husband. You should've thought about that beforehand and tried to get a message to him or something, not to eat before he got home. So don't be blaming me."

Estelle breathed a heavy sigh. "I'm not blaming you. I'm just so mad. That's the last time I ever go outta my way for him. And to top it off, he acted like it wasn't even a big deal that I'd gone to all that trouble."

Gloria unsympathetically stated, "Well, Estelle, I don't see what all the fuss is about. You cooked a meal. You had to eat, too, so what's the problem? I mean, I can see you being upset if he'd known you were cooking a special dinner for the two of you and then he went and ate before he got home."

Estelle was offended by her friend's remarks. She hastily muttered, "I don't need to hear this. I'll talk to you later." She slammed down the phone.

Chapter 4

It was Saturday, and Estelle was enjoying the meal she and Roger were sharing. Gloria's words from a few days before were still ringing in her head. Since she and Roger had gotten away from their quiet ritual of eating dinner together, Estelle supposed she had overreacted.

As they sat eating the breakfast he'd prepared for them, Roger noticed his wife seemed to be in a much better mood today.

Batting her beautiful brown eyes, Estelle asked, as though she didn't know, "You going fishing today?"

Roger studied his wife's face curiously, expecting her to start complaining again about his weekly ritual. "Yeah. Why?"

Estelle grinned sheepishly. She didn't know why, considering how mad she'd gotten at him a few days ago, but she was in a good mood. "Can I come?"

Estelle had never gone fishing with Roger. In fact, to his

knowledge, she'd never fished at all. Fishing and hunting were his outlet. A means of escape from the painful realities of life, and he didn't want her encroaching on it. "Stelle, you've never gone fishing with me. Why on earth do you want to come now? You usually go out with Gloria."

Her smile grew bigger. "I know, but I wanna do something with you today."

"You've never even been fishing. You wouldn't know the first thing to do."

"Well, you can teach me."

Roger's throat grew tight as he shook his head. "Nah. Fishing helps me relax. I can't do that if I've gotta concentrate on teaching you. Find yourself something to do."

He seemed to have blurted out his last sentence without any remorse whatsoever. Estelle felt a sensation of intense heat blazing along her spine, but much to her surprise, she maintained control of the anger she felt brewing. "I want to go with you. We never do anything together." Rising, she took her dishes to the sink, rinsed them off and placed them in the dishwasher. "I'm coming," she stated firmly as she walked past her husband.

Roger turned around in his seat, glared at Estelle and shouted, "No, you're not!"

"Yes, I am!" Estelle answered.

Was she going insane? She wasn't going to spoil his Saturday, one of the few occasions he could get away from her and her mouth. Roger leaped from his chair and followed her into their bedroom. "No, you're not," he sternly repeated.

"Yes, I am," she echoed in a tone similar to his, as she started to dress.

Roger stopped by her side. "Are you deaf? I said you're not coming."

Ignoring her husband, Estelle zipped up her khaki jeans. Next, she grabbed a white pullover from the bed and tugged it over her head.

With fire blazing in his eyes, Roger asked brazenly, "Did you hear me? I said you're not going."

When she didn't respond, he quickly thought of a way to bring her to her senses. "What about the shop? You just gonna close it up for the day? You're not gonna keep customers that way, you know."

"Lidia can run the shop. She's done it before."

Not knowing what else to say, Roger shouted, "You're not coming with me!"

For a brief moment, Estelle felt a tinge of fear. Roger looked like a madman. She'd never witnessed the expression before, but she had no intention of backing down. She was fed up with him acting as though she didn't exist. "And I told you I am."

"No, you're not!" Roger roared. "When I go fishing, it's my time to relax and have some peace and quiet, and you're not gon' spoil it."

That was it! She'd tried to be nice, and he was acting like a crazed lunatic. Her woman's intuition kicked in. "And why don't you want me to go, Roger?"

"I told you it's my time to have some relaxation."

Estelle stared him square in the face. "Are you sure that's it?" Afraid of what he might say, she could only insinuate. What would she do if he just confessed right now and confirmed her fears to be reality?

"What are you trying to say?"

"Don't play dumb with me. I know you're seeing someone else. What's wrong? You got a lil' stop to make along the way? Why else is it you can never spend any time with me? You never hug or kiss me. We haven't made love in God knows how long." Estelle threw her hands out to her sides.

"I feel like I don't even have a husband." She suddenly dropped down onto the bed with her face in her hands and started sobbing. Mentally, she scolded herself for breaking down in front of him. But perhaps when he witnessed how hurt she was, he'd be more loving toward her. "I just want you to love me like you used to. I want us to spend time together. We live under the same roof, but it's like we're total strangers."

Roger could listen no more and simply walked away.

All Estelle could do was fall back on the bed and sob harder. He never responded to her cries for his affection, not even when she tried to express to him how much she needed him.

Evan didn't want Justine to move from the warmth of his embrace. He had a deep desire to stay in bed with his wife at least until noon. After all, soon they would be having a baby, and when they did, peaceful mornings to themselves like this would be a thing of the past. He didn't care, though. He wanted them to have a child so much that he could taste it.

As Justine made an effort to escape the strong arms she loved being swallowed up in, Evan sleepily mumbled, "Where're you going?"

As she grabbed her robe and covered her unclad body, Justine, replied drowsily, "Gonna take a shower. You know I've gotta go to the office today."

Yes, Evan was aware, but couldn't she make an exception just this once? In the most pathetic voice he could, he moaned, "Stay home with me," as he reached out and grabbed Justine's hand and gently pulled her back down onto the bed beside him.

He was acting like a big baby. Every now and then, she had to pamper him, for he seemed to relish her attention. Justine playfully reprimanded, "Don't even start. You know I've gotta work."

Jokingly, he added, "Yeah, go on to your ol' job. Don't worry about me. I guess I'll have to find some stray dog or cat to keep me company."

"Oh, *please*. You are so pathetic," Justine teased. "And my ol' job helps put food on the table, clothes on our backs and a roof over our heads. Besides, you told me you and the guys were gonna hang out at Darryl's while I'm gone, and now you want to act all pitiful."

Evan hung his head. "See? I get no sympathy. Can't you just call the office and tell 'em you're not coming in and stay home with me?"

Justine grinned proudly. Though it was somewhat irritating at the moment, Evan's need and desire for her stirred her emotions. She sat on the side of the bed and placed her hand tenderly on the back of his head. "You just want to be babied, don't you?"

"Yeah," he agreed, grinning, as their faces meshed together so that their lips met perfectly.

Several moments later, Justine took her shower while Evan whipped up a quick breakfast of grits, eggs and toast. As they finished eating, the telephone rang, and Evan answered it.

Handing the cordless phone to his wife, he whispered, "It's Mom. She sounds upset."

Justine quickly took the phone and walked away as she spoke into the receiver.

When she returned to the kitchen, Evan inquired, "Is everything okay?"

With a shake of her head, Justine replied, "Not really. Mama and Daddy had a fight."

Evan's eyes flew open. "He hit her?"

Justine grimaced. "No-o-o. Daddy's never hit Mama. He'd never do that. I think they just had an argument. Anyway, she's upset. I'm gonna meet her at the shop for lunch today. Sounds like she just needs a shoulder to cry on."

Evan nodded in understanding. "Okay. Where's Dad?"

"Fishing. Where else?"

Estelle had told Justine that she desired to eat in the shop today. After Justine had gotten off work at noon, she'd stopped by a local Chinese restaurant and picked up their lunch.

After her spat with Roger that morning, Estelle felt as if she could eat a horse. She had some strange eating habits. Most of the time when she was depressed or angry, she ate like a pig. Then there were rare moments when she lost her appetite.

"Maybe if you and Daddy go away somewhere—just get away from everything and everybody—so you can enjoy yourselves and talk, things'll get better. I could hook you up with a trip anywhere you'd like to go." Justine looked at her mother worriedly, her eyes pleading with her to accept her offer.

Estelle's voice was placid. "Sounds nice, honey, but you know I have a hard enough time getting your daddy out of the house for family events and social gatherings. And I already told you me wanting to go fishing with him this morning is what started the whole thing. Besides, I've mentioned trips to him before, and he's never interested."

Panic flooded Justine's chest as she contemplated what her mother had shared with her earlier. "Mama, you don't really think Daddy's having an affair, do you?"

All Estelle could do was shrug her shoulders and answer,

"I don't know if he is or not. He certainly didn't deny it." She took a bite of her egg roll. She and Justine sat in silence for a moment.

Justine didn't know what else to say or do. "So do you want to see a movie when you get off work later this afternoon? I can call the theater and get the show times."

Estelle wrinkled her brow. "I don't care. I guess so. I don't even know what movies are out now. We like the same thing. Whatever you pick is fine." As an afterthought, she added, "Let's see an early afternoon one."

Justine gazed at her curiously. She'd never known her mother to leave work early for any sort of amusement or diversion. "Are you sure?"

"Yeah. Lidia'll be back from lunch in a few minutes. She can keep the store open. She won't mind. She's done it before."

"Okay. If you're sure, but let me call Evan first." Justine quickly wiped her fingers on her paper napkin and dropped it beside her plate on her mother's desk.

She grabbed the cordless phone. First, she placed a call to Evan. Next, she pressed the speed dial button for their favorite neighborhood theater. "Line's busy." Putting the phone back in its stand, she offered, "I'll try again in a few minutes."

The two women chatted while they finished their meal. When Justine got another busy signal, her mother suggested, "Why don't you just use the computer here and go on the theater's Web site to see what's playing? Today's Saturday. Everybody's probably calling, like us, and keeping the line tied up."

"That's a good idea," Justine concurred.

Minutes later, they found a movie that suited them both. As they put away their trash, Estelle said, "The two-thirty show sounds good. I'm an old woman, and I can't stay out as late as I used to." She flashed a grin.

It was good to see her mother break into the smile Justine adored. She laughed. "Oh, Mama."

Chapter 5

"Hey, man," Darryl Jones breathlessly exclaimed as he invited his friend into his house. "I've been trying to call you and the guys for over an hour at home and on your cell phones. Now I know why they're not answering, but what's your excuse?"

Evan couldn't reply right away for wondering where his friend had suddenly gotten the baby he was carrying. When Evan finally glanced down at his cellular telephone, which was clipped to the waist of his relaxed-fit blue jeans, he replied, "I forgot to turn it on." As he followed Darryl into the den, he asked jovially, "Who's the lil' lady on your hip?"

The two men sat down on a plump leather, royal-blue sofa. Darryl was a year older than Evan. A lot of people thought they were brothers. They could almost pass for such.

Darryl flashed a smile and looked proudly at the child. "This is Misha. I call her Mee-Mee." Then to the baby, he said, "Say hello, Mee-Mee. Say hi to Uncle Evan."

The little girl let out an excited squeal as she wiggled on Darryl's knee.

Evan was full of questions. Darryl was truly like a brother to him. Why was he telling this child to call him *uncle?* "Hey man, you been keeping a secret from us?"

Initially confused, Darryl asked, "A secret? What are you talking…?" As soon as he realized what his friend was thinking, he quickly offered an explanation. Shaking his head, he said, "Naw, man. Mee-Mee's my niece—my sister Shantel's baby. You know I don't have any kids."

Evan shrugged his shoulders, snickering. "Hey, you never can tell nowadays. I come by, and all of a sudden you're walking around carrying a baby. What was I supposed to think?"

Darryl cracked a smile. "That she's my niece."

"Well, how was I supposed to know? She's cute. You're right. I should've known she didn't come from your loins."

Darryl burst out laughing. "Man, that's cold. I'm gon' let you have that one."

Evan almost fell over from laughing. "Will she let strangers hold her?"

"Yeah, as long as they're not too hideous looking," Darryl replied, grinning.

Evan retorted, "Well, she's sitting on your lap so she oughta be used to that by now."

Misha grinned as the two men let out another cackle.

Evan asked, "Can I hold her?"

"Yeah," Darryl agreed, offering the child to his friend.

Evan cautiously removed the little girl from his friend's hands. "How old is she?"

"A year."

Evan began to murmur to her. "Hey, Mee-Mee. Can you talk? Can you say 'Uncle Evan'? You're cute, you know that?

When my wife and I have a baby, I hope it's a girl and she's pretty just like you."

The little girl laughed and patted Evan's cheeks with both hands. "Eeh. Eeh."

Evan's eyes lit up like the moon. "Did you hear that, man? She said Evan!"

Darryl teased, "Actually, she said 'Eeh. Eeh.'"

"Man, you know she said Evan."

There was a loud knock on the front door. Darryl got up to answer it, agreeing obligingly, "Okay, man, if you think she said Evan, she said Evan."

As soon as the door was open, two men, one tall and the other a little shorter, entered, yelling, "What's up?"

Darryl said, "Hey, guys. Keep it down. My one-year-old niece is here. You'll scare her."

The shorter one replied, "We didn't know you had a niece."

Leading his friends to the den, Darryl stated, "Yeah, Jarrod, I do. She's my sister's little girl."

The taller one asked, "Is your sister here? I thought we were playing cards tonight."

"Ray," Darryl said, "I've been calling y'all all afternoon to tell you the game's off."

When Evan spotted the trio, he called, "Hey, fellows, look at her. Isn't she cute?"

"Oh, no, man," Ray moaned, slapping his forehead with the palm of his hand. Eyeing Darryl, he said, "Why'd you let him hold her? You know how he gets around babies. Now that's all we gonna hear for the rest of the night." Mimicking Evan, he crooned, "'I want a baby. I'll be so glad when me and Justine have a baby. I don't know what's taking so long.' If I hear him say it one more time, I'm gon' throw up."

Evan just laughed. They always threw flippant remarks at

each other, comments they couldn't get away with around the opposite sex. "But just look at her. Now doesn't she make you wish you had one just like her?"

Jarrod and Ray immediately grunted, shaking their heads. They were both married but had no children, and didn't seem to want any.

"Guys, didn't you hear what I said?" Darryl repeated, "The game's off for tonight. I'm babysitting for my sister. Her husband's mother had to be rushed to the hospital for emergency surgery. They needed someone to watch the baby, and she asked me. I tried calling to let you know before you got here. I called you at home and on your cell phones."

Jarrod replied, "Man, you know we turn the cell phones off as soon as we hit the door when we leave home. Otherwise, the wives call every five minutes wanting us to do something."

Evan thought it was terrible how they treated their spouses. While he loved joking and playing around with them, their disrespect for their wives was one of the areas where he drew the line. His cell phone had been off earlier, too, but not because he was trying to avoid any calls from Justine. He'd talk to her all day and night if he could. He focused all of his attention on little Misha in order to avoid his friends' present conversation.

Ray plopped the twelve-pack of beer he'd brought in with him onto the coffee table. "Well," he suggested, "can't you just put her to bed? We can play while she's sleeping."

Darryl quickly asserted, "Naw, man, I'm not gon' do that." Eyeing the beverages Ray had just set down, he added, "And get that beer outta here. My sister and her husband won't allow any drinking around her."

Jarrod asked, "Why not, man? She's just a baby. She won't even know what we're doing."

Darryl firmly stated, "If I get caught, that's it. I told you, everything's cancelled. If you wanna stay and watch TV or something, that's fine, but there'll be no cards and no beer."

Jarrod complained, "Aw, man, that's messed up. You're scared of your sister. You think we're gon' sit 'round here with you and a baby watching TV on a Saturday night? You can forget that."

"Well," Darryl said, "let the doorknob hit cha where the good Lord split cha."

Ray said, "Oh, so it's like that? Okay, man. We'll holler at your whipped behind later."

Jarrod added, "Yeah, when you're not *babysitting*."

Ray asked Evan and Darryl, "Y'all want me to leave you a beer or two in the refrigerator for later?"

Evan and Darryl looked at each other and nodded.

Darryl answered, "Yeah, put a couple in there for us. Thanks, man."

Ray said, "See, I ain't mad at ya. You throw me outta your house, but I'm gon' still leave you some beer. No hard feelin's, man."

The four friends shared another laugh and knocked their fists together.

After Ray and Jarrod had gone, Evan played with Misha while he and Darryl talked. Evan couldn't believe how much fun he was having. He never would have thought he'd pass up a night playing cards with his buddies for an evening babysitting with his friend.

When Justine got home later in the evening, she found Evan watching television. Tiptoeing up behind him, she leaned over and kissed his cheek, after which he tenderly took her by the arm and pulled her around to join him on the sofa.

Wrapping his arms around her, Evan asked, "How's Mom?"

Justine laid her head back and relaxed, enjoying the rise and fall of Evan's chest. His breathing was soft and shallow. Smiling, she answered, "I don't understand how two people who were so in love and have been through so much together could draw so far apart. She thinks he's cheating on her."

"Really? Why does she think that? Has he given her reason to believe he is?"

"I don't know. I think she feels that since he doesn't want to spend time with her, he must be seeing someone else."

Evan simply nodded and kissed the top of his wife's head.

Justine asked, "So how was your day?"

Evan perked up. Smiling, he asked, "Would you believe I spent my evening at Darryl's with him and his one-year-old niece, Misha, nicknamed Mee-Mee?"

Justine moved her head to the side, reared back a little and looked at him, impressed. "Are you serious? You, Ray and Jarrod spent your Saturday afternoon babysitting with Darryl?"

"Well, not Ray and Jarrod. You know those characters. I don't think they'd babysit their own kids if they had any. They left, but I stayed. Darryl's sister and brother-in-law had to go to the hospital. Her husband's mother had emergency surgery. Oh, Justine, you should see the baby," Evan exclaimed. "She's the cutest little thing. And guess what? She said my name."

Surprised, Justine queried, "She did?"

Evan chuckled. "Well, what she said was, 'Eeh. Eeh.' But doesn't that sound like she was trying to say Evan?"

Looking into her husband's happy face, Justine pecked his lips. "Sure, honey."

Evan said, "I can't wait for us to start a family."

Justine began to feel peevish. She should have known

where the conversation would end. She felt guilty for participating in this discussion about Darryl's niece and getting Evan stirred up again.

Trying not to arouse any suspicions within him, she pulled back from his embrace, stood and said, "I'm sleepy. I'm gonna get a drink of water and go to bed."

"Okay. I'll join you in a few minutes."

"Okay," Justine answered as she went toward the kitchen. "Good night."

"Good night."

In the bedroom, Justine put on her nightgown. Then she pulled open her lingerie drawer and fumbled underneath the delicate pieces of clothing until she had grasped what she was searching for. After removing the birth control dispenser, she popped out the day's pill. Quickly, she put the remaining contraceptives back in their place, rushed into the bathroom and poured a cup of water to wash the pill down.

On Sunday afternoon, Estelle took a moment to confide in her best friend, Gloria Edmonds, while their husbands went to the store. In the kitchen, the two women ate some red velvet cake that Estelle had baked, and washed it down with cold milk.

Gloria firmly stated, "Girl, you know Roger isn't having an affair."

Estelle replied, "I don't know that. Why else can't he stand to be around me, be with me?"

"That doesn't mean he's having an affair."

Estelle let out a huff and stared vehemently at her friend. "Well, Gloria, how d'you think you'd feel if Donald acted toward you the way Roger does toward me?"

"I wouldn't like it, but look. You've been married for thirty-seven years, a year longer than Donald and me. All marriages have problems."

Ignoring her friend, Estelle stated flatly, "Roger and I haven't had sex in I don't know how long. I have needs, and I know he does, too. After all, he's a man, and men usually have a stronger sex drive than women. So if he's not getting it from me, he's getting it from somewhere."

Gloria quickly rebutted, "Just because you and Roger aren't sexually intimate with each other doesn't mean he's being unfaithful. Do you have any proof that he's seeing someone else?"

"No, and it's not just about sex. It's also the way he acts toward me, like he doesn't wanna be with me in any shape, form or fashion, like I don't exist. Sometimes he makes me wish I'd married someone else."

Estelle's confession caused a question to surface in the back of Gloria's mind. She eyed her friend suspiciously.

Her expression of disapproval caused a scowl to erupt on Estelle's face. "What?"

"Nothing," Gloria lied.

"Why'd you give me that look? What are you thinking?"

Gloria shook her head. "Nothing," she repeated.

A light suddenly clicked. Estelle said, "You think *I've* been unfaithful to Roger just because I said sometimes I wish I'd married someone else."

"I didn't say that."

"But you're thinking it. You won't believe something like that about Roger, but you do about me, your best friend— or so I thought."

"Estelle, I didn't say that."

"Then why won't you tell me what you *were* thinking?"

The two women sat in silence for a few seconds before

Gloria admitted, "Okay. I did wonder for a brief moment if you had. I'm sorry."

Estelle shook her head sadly. "Roger isn't a saint. I'm not saying I am, either. I'm the only one who puts forth any effort to make this marriage work. I feel so miserable."

Gloria's heart went out to her friend. "I know, but like I told you, *all* marriages have problems."

Estelle quickly asserted, "Yours doesn't. You and Donald have the perfect marriage. You're our friends, and I love you both dearly, but sometimes I envy you."

"There's no such thing as a perfect marriage. There are good marriages. That's what Donald and I have, but we have our share of problems just like everybody else."

Estelle let out a fake chuckle. "Yeah, right."

Gloria said, "Estelle, you can't base your marriage or your life on what you think everybody else's is. You'll only make yourself more miserable. You know how to have a happy marriage. You know what the Bible says, if only you'd apply it."

Estelle glared across the table at her friend. "Gloria, why do you always have to bring that up?" Gloria and Donald had been trying for a while to get her and Roger back to church, but neither of them were interested at the moment. The spiritual aspect of their life was a thing of the past, just like their happiness. "You're always telling me *I* need to apply it. What about Roger? A marriage is made up of two people. It's give and take, and I'm tired of always being the one to give."

"I'm just saying two wrongs don't make a right. You can't control what another person says and does. You can only control yourself, and even that's hard to do. The Bible has the answers to all our problems if only we pay attention."

Estelle thought back to the time when she and Roger had

been happy like Gloria and Donald—fifteen years ago, prior to the death of Roger's mother. After having undergone routine surgery, Hannah Brickman had suffered a stroke and never regained consciousness.

Roger was never the same after the passing of his mother. He had been very close to her, and was shattered by her death. Alcohol took control of him and his life. No longer was there any room for Estelle and their two young children, Justine and Justin, who were fifteen and ten, respectively. Gone was their spiritual, emotional and physical support.

Estelle had attempted to stay by her husband's side. God knew she had tried with every fiber of her being. If it hadn't been for Gloria and Donald, she didn't know where she and the kids would have gone when she finally gained the courage to walk away.

She and Roger had stayed separated for eight months. When Estelle returned to him, it had been with the ultimatum that he never drink another drop of alcohol. If he did, she would leave for good.

Estelle had been so happy that her family was back together. However, after she'd returned home, she'd noticed how distant Roger had become toward her. He'd claimed to want her back, yet his actions said just the opposite. He didn't drink; she was thankful for that. But the man she'd met and fallen in love with seemed to have disappeared.

Hoping that things would soon get better between them, Estelle had pushed aside her fears. The next thing she knew, months of sadness and loneliness had turned into years. And once the children grew up and moved out, things got worse.

But that was in the past. Some things were better left there. No one ever talked about it.

Now, here was Gloria telling her that the Bible had the

answers to everybody's problems. The Bible said to throw one's burdens on God and he would hear your cries for help. If that was true, why hadn't he heard Estelle's pleas regarding her marriage?

She heard herself admitting out loud what, in times past, she'd only yearned silently within the depths of her soul. "I wish I'd never gone back to Roger."

Gloria gently touched her friend's hand as it lay on the table. "You don't mean that."

With tears in her eyes, Estelle looked at Gloria and nodded slowly. "Yes, I do. I hate feeling this way, but I do."

Gloria felt there was nothing more she could say at the moment. Moving closer, she wrapped her arms around Estelle while her friend cried.

Chapter 6

Southern Comfort was one of the finest restaurants in Savannah, and Justin was the head chef. Five days a week and occasionally on weekends, he delighted guests with his mouth-watering dishes.

Today was Saturday, his day off. However, two of their best customers were celebrating their twenty-fifth wedding anniversary and had specifically requested that he prepare their meal. Therefore, he had come in just long enough to oblige them. They simply adored his grilled salmon with grilled vegetables and brown sesame rice. Their favorite dessert was Justin's caramel apple-pecan empanada topped with a scoop of vanilla bean ice cream.

Relieved that the couple had chosen the same dish, Justin arranged the succulent main course on plates and garnished each piece of fish with a sprig of parsley before they were taken away to be devoured by their dinner guests. In the middle of their meal, the couple asked their waiter if Mr.

Brickman could come to their table so they could personally thank him for coming in on his day off to prepare for
them such a delightful feast.

Justin spoke with them briefly, then hurried back to the
kitchen to prepare their pastry dish. As soon as he was done,
he handed the desserts to the waiter and rushed home from
the restaurant for his evening out with Shayna.

He and his wife were just about to step inside his car when
his pager vibrated.

Seeing the frustrated look on his face, Shayna asked,
"What is it?"

"The restaurant. They're paging me."

Shayna frowned. "You just left there. What can they
possibly want now? Can't you just ignore them?"

The two of them were going to a nice hotel for dinner
and dancing, and had made their plans two weeks ago.
They'd only been married for six weeks and were still
wrapped up in the passion of being newlyweds.

"No. It's on the way to the hotel. I'll stop by, run in and
see what's up."

Shayna buckled her seat belt and folded her arms across
her chest.

Justin glanced her way. "I promise. I'll run in and right
out."

"You don't even know what they want, so you don't
know how long you'll be. You already went in on your day
off, and now they're calling you for something else."

Justin backed out of the driveway and maneuvered the
car down the well-lit street and onto the highway, heading
toward the restaurant.

Pulling into the closest parking space he could find, he
said, "I'll be right back. I promise." Before Shayna could say
anything, he was out the car.

Shayna was fighting mad. After ten minutes of sitting in the car, she climbed out and ventured into the restaurant. Before she could get past the foyer, she caught sight of Justin walking toward her at a fast pace, and he didn't look happy.

Shayna's brow wrinkled in confusion. "What's wrong?"

Grabbing her by the hand, he pulled her along with him as he headed for the exit. "Come on. Let's get outta here."

All the way to the car, Shayna kept asking, "What's wrong?"

It wasn't until they got into the vehicle that he turned to her and said, "My boss is really angry with me."

Shayna shook her head. "What?"

"He yelled at me and embarrassed me in front of the staff."

"Why?"

"The couple I fixed dinner for said I put peanuts in their dessert."

Shayna wrinkled her brow and shook her head again. "What?"

"They said I put peanuts in their empanadas."

"Well, what's wrong with that?"

"Mrs. Wilder's allergic to peanuts."

"How were you supposed to know that?"

"She and Mr. Wilder are two of our best customers. I know she's allergic to peanuts, but I didn't put peanuts in the empanadas. The recipe calls for pecans. I used pecans."

"Well, aren't pecans and peanuts both considered to be the same thing—nuts?"

Shaking his head, Justin rattled in an impatient tone, "No, Shay. You don't understand. Peanuts belong to the bean family, not the nut family, like pecans, walnuts and things like that. They're not the same as pecans."

"Well, what happens when a person has an allergic reaction to peanuts? Is it that serious?"

Justin's brow was sweating profusely. "Yes, it can be deadly."

Shayna threw her hands up to cover her mouth. "Oh, my God, is she dead?"

"No, she had her allergy kit with her so they were able to reverse the breathing problems she was having."

"Oh, this is terrible."

"I know." Justin looked at his wife, wide-eyed. "But I didn't do it, Shay. I didn't do it. I kept telling them I didn't, but they don't believe me. Mr. and Mrs. Wilder are extremely upset with me. They're my favorite customers. They really liked me and my food. That's why they specifically asked if I'd come in and prepare their meal. This'll ruin my career as a chef.

"I kept telling Manuel I didn't do it. I've been working for him ever since I graduated from culinary arts school. He had just opened the restaurant when he hired me. He thinks I did it, not on purpose, but by accident because I was rushing to finish so I could leave. I kept telling him over and over that's not what happened. I used pecans, not peanuts. I know it, but nobody believes me."

"Well, couldn't Mrs. Wilder tell the difference between the two before she ate 'em?"

"Evidently not. They were both chopped. The peanuts were mixed in with the pecans in the caramel sauce, and she ate 'em." Justin hung his head and shook it again as he repeated, "I didn't do it."

Shayna had never seen him so upset. She truthfully stated, "I believe you." Reaching over, she pulled him toward her and held him. "Don't worry, we'll get to the bottom of this."

Pulling out of his wife's embrace, Justin said, "Don't say anything to my family about this. I don't want them to know."

"Okay, baby. Whatever you say."

★ ★ ★

Justine spoke to her coworker from her cubicle. "Hey, Catina, what are you doing tonight?"

"Nothing. Why?"

"Now, don't yell at me. Evan has a friend I want you to meet."

Catina rolled her chocolate-brown eyes toward the partition that separated her and Justine's office spaces. "What did I tell you?"

"I know. I know. You don't want to get involved with anybody right now. I just hate the thought of you being home alone on a Saturday night."

"If it doesn't bother me, why is it such a problem for you?"

"I just worry about you being by yourself. Don't you ever get lonely?"

"Why is it everybody thinks a woman has to have a man in order to feel complete? I *do* have other people in my life, you know—friends, family. Will you please stop trying to set me up already?"

"But, Catina, I told you this guy is nice. He's a real gentleman, not like the other guys you've dated. He has a good job. He's down-to-earth."

Catina responded nonchalantly, "I don't care if he's the prince of Egypt. I'm not interested. Okay?"

Justine playfully shivered as she turned around in her chair and spotted Catina in her doorway. "Okay. Okay. Woo, somebody's in a foul mood today."

Catina said, "You think that was foul. You ain't seen nothing yet. Just keep on."

"Oo-ooh, I'm scared o' you."

The two friends burst out laughing.

Evan and Darryl had teamed up to play a game of basketball against Ray and Jarrod at Evan's house. Jarrod dribbled the ball in for a slam dunk, gaining his two points and landing in Justine's nearby hydrangea bushes.

Evan quickly cautioned his friend, "Man, watch what you doing. You trample all over Justine's flowers, she'll have your head on a platter."

With the palms of his hands against the house for support, Jarrod tried to push himself away from the plants without doing any more damage. "Man, why'd she put 'em right here beside the goal?"

"She didn't put 'em there. I did."

Jarrod snickered. "Figures. I shoulda known. You ain't got the sense God gave a gnat."

The friends' laughter echoed throughout the air as Evan grabbed Jarrod in a headlock. "Oh, is that right?"

Jarrod managed to get free, then lifted Evan up and dropped him onto the lawn, where he held him down.

Evan asked, "Man, what you trying to do, kill me? You better get off me before I hurt you."

Darryl yelled from where he and Ray stood laughing, "Okay, you two, y'all wanna play ball or act like monkeys?"

Evan stood, and the two of them rejoined the game. Ray made the final shot, thereby breaking the tie and making him and Jarrod the winners.

The four men went inside to drink a beer and cool off from their strenuous activity. After taking a long swig of his brew, Ray let out a long, loud belch, filling the air with one of the most horrid smells any of them had ever experienced. The other three men starting fanning their hands in front of their faces.

Evan said, "Man, that was nasty."

Darryl asked, "Woo! What you been eating?"

"Yeah," Jarrod said, "it smells like something crawled down your throat and died."

Evan added, "Man, next time you need to let something that foul out, go outside. Don't be stinkin' up my house. If Justine comes home and smells that, she'll run you outta here."

Ray grumbled, "Aw, man, there you go again. Justine's got your butt whipped. I bet you can't even take a pee without her permission. You not even potty trained yet."

Jarrod was laughing so hard he kept jiggling his left foot up and down, while shifting his torso forward and back.

Grinning, Darryl hung his head and shook it from side to side while Ray rambled on in jest. Darryl liked the way they were able to joke around with each other, but he had a feeling that one day, one of them would go too far. He wanted to tell Ray to shut up, but since Evan was smiling, too, and didn't seem upset by their friend's comments, he kept quiet.

Ray asked Evan, "Does she let you cross the street by yourself? When are you gon' grow up and be your own man? It's always Justine this and Justine that. Who wears the pants in this house—you or Justine?"

Evan laughed and took another sip of beer before saying, "You don't worry 'bout who wears the pants. You just do something 'bout that funky odor you just let out in here."

Jarrod put in his two cents. "That's right, Ray. Besides, Evan always has the last word." Quickly, he added, "*'Yes, ma'am.'*"

The roar of laughter spilled throughout the room. Evan was laughing harder than anybody.

Gloria placed a crystal water goblet on the dining room table as she and Donald prepared for Estelle and Roger's visit. "I'm glad you were able to finally convince Roger to come with Estelle for dinner. I wish he would've agreed to all four of us going out for the evening. Estelle misses that. She wishes he'd spend time with her sometimes, just the two of them." After pausing, she said, "Does Roger ever talk about her or them?"

"No."

Gloria raised an eyebrow. "Never?"

Donald repeated, "No."

"Well, what do y'all talk about, if you don't mind my asking?"

"Work, fishing, hunting, sports. You know, the usual stuff men talk about."

Gloria awarded her husband a flirtatious grin. "You don't ever talk about me?"

Donald's smile was impeccable. "Sometimes."

Gloria waltzed up behind him, placed her arms around him and whispered in his ear, "What do you say?"

Just as Donald was about to answer, the doorbell rang. Instead, he said, "I'll get back with you on that."

Gloria lightly pecked his cheek. "Yeah, you got off this time, but like you said, we'll take this up later," she said, as she made her way to the door to greet their friends.

During dinner, Estelle saw a side of Roger he hadn't granted her the privilege of witnessing in quite some time. His laughter sent chills down her spine. Just hearing him talk had a profound effect on her, for conversation between the two of them was very limited unless they were arguing. Even on the ride over, as usual, she'd done most of the talking. When they were alone, it was as though they didn't know how to act toward one another.

After dinner, Estelle offered to help clean the kitchen, but Gloria said, "Donald and I'll do that later. We invited y'all over for us to have some fun, and that's what we're gonna do, so come on."

They teamed up and played an assortment of card and board games, alternating between the women against the men and one set of spouses against the other. When it came time to leave, Estelle felt her heart drop.

On the ride home, Roger regressed back to his old self. Estelle was in the mood for romance. Fear trickled through her body as she tried to think of the words to express to him how she was feeling. It seemed that everything she said made him angry. Her daring heart forced her panic aside. She gazed at him, her eyes warm with adoration. "I really had a good time tonight."

Staring straight ahead, Roger said, "Yeah, it was nice."

Estelle whispered, "Thank you for coming."

With no emotion whatsoever, he said, "You don't have to thank me."

His insensitivity tugged at her. "I just wanted you to know how much it meant to me that we did something together."

Roger said nothing. Every few minutes, Estelle would rack her brain for something to talk to him about, but held back. They drove the remainder of the way home in silence. As soon as they were in the house, Roger informed Estelle that he was tired and was going to bed. A few minutes later, she joined him.

Nervous tension raced throughout Estelle's body as she slowly slipped her hand around Roger's waist. His back was toward her, as usual. He didn't move or say a word.

Estelle whispered, "Roger."

Believing the best thing to do was pretend to be asleep, Roger said nothing as a feeling of vexation rippled throughout him.

Estelle shook him and said his name again.

"What?" he answered gruffly.

"Hold me, please," she replied gently.

She just couldn't leave well enough alone. They'd gone

out like she'd been bugging him to do, and that wasn't enough. "Stelle, I'm tired. I'm trying to sleep here."

"I know," Estelle whispered. "All I want you to do is hold me. We don't have to do anything else. Just hold each other."

When Roger didn't respond, she said, "Please."

Still he lay there as though she'd said nothing.

"Roger, don't you love me?"

Roger didn't think he could deal with any more of his wife's whining. He had been putting up with it for the past fifteen years, ever since they'd gotten back together. She'd given him an ultimatum back then—never take another drink of alcohol, or she'd leave him again and not return. They had built a nice home together and had two wonderful children. Yet Estelle was always pestering him about something. He didn't know how much more he could take. Had it been a mistake for them to get back together?

Roger gritted his teeth. "Stelle, don't start that."

"Start what? All I want to know is if you love me. Is that so hard a question to answer? Do you love me?"

Raising his head slightly, he practically yelled, "You're still here, ain't cha? *I'm* still here. Now will you hush and go to sleep?"

Estelle jumped from the bed. "All I did was ask you a simple question, and you get bent all outta shape. Why is it so hard for you to show me some affection?" She took off to an empty bedroom, her heart feeling as though it had been ripped to shreds.

Chapter 7

As Estelle sat observing everyone at Alabama Power's annual Memorial Day company picnic at Buffalo Park, she wished she'd stayed home. It was thoughtful of Gloria and Donald to invite her to accompany them, although Estelle had been unable to convince Roger to come with them.

She had finally been able to persuade her friends to take a much desired stroll down by the lake. Estelle watched the children playing nearby and the couples walking hand in hand.

Out of nowhere, a stranger came up and sat down at the opposite end of the picnic table where she was sitting. She decided to ignore him, as she was in no mood for conversation. She briefly contemplated getting up and walking away; however, she did not want to offend anyone.

"Sure is a pretty day," the stranger said in a warm baritone voice.

For a moment, Estelle wondered who he was talking to.

Then she realized it was her. She looked at the man and offered him a slight smile. "Hmm, yes, it is." She refused to say more.

"You by yourself, too?" He knew she was alone because he'd been observing her with her friends ever since he'd arrived. He was mesmerized by her. She was an extremely attractive woman with a very beautiful smile. The gap between her teeth made her appearance more intriguing. He casually dropped his gaze to her left hand. She was married. Too bad. He respected that, though he envied her husband.

"'Scuse me?"

"I was just wondering if you came alone."

"Oh. No, I'm with a couple of my friends."

The man nodded. Suddenly, he heard himself saying, "I don't mean any disrespect, but you're the most beautiful woman I've ever seen."

Estelle couldn't believe her ears. No one had ever told her that, and she certainly didn't feel beautiful. Aware that she was blushing, she smiled and replied, "Thank you."

"You're welcome. I hope you don't think I'm trying to flirt. I know you're married. I see your ring," he said, nodding toward her hand. "I just had to tell you that."

"That's very sweet. Thank you," Estelle said again. She had to admit to herself that she felt both uncomfortable and flattered at the same time. She didn't think she appealed to Roger any longer, as he certainly never told her she did or even acted that way.

Guilt consumed Estelle's soul. She was a married woman who had no right to be sitting here talking to another man. Then she reminded herself that she wasn't doing anything wrong. They were just two people having a conversation.

"Hey, would you like to play volleyball? Looks like they're fixin' to start another game."

With the sunlight blinding her vision, Estelle squinted, shaking her head. "No, I don't think so."

"You sure?"

"Yes, but thanks."

The man stood. "Oh, by the way, my name's John—John Sinclair," he said, holding out his hand.

Estelle shook it. "Estelle Brickman. It's nice to meet you, John."

"You, too, Estelle. I enjoyed talking to you. So long."

Estelle's heart dropped. She didn't want him to leave. "Bye."

"Enjoy the rest of the picnic."

"You, too."

Then he was gone. Estelle's heart was racing. She felt like a foolish teenager. John had boosted her confidence in herself, yet she longed for Roger to make her feel beautiful the way the stranger she'd just met had.

Gloria interrupted her thoughts. "Who was that?"

"Hmm?"

"The guy you were talking to—who is he?"

Gloria and Donald were looking at her as though she'd grown an extra head. Why was she feeling so nervous? She hadn't done anything wrong. "Some guy who just came over and started talking."

Estelle took note of Gloria's piercing eyes but decided not to make any comment.

"So how was your day?" Estelle asked Roger when she got home later that evening. "I brought you a plate."

Not looking away from the television, Roger answered, "Okay. Thanks."

She stood there a few minutes, hoping he'd ask her how her day had gone. What was she thinking? He never did, so why would he start now? A part of her wanted to tell him about John. Maybe then she'd get his attention. Perhaps if he thought another man was interested in her, he'd get up off his rump and start treating her like he was supposed to. However, after mulling the idea over for a moment, she decided against it.

Sitting on the sofa, Estelle said, "There were a lot of people at your company picnic. It was nice. I wished you'd come. Gloria and Donald had a good time, too."

Never once turning his head away from the television, Roger said, "That's good."

Estelle attempted to converse with her husband a few minutes more, but it was a one-sided effort. Finally, she gave up and went to bed.

The next day, Gloria came to assist Estelle in the flower shop. Estelle thanked her friend for helping her out during part of her summer break from teaching high school.

"Girl," Gloria said, "you know I don't mind. Since school's out, I'll be able to help out a lot more. Besides, I love it."

Estelle nodded at the project her friend was working on. "You're doing a wonderful job with that wreath. We've got one more to make for the Williams funeral today."

Gloria nodded. "What time is the funeral again?"

"One o'clock, but we need to have the wreaths at the church by twelve."

Gloria checked her watch. "So we've got two hours. Let's get busy."

The women worked steadily and talked while they finished the wreaths. Then they loaded them into the van, and Estelle took them to the church while Gloria minded the store. Afterward, they closed the shop while they went for a bite of lunch. As they ate, Estelle told her friend more about the man from the picnic.

Gloria said, "I knew something was up with you when Donald and I came back and saw that look on your face."

Estelle's heart began to palpitate. *What look?* Had her expression indicated how flattered she was by the compliment and attention John had heaped upon her? Was that why Gloria had given her that definite glare of disapproval? She gazed at her friend. "What look?"

Gloria narrowed her eyes at Estelle. "The same one you have on your face now—like you're in love with the man."

Estelle quickly tapped her friend's hand. "You oughta be ashamed of yourself for even thinking something like that."

"*I* oughta be ashamed? You're the one lusting after another man."

Estelle's mouth fell open. "Gloria, I can't believe you would think, let alone *say,* something like that to me. I'm not lusting after anybody. Just because I'm unhappy with Roger doesn't mean I wanna be with somebody else."

"Well, you're the one who said sometimes he makes you wish you'd married someone else."

"Yeah, I said that, but it doesn't mean I'm gonna be unfaithful to him. You think just because I don't go to church anymore that I've forgotten what the Bible says about fidelity. Why do you always think the worst of me when it's clear that Roger's not putting any work into our marriage? You always wanna blame me for everything."

"That's not what I'm doing. It's just that I know how unhappy you are, and I guess I'm afraid of what you might do one day in order to feel loved."

"And you think I would be with anyone other than Roger just to feel loved? Gloria, I'm not a child. I've got more sense than that. You know what? When John told me I was the most beautiful woman he'd ever seen, it made me feel good. I won't lie. For the first time in a long while, I felt attractive. But that doesn't mean I'm gonna cheat on Roger. Despite our problems, I still love him. I try to show him I do, but I get nothing in return.

"Just like last night, when I got home from the picnic. I asked about his day, sat down and tried to tell him about mine. You wanna know what he did? Kept his eyes glued to the TV and responded to me in as few words as he possibly could. Finally, I got up and went to bed. You don't know what it's like day in and day out to be married to someone who's a stranger to you. We live in the same house and sleep in the same bed, but that's all we share. I feel bad enough as it is about my life, so I don't need you judging me."

Gloria's heart ached for her friend. She reached out and touched Estelle's hand as it lay on the table. She whispered, "I'm not trying to judge you. I just know you're very vulnerable right now because of what you're going through. This is the time when you might be tempted in the wrong direction.

"I'm not saying you are or will be unfaithful to Roger. It's just that I realize there's a void in your life that you need filled, and things happen when we least expect them to. I admire you so much for staying in your marriage despite the difficulties. Many times, I've asked myself if I could do the same. Let's not be mad at each other. You're my best friend."

"You're mine, too." Estelle didn't know what she'd do without Gloria. She wasn't sure how she felt about Gloria's admiration for her, though, because she didn't know how much longer she could stay with Roger.

"All I'm saying," Evan said, "is let's at least get tested. It's June now, and you're still not pregnant."

Justine nestled deeper into his arms as they lay in bed.

"I've been doing some research on the Internet." Evan was

excited. "Did you know there are tests you can do at home now? There's an at-home sperm test that just recently became available. There are tests women can do at home, too. But I think we should go to the doctor and get a basic physical, just to be on the safe side. What d'you think?"

"Honey, you're throwing too much at me at once. I hate going to the doctor as it is once a year, just to get my Pap smear. This sounds like it'll be long and drawn out. I don't know if I'm ready to go through all that." Justine's words tasted bitter and deceitful.

"You want a baby, don't you?"

"Yes," she lied, "but…"

"Then it'll be worth it."

She pressed her body against Evan's but didn't respond.

He asked, "Won't it?"

"I don't know," she whispered. "Can't we just keep trying and see what happens?"

"We've been trying for over a year now. If it was gonna happen by itself, it would've already. We need help. What are you afraid of? Are you scared of what we may find out? Do you think it might be you? It's probably me. And if something is wrong with me—if I'm the reason we haven't had a baby—I need to know so we can do something about it.

"Justine, men have biological clocks, too. I read that a man's reproductive capabilities may start deteriorating as early as his mid-thirties. I'll be thirty in four months. I can't waste any more time."

Justine said nothing. She had to think of a way to get out of this testing Evan was so enthusiastic about them having done.

Chapter 8

As soon as the waitress left their table, Justine said firmly, "Honey, don't you think you've had enough?"

"What?" Evan said. "I've only had one. This'll be my second and last."

Justine gave him a disapproving gaze. "You really shouldn't be drinking at all."

An irritated expression filled Evan's eyes. He always tried to be a loving and supportive husband, and because of that, Ray and Jarrod were always giving him a hard time. Now here she was on his back about him having a couple of drinks. "Why are you having a fit?"

Justine decided to keep quiet for now. As she drove home, Evan was talking a mile a minute. "How are Mom and Dad?" he asked.

Justine was still ticked off at him. "Fine," she lied.

Evan glanced at the digital clock on the car's dash. "Hey, it's only eight-thirty. Why don't we stop by and see 'em?"

"Not tonight. I'm tired. I just want to go home and go to bed."

"You're not going to the office tomorrow, are you?"

"No, but I need to get to bed early. I told you I'm tired."

"Okay. That's fine. Maybe we can see 'em tomorrow."

When they got home, Justine put on her nightclothes and went to bed. Around ten o'clock, she woke up to go to the bathroom, and heard the loud roar of laughter coming from the den. She snatched up her robe, threw it on and went toward the sound. She found Evan, Darryl, Jarrod and Ray laughing up a storm.

When Evan spotted her, he yelled out, "Sorry, baby. Did we wake you?"

The room grew quiet. As Justine looked with an evil eye at the beer bottles in Ray's and Jarrod's hands, she answered, "No. I just got up to go to the bathroom and heard noise."

Darryl said apologetically, "We're sorry if we woke you, Justine. We'll keep it down."

She tried to smile. "It's okay, Darryl."

When her eyes met Jarrod's, he nodded and said, "Hey, Justine. How ya doing?"

"Fine, Jarrod. You?"

"Fine."

Ray nodded his head. "Hey."

"Hey, Ray. Y'all's family doing okay?"

Jarrod's and Ray's heads were bobbing up and down like those little fake felt puppies that people put in the backs of their car windows. "Yeah," they said in unison.

Justine stated, "Well, that's good. See y'all later. Good night."

"Good night," Evan's three friends hollered.

Evan said, "'Night, baby."

The next morning when Evan attempted to kiss Justine as she stood at the bathroom mirror combing her hair, she was a little aloof toward him. "What's wrong?" he asked.

"Nothing," she said as she pulled the comb through her locks. Her expression reeked of vexation.

Evan placed a gentle arm around her waist, staring at their reflection in the mirror. "Are you mad at me about something?"

Justine tossed her comb down on the counter and brushed past him into the bedroom.

Following her, he asked, "What did I do?"

Justine still refused to answer, and headed toward the kitchen, with Evan close behind. "Justine, what's wrong with you?"

When she opened the refrigerator and spotted a beer, she blew a gasket. "What's wrong with me? I'll tell you what's wrong with me," she said, as she grabbed the malt liquor and shoved it in his face. "*This* is what's wrong with me. I don't appreciate you and your friends sitting around our house guzzling down beer."

Evan had never seen her pitch such a fit. "Justine, we weren't sitting around guzzling beer."

Justine shook the bottle in his face again. "Well, what d'you call this?"

"Me and Darryl didn't even drink any, just Jarrod and Ray, and they only had one. They gave me one—that one—and left the rest in the car."

"I don't like you hanging out with them."

Evan drew back his head and frowned. "Who? Darryl, Jarrod and Ray are my friends."

"Not Darryl. Jarrod and Ray. I like Darryl. I don't care for Jarrod and Ray. They're a bad influence on you."

"A bad influ— Justine, wait a minute. I'm not ten years

old. You don't pick my friends. I don't say anything when you bring people home."

"Well, the people I bring home aren't drunkards."

"My friends aren't drunkards. They like to have a few beers, but that doesn't make them drunkards."

"You can say what you want. I don't want them back here. Darryl I don't mind, but those other two I do."

"You don't tell me who I can have in my own house."

"It's my house, too."

"You know what? I think we both need to take a moment to calm down." Without saying another word, Evan turned on his heel and left Justine standing there, still holding the beer in her hands.

Chapter 9

Roger walked through the kitchen door with his chest puffed out and a big Cheshire cat grin on his face.

He dropped his keys on the table and merrily announced, "I bought a boat."

Estelle quickly turned around from washing dishes. Drying her hands on a red gingham dishcloth, she said, "You what?" and dropped the towel onto the counter.

Roger repeated, "I bought a boat." Grabbing her by her arm and heading toward the door, he said, "Come on. Let me show it to you."

Estelle stopped dead in her tracks, lifted her chin and focused her eyes squarely on Roger's face. "You didn't tell me you were buying a boat."

"Well, I wasn't planning to. I just went looking and decided to get it." Taking her again by her arm, Roger urged her once more toward the door. "Come and see it."

Estelle pulled herself free. "I can't believe you went out and bought a boat without talking to me about it first."

"I told you I decided at the last minute," Roger stated, again trying to defend his impulse.

"Without discussing it with me," Estelle reminded him.

"Why are you so mad?"

"Why am I so mad?" she echoed. "I just told you. You made a major purchasing decision without consulting me."

"Are you coming to look at it or not?"

"No, I'm not coming to look at it. You shouldn't have bought it."

Roger yelled, "I work just like you. I can buy whatever I want." Then he turned and walked away.

Estelle trailed behind him to the bedroom. "I can't get you to do anything with me as it is." Waving her hand in the air, she added, "Now you went off and bought yourself another toy to play with. Every time I turn around, you'll be out on the lake somewhere, and I'll be stuck here at home. I'm tired of it. I'm fed up with you treating me like I don't exist."

"Stelle, do you have to start this again?"

"Yes, I have to start this again. Until you begin treating me like your wife, I'll start it over and over. You are so selfish. You never think about what I want. Everything is always about you."

"I don't want to hear this."

"No, you don't want to hear it 'cause you know it's the truth. What are you running from? Why won't you talk to me? I try to talk to you, and it's like speaking to a brick wall. I need you to talk to me. Our marriage is in serious trouble, and you won't face up to it."

"Our marriage is no more worse than anybody else's," Roger lied.

Estelle threw up her hands. "Will you stop telling me that? How many times do I have to tell you I don't care about anybody else's marriage? I care about ours. Are you happy with the way things are?"

Estelle's constant nagging was getting on Roger's nerves. He hadn't had a drink in years, but sometimes he felt like taking a swig just so he could block out her persistent bickering. He rushed through the bedroom door.

Estelle followed him. "Did you hear me? Where're you going?"

"Out."

"Out where?"

"Just out."

"Oh, are you going to see your woman? Or are you one of those men on the down low?"

Before Estelle knew what had occurred, Roger had spun around and pinned her up against the living room wall. He had a crazed look in his eyes that frightened her. She'd never seen it before, but she didn't allow it to silence her.

She yelled, "You gonna hit me? Go ahead so I can hit you back." She wanted to fight. She needed to release the anger, hostility and resentment welling up inside her.

After a brief moment, Roger released her, went to his truck and drove away.

Justine was still feeling the tension between her parents. She and Evan had seen the boat parked at the side of the house just outside the garage when they'd arrived for Sunday dinner. As soon as her mother had gotten her alone, she'd told Justine about how her father had purchased the boat without her knowledge and had come home with it the day before.

Justine prayed for the couple to make peace with one another as she attempted to ease the strained relations that existed between her parents.

"Mama," she said, "*that* was delicious."

Estelle smiled as she got up from the table. "Thank you, honey."

Evan wiped his mouth with his napkin and added, "Yeah, Mom, it was good. Thanks for having us over."

Estelle turned slightly to smile at her son-in-law. "You're welcome, Evan. It's nice to be appreciated," she added, cutting her gaze to her husband, who said nothing, but simply got up from the table and walked away.

Justine and Evan eyed one another briefly. Justine was very disappointed in her father's attitude. She never heard him compliment her mother on anything anymore. He didn't use to be that way. She remembered how affectionate he once was toward Estelle, before everything had gone haywire.

Justine knew how hard marriage could be. She and Evan had had their own little spat yesterday, and he'd walked out on her. He'd actually left her standing in the kitchen like a raging lunatic, with a beer in her hand. All the while she was yelling at him, her brain was instructing her to shut up, but her mouth kept telling her to let him have it. When he'd returned home, Evan had tried to talk to her about what had happened. She couldn't share her fears with him and pretended everything was okay.

Justine stood and started helping her mother straighten up the kitchen.

Evan took his dishes over to the sink. "Do you need any help?"

Justine said, "No, we got it. Thanks, though."

Evan nodded and joined Roger in the den, where he was watching a nature show on television.

Evan asked, "Have you talked to Justin and Shayna lately?"

"A couple of weeks ago."

"How are they?"

"Fine."

"That's good."

"Maybe you and me can go down one weekend, take the boat, and do some fishing while we're there."

"That sounds great. Maybe Mom and Justine will want to come, too."

"I was thinking of just us guys getting together."

Evan nodded. "Oh, yeah, sure. Sounds good."

They chatted until Estelle and Justine joined them. Justine attempted to lighten the mood between her parents.

"Daddy, do you remember when I was little and used to sneak in bed in the middle of the night between you and Mama? You'd wake up and find me and take me back to my bed, and I'd be so mad at you."

For the first time since he'd brought home that stupid boat, Estelle observed a smile lighting up Roger's features. How many times had she craved the tender look he now displayed?

"Yeah, you'd lay there in the dark with your big eyes wide open," he said, "telling me you weren't gonna go to sleep, that you were gonna stay up all night."

Justine said, "Then you'd leave and Mama would come in and sit on the side of the bed until I fell asleep, or until she *thought* I'd fallen asleep."

Estelle let out a laugh. "Yeah, you were a great pretender. As soon as I eased up off the bed, you'd open those big ol' eyes, and I had to start all over."

Roger and Evan were laughing.

Roger said, "And what about the time she gave Justin a haircut?"

Estelle said with a yelp, "Oh, yes! Evan, Justin had this big plug of hair cut out of his head right on the top. She got a whipping for that."

Justine said to Evan, "They were wrong for that. I told them Justin wanted me to cut it. Of course, he denied it.

Then he got mad at me 'cause he didn't like the way his hair looked, and cut the hair off one of my dolls."

As they talked and laughed about the good old days, Estelle felt as though she'd gone back in time to a period where everything between her and Roger was good. Their children had always brought out the best in them. Perhaps that was why it seemed that after their nest had become empty the problems between them had resurfaced.

Chapter 10

Evan pulled back the bed covers. "I'm going to make our appointments tomorrow for the fertility tests. What's a good day and time for you?"

Justine grabbed her novel from the nightstand and climbed into bed. "I don't know. Where's this doctor again?" She couldn't remember any of the stuff he'd been telling her. Half the time, she wasn't even listening.

"In Birmingham."

Justine had to get out of this. "Evan, I don't feel comfortable going to some strange doctor I've never been to before."

Evan joined her in bed. "Well, I've checked him out, and he's very reputable."

Justine turned to face her husband. "*He*. I don't want some man poking around private areas of my body. My gynecologist is female."

"This doctor specializes in fertility issues, so I thought it'd be a good idea to see him. I think we should do this together, but if you don't want to, I guess you can go to your own doctor. Has she ever said anything to you about why you haven't been able to get pregnant? I mean, I'm not saying there's something wrong with you. I was just wondering, since she's your doctor, if she's ever mentioned anything to you."

Justine frowned. "Evan, if she had, don't you think I would've told you? Gee."

"Yeah. I was just wondering. So you want me to just make my own appointment and you'll make yours to see your doctor?"

"Yeah, I guess."

Turning on his side, Evan looked at her innocently. "What's wrong? You sound as if you don't care about doing this. Don't you want us to have a baby?"

Justine kept her eyes glued to her book. "I don't know. Maybe we should wait."

"For what? Justine, we've been married for five years. We've had plenty of time to ourselves. I'm not getting any younger, and neither are you."

When Justine raised her eyes from her book, her chiding look told him he'd offended her.

Evan was quick to respond, "That came out wrong. Just 'cause you're a few months older than me doesn't mean you're old. You look good for your age."

Their six-month age difference didn't bother her. However, Justine was sparing him no mercy with the looks she was casting his way.

Evan tried to redeem himself again. "I didn't mean *that* the way it sounded. You know you look good. I think you're beautiful. You always have been and you always will be. I hope our children look just like you."

Despite her apathy, Justine couldn't help but laugh as she

let Evan off the hook. "You dug yourself out of that hole real quick, didn't you?"

Evan laughed as he wiped a hand across his brow. "Whew. Yeah. I could tell from the look on your face you were getting ready to shovel the dirt over me."

Justine giggled.

"So what about the appointment? Do you want me to make my own and you'll set up yours with your doctor?"

Not wanting to discuss the matter any further, Justine simply replied, "Yeah."

Catina kidded her friend during lunch the next day. "Why are you so quiet today? That mouth is usually going ninety miles a minute. 'Course, I guess I better enjoy the peace and quiet while I can." She used her fork to cut off a chunk of pineapple from the slice on her plate.

Justine faked a smile. "Very funny, Catina. If you were any funnier, I'd be rolling around on the floor."

"What's wrong?" Catina popped the piece of sweet, juicy fruit into her mouth and savored the flavor.

"Evan found some fertility doctor he wants us to go to."

"What's wrong with that? Don't you want to have children? You've been married for how long now?"

"Five years."

"So what's the problem?"

Anxiety laced Justine's chest. "Catina, what I'm about to tell you—you have to promise me you won't mention a word of it to anyone. My family doesn't know—not even my mother—and you know how close she and I are."

Catina's eyes lit up the entire restaurant. "Is it something bad?"

"Just promise me you won't tell anyone. I have to have your word before I tell you."

Catina laid her fork on her plate and wiped the corners of her mouth with her napkin. "Justine, you're scaring me. What is it?"

"You have to promise, Cat."

Justine had called her *Cat*. So Catina knew whatever it was, it was serious. "Okay. Okay. I promise I won't say a word to anybody."

Justine's eyes darted around the restaurant in search of anyone who might know her or her family. When she spoke, she leaned forward a little and kept her voice low. "Evan wants us to have a baby. I'm not ready yet. He thinks there's something medically wrong that's preventing me from getting pregnant. He doesn't know I'm taking birth control pills."

Catina bent forward as she whispered back, "Well, why don't you just tell him you're not ready to start a family yet? Why sneak behind his back and take the pills?"

Justine sighed. "It's a long story, Catina, and I don't care to get into it right now."

"Okay. I just don't understand why you don't just tell him how you feel. I mean, after all, he's your husband. What if he finds out you've been lying to him?"

"He won't find out, and besides, I'm not lying to him. He just doesn't know I'm on the pill."

"I don't know about you, but where I come from, that's the same as lying."

"Catina, don't you think that sometimes in order to keep from hurting someone, we should just keep our mouths closed?"

"Sometimes the truth hurts. I'm saying we shouldn't intentionally hurt anyone, but if we're keeping something from someone that could destroy their trust in us, that's serious. Remember, that's why I'm alone now—because the person I loved betrayed me. Once trust is lost, it's hard to get back."

★ ★ ★

"I tell you, Gloria," Estelle was saying, "Roger turned into a totally different person yesterday when Justine got us talking about when she was a little girl. He never speaks to me like that."

Gloria bit off a huge piece of the pizza they'd had delivered to the shop, and listened while her friend filled her in on the details of the day before.

"Well, you know, some men don't talk a lot. We're more verbal than most of them are."

"I don't buy that where Roger's concerned, because he talks to other people, just not to me. So what d'you have to say about that, Miss Smarty Pants? You're always trying to make excuses for him. Sometimes I wonder whose side you're on."

"I'm not on anybody's side. You're both my friends. And Donald's," Gloria added. "Roger's just his own person. I know it's hard on you. You know, Estelle, we can't change people," she reminded her friend. "We can only change ourselves."

Estelle quickly shook her head. "I don't believe that. I think if we try hard enough, we *can* change people. One day, Roger's gon' come around. He'll change back into the man I fell in love with and married."

She hesitated for a moment, gazing at her friend solemnly. She was almost too embarrassed to share what had happened Saturday. "I guess you know he bought a boat."

Gloria nodded. "Donald told me."

"I got so mad at him 'cause he didn't even discuss it with me. I feel like he's just trying to find things to fill his time to keep from spending any of it with me. I still feel like he's messing around with somebody."

Estelle was on the verge of telling her friend about the spiteful accusation she'd thrown in Roger's face Saturday afternoon. She'd only done it because she was so full of anger and resentment toward him for neglecting her. If he was messing around, she didn't know if it'd hurt more if it was with another man instead of a woman. Just the thought of either tore her to pieces.

Gloria rolled her eyes. "You didn't throw that in his face again, did you?"

Before Estelle realized it, she was disclosing her allegation. "We were arguing, and he started to leave. I asked if he was going to see his woman. Then I asked him if he was one of those men on the down low."

This time, Gloria dropped her pizza back onto her paper plate. "What'd you say that for? Estelle, if I've told you once, I've told you a thousand times, you gotta stop flying off the handle and hollering out the first thing that comes to your mind. You're gonna really make him mad one day. Men don't like that kinda stuff. One of these days, you'll gonna push him too far."

Estelle glared at her friend. "Sounds to me like you're saying one day he's gonna hit me, and it'll be well-deserved."

"I'm not saying that. No one has the right to abuse anyone in any shape, form or fashion, but you know, there's such a thing as verbal abuse, too."

Estelle held her head high as she stated boldly, "Well, I'm the type person who says what's on my mind. And how many times do I have to tell you I've tried it your way? I talk nice and sweet to him, and it doesn't work. I get nothing back but more heartache. I'm tired of doing all the giving and him doing all the taking. You're supposed to be my friend. You know what I'm going through, and you always side with him. I'm sick of him, and I'm sick of *you.*"

Estelle's last few words threw Gloria for a loop. Throughout their lifelong friendship, they'd never had any serious disagreements until lately. Despite the jolt to her heart, Gloria said sympathetically, "I'm not saying he's right to treat you the way he does, but you're abusing him verbally. Verbal abuse can hurt just as badly as emotional neglect. You're both hurting each other, but the only person you can change is yourself. You have every right to be angry and upset at him for the way he treats you, but think about what you're doing to him. After all these years of telling him off, has it made things better between you?"

Gloria had said a mouthful, and Estelle felt like shoving every single word back down her throat. Refusing to reply to her question, she said, "You know, it's easy for you to sit there on your high-and-mighty throne and judge me when you have a husband who shows that he loves you. You wanna try walking in my shoes and see how *you* feel? Until you do, keep your judgmental comments to yourself."

"Estelle, I wasn't being judgmental."

"Yes, you were, and I don't care to talk about it anymore."

Though Gloria attempted to lighten Estelle's mood by engaging her in conversation not related to her marriage, things were extremely tense between the two friends for the remainder of the afternoon.

Chapter 11

"How's Mee-Mee?" Evan asked Darryl as they sat in Darryl's living room Saturday evening.

Darryl's grin lit up the room. "Man, she's fine. Growing like a weed."

"She sure is cute," Evan acknowledged.

"Thanks. She likes you."

"You think so?"

"Yeah. I mean, she did call you 'Eeh Eeh.'"

Evan laughed. "Yeah, she did, didn't she?"

The two men grew quiet. Then Evan said, "Did I tell you I'm having some fertility testing done next month?"

Darryl leaned forward. "Naw, you didn't. Are you nervous?"

"A little. Not about the tests, but the results. I think I might be the reason me and Justine can't have kids."

"Well, it's good y'all are going to get tested. Then you'll know for sure what's wrong."

"Well, Justine wants to go to her own doctor even though the one I found is a fertility specialist. But I don't care what doctor she sees as long as we can pinpoint what and where the problem is."

Darryl nodded in understanding, just as a loud banging sounded. He got up and opened the door to their two other friends.

As Jarrod and Ray entered, Darryl said, "Y'all sounded like a bunch of wild horses out there. And how many times have I told you to use the doorbell? You need some good home training."

All four men laughed.

"Aw, man," Ray said. "You and Evan tryin' to sit up in here like you're so sophisticated with your big-head selves. Evan, it's good to see Justine let you off the chain for a while. What time's curfew?"

Evan laughed. "Man, you can't even spell *curfew*. Why don't you hush?"

Jarrod asked Darryl, "Where's Pee Wee?"

Darryl chuckled. "Mee-Mee," he corrected. "I don't know. I guess she's with my sister."

Ray asked, "You mean you're not babysitting?"

"Naw, not tonight. You guys ready to play cards? Stop running your mouths and come on."

The four friends sat down at the kitchen table and started playing their first round of cards while Darryl, Jarrod and Ray sipped their beers.

Darryl tapped Evan's arm. "You want a beer? There's one more six-pack in the fridge."

Evan rested his elbows on the table and threw down his card. "Nah. I'll pass."

Ray came close to uttering a rebuttal, but decided not to as he attempted to focus on his cards.

A little after ten, Evan's cellular phone rang. As he answered it, he stood and walked to a corner of the kitchen with his back to his friends.

When he got off the phone, Evan told them, "Hey, guys, don't deal me in this one. I'm leaving."

Ray complained, "Man, it's ten o'clock. What's wrong? The lil' wife wants her baby to come home? Does she spoon-feed you, too?"

"Yeah," Evan answered, grinning, "and I love it."

Jarrod remembered the dirty looks Justine had given him and Ray the last time they had visited Evan. She never gave Darryl the disapproving stares she gave him and Ray. He didn't like her any more than she liked him.

Jarrod stood, went to the refrigerator and grabbed four beers, two bottles in each hand. He set his on the table and put Darryl's and Ray's in front of them. He offered the last one to Evan and said, "Here, man. You need to loosen up. Have a beer before you go."

Evan held up his hand. "I don't want it. I'm not drinking tonight. I've got to drive home when I leave here."

Jarrod glared at his friend. "Is that it, or are you just scared of what Justine'll say? Man, you need to put your foot down. Let her know who's the boss. You keep being her puppet and she'll have you jumpin' through more hoops than a trained seal."

Evan liked joking around with his friends, but he hated how Jarrod and Ray always made it seem as if Justine ran things with him. The truth was he didn't even want a beer. He drank every now and then, but sometimes he just didn't have a taste for it. However, in an effort to prove that he was his own man, he agreed to drink one beer.

Ray grinned and said, "Yeah. That's what I'm talkin' 'bout. Sometimes you just gotta put your foot down. Let 'em know who's boss. I wish Connie would call over here, telling me to come home. I'll tell her I'll come home when I'm good and—"

"Ray," Darryl said as he held out the phone to his friend, "telephone. It's Connie," he whispered.

As Ray spoke into the mouthpiece, his voice was velvety smooth, yet nervous. "Hey, baby, what's up?"

However, the voice he heard wasn't that of his wife but a voice recording that said, "The time is now 10:13 p.m."

Ray thrust the phone back at Darryl. "Man, I'm gonna kill you."

Evan imitated Ray in a deep, masculine voice. "I wish Connie would call telling me to come home. I'll tell her I'll come home when I'm good and…"

Holding the phone to his ear, Darryl took his turn at mimicking their friend. "Hey, baby. What's up?" he said in a timid voice. He didn't like the way Jarrod and Ray were always teasing Evan. Evan was a loving, supportive husband to Justine. That didn't mean she dominated him. Darryl had to do something to take the heat off.

They all started laughing.

Chuckling, Ray said, "Y'all wrong. Man, you almost gave me a heart attack."

"I bet," Jarrod retorted. "You're all talk and no action. I wish you coulda seen the look on your face."

Ray snorted. "Jarrod, you can't talk. What about that time Nancy came to our house looking for you? Man, if she'd found you, she'd have bit off what lil' bit of behind you got, chewed it up and spit it out."

Through his laughter, Jarrod said, "Ah, naw, man, you're exaggerating."

"If I'm lying, I'm flying," Ray exclaimed.

Jarrod said, "Well, get to flying, liar."

"Darryl, just wait. Your turn's coming," Ray warned. "Just wait till you go crazy enough to get married. Enjoy that healthy head of hair 'cause when you get married, it's history. Look at us. Evan's already bald. Me and Jarrod are headed that way."

"Y'all are crazy," Darryl said.

As Evan made his way home, he felt guilty for driving after drinking a beer. If he had an accident and hurt or killed someone, he would never forgive himself. He shouldn't have let Jarrod's and Ray's taunts get to him. His next thought was of Justine. He prayed she wouldn't jump all over his case about drinking when he got home. Maybe she wouldn't notice. *Yeah, fat chance. That woman's got a nose like a bloodhound.*

Chapter 12

The following Saturday, Justine and Catina decided to go shopping when they got off work.

As Justine carefully maneuvered her white Malibu toward her house, Catina told her, "I could've loaned you some money. You didn't have to make this trip home."

Glancing at her friend and smiling, Justine said, "I know you would've, and I appreciate it. But you know I don't like borrowing money. I've got a few dollars I put away recently, and I need to get it." She pulled into her driveway, past a sleek black Rodeo parked at the curb. "It'll only take a minute."

The Rodeo belonged to Darryl. Justine wanted Catina and Darryl to meet. As she climbed out of the car, she noticed that her friend was making no effort to get out, so she asked, "Aren't you coming in?"

Catina shook her head. "No. You said it'd only take a minute, and besides, it looks as though you have company. I'll stay in the car."

"Ah, girl. Come on."

Catina looked at her friend. "What are you up to?"

Leaning down, Justine peered at her girlfriend through the car window. "Nothing. Will you come on?"

Catina had a distinct feeling that Justine had something up her sleeve, but she followed her inside. As they made their way through the house, Catina could hear male voices booming from the family room. She stopped beside Justine when they entered. Evan and his companion looked up immediately.

"Hey, baby!" Evan exclaimed.

Justine smiled. "Hey. Hey, Darryl."

"Hey," Darryl said in greeting, hoping that the pretty lady with Justine was aware it was meant for her as well.

Evan said, "Hey, Catina. How ya doing?"

"I'm fine, Evan. And you?"

"Great." Looking at Justine, he said, "I thought y'all were going shopping."

Justine answered, "We are. I just had to stop and get some more money."

Rising, Evan reached into his back pocket. Pulling out his wallet, he opened it, took out several twenty-dollar bills, and asked, "How much do you need?"

"That's okay, honey. I've got some money I saved back a week or so ago. I've got enough."

"You sure?"

Justine smiled again. "Yes, but thank you."

Evan suddenly remembered that neither he nor his wife had introduced Catina and Darryl. "Darryl, this is Justine's friend and coworker, Catina James. Catina, this is my friend and coworker, Darryl Jones."

Justine and Evan grinned as their friends spoke to one another and shook hands. When Justine slyly turned to go retrieve her money, she was disappointed to discover her friend right on her heels as she made her way into the master bedroom.

Catina quickly shut the door and stood with her back to it. Gritting her teeth, she whispered, "I'm gonna kill you. I knew you were up to something. I told you I'm not interested in meeting anyone right now."

Justine started laughing as she removed five twenty-dollar bills from her lingerie drawer. "I didn't plan this. I know that's what it looks like, but that's not what happened. I didn't know Darryl was here till we pulled into the driveway and I saw his car."

"Yeah, right."

"So what d'you think? You like him?"

"Do I like him? I just met him. I don't even know him."

"Well, we can change that. Y'all can double-date with me and Evan tonight."

"Oh, sure. I'll just go back out there and ask him if he wants to go on a date with me tonight with you and Evan. Justine, get real," Catina said with a chuckle.

"What's wrong with that? This is the twenty-first century. Women don't wait on men to make the first move like they used to. Remember, you snooze, you lose. If you don't step on it, someone else might beat you to him. He's a good catch."

"If he's such a good catch, as you say, why hasn't somebody already hooked him?"

"I think he just hasn't found the right person yet. He's a good Christian guy. He's very particular about the type of woman he wants. You know, you've been complaining lately about the jerks you've been dating. Maybe Darryl's the guy for you."

Catina opened the door and whispered to her friend, "I'll see you back in the car."

"Catina, don't go. He's probably the guy I've been praying for you to meet."

Catina said, "See ya," before making her exit.

As Justine and Evan ate dinner at one of their favorite restaurants later that evening, she inquired excitedly, "So, what did Darryl think of Catina? He like her? Did he say anything about asking her out?"

Holding up his hand as he downed a swig of his ice-cold blackberry lemonade, Evan said, "Slow down, baby. They just met."

He remembered Catina's recent breakup with her boyfriend. As much as Evan cared about Darryl and inwardly agreed that he and Catina would make a charming couple, he didn't want Justine forcing the situation. His wife could at times be annoyingly persistent and aggressive.

"Well, he had to say something about her. What'd he say? Tell me."

Evan grinned. "He thinks she's pretty and wanted to know if she's committed to anyone."

Justine smiled and squealed, "Yes! I knew it! I knew the two of them would hit if off."

"Hit it off? Justine, they just met. All they said was 'Hey, how ya doing?' Baby, you gotta slow down now. Don't push it. Let them do this themselves. If it's meant for them to get together, it'll happen."

"I know. I just worry about Catina, you know."

"Yeah, I know you do."

"She's had such a hard life. And all the men she's dated so far haven't helped any. I just want her to be happy like us." Justine smiled adoringly at her husband. "You know, since Monday's the Fourth of July and most everybody's off work, maybe we can have a little get-together at our

house. We could invite a few people over and have a barbecue."

"Well, that sounds nice, but it's kinda short notice. Everybody probably already has plans."

"Well, I know Catina doesn't. Maybe Mama can get
Daddy to come with her. You can invite Darryl. What d'you
say? It won't hurt to ask."

"I guess you're right. It won't hurt to ask."

Everyone seemed to be having a great time, but as
expected, her mother hadn't been able to convince her
father to come. Justine was disappointed about his absence,
but ecstatic that she and Evan had gotten their two friends
to accept their invitations.

As Justine stood at the sink, rinsing off the hot dogs Evan
was about to put on the grill, she peeked at the couple
through the kitchen window. She beckoned to her husband.
"Look, Evan, I told you they'd hit it off. Look at 'em. They're
both grinning like Cheshire cats."

As Evan grabbed a bottle of barbecue sauce from the door
of the side-by-side refrigerator, he kindly warned his wife,
"Justine, stop spying on them. How would you like it if
someone did that to you?"

"As long as I was enjoying myself, I wouldn't mind.
Come and look."

Taking the platter of hot dogs from her, Evan kissed her
cheek and warned her again, "Stop being nosy," before
heading out the kitchen door.

As Catina and Darryl sat talking at the picnic table near
Justine's zinnia bed, Catina asked, "Do you have the feeling
that our two friends are trying to set us up?"

Darryl let out a chuckle. "I'm not sure about Evan, but I

wouldn't put it past Justine. She and Evan have a good thing going. She wants everybody to be as happy as them."

"Yeah. I know she has good intentions. But I need to let you know I've been burned by several bad relationships. I'm not ready to get back in another one."

Darryl grinned. "Well, if we did start a relationship, what makes you think it'd be bad?"

Catina laughed as she lowered her head to hide the embarrassment she was feeling. Darryl was nice. She hoped she hadn't offended him. "I'm sorry. That's not what I meant. I meant any kind of relationship."

"I know what you meant. I was just teasing."

Catina nodded. "Oh. Good. 'Cause I wouldn't want to offend you."

There was a brief silence before she stated solemnly, "Maybe we'd better do a little mingling."

"Mingling," Darryl repeated. "There's nobody here 'cept us, Evan and Justine, and Justine's mama."

"I know. I just don't want to seem rude."

"You're right. Besides, I guess I have been sort of greedy, hogging all your time since you got here."

"It's okay. I've enjoyed your company."

Darryl was certainly fun to be with. Although Catina felt there was still a lot about him she didn't know, he was different from any other man she'd ever met. Polite. Funny. Refined. Yet something deep within her warned her not to get serious about anyone again. She'd already been hurt too many times.

Chapter 13

That night, Darryl called Catina and asked if she'd go out with him Friday evening to dinner and a movie.

The next morning at work, Catina informed Justine that she'd turned down his invitation.

"What? Girl, are you crazy? He's interested in you. Otherwise, he wouldn't have asked you out."

"I like him, but I'm not ready for another relationship yet."

Justine plopped down into a vacant chair in Catina's cubicle. "The two of you are so right for each other. Of all Evan's friends, Darryl is the one who suits you best."

Catina was becoming a little irritated at her friend. She knew her intentions were good, but Catina had been hurt enough and needed some time to heal. She stared Justine square in the face when she said, "You make it sound like I'm in the market for a man. Stop trying to push what you want off on other people."

"I know you've been hurt in the past, Cat, but how long are you gonna hang on to that?"

"It's my decision to make—not yours."

Justine could see the determination in her friend's face. "Okay. Okay. I'll back off."

"Thank you," Catina whispered as she batted her eyes and nodded her head.

As Evan and Darryl prepared to take their trucks out on the road to make their soda deliveries, they chatted in the men's locker room.

"Man," Darryl said, "I really like her, but I don't think the feeling's mutual. I thought it was till I called her last night and asked her out, and she turned me down."

"You think just 'cause she said no the first time you asked her out, that means she doesn't like you? Man, it has been a long time since you asked a girl out. When's the last time you went on a date?"

"I don't know. A year, maybe."

Evan spun around quickly to face his friend. "A year! Are you serious?"

"Yeah," Darryl chuckled. "I just haven't found anybody I'm interested in. All the sisters at my church are already spoken for. I don't do leisurely dating. Man, I'm eight months older than you, and you been married five years and now you're planning to start a family. I'm ready to settle down with a good Christian woman and maybe have some little Darryls running around one day."

Evan pretended to choke up and shed fake tears. "You growing up, man. I'm proud of you. Real proud."

Darryl swatted his friend's cap off his head. "Get outta here."

The two friends laughed as they made their way to their trucks.

★ ★ ★

As soon as Shayna pulled into the driveway and saw Justin's car, she knew she was not going to like what she saw. It was a few minutes after noon. She wasn't feeling well and had decided to come home during her lunch break to lie down. A loan officer at one of Savannah's largest banks, she had to be back at two to go over an application with one of her clients, and had thought a quick rest would do her good.

When she walked into the bedroom, she found Justin lying in bed. A few days ago, they'd gotten the official news that he was being let go from his job. After the Wilders threatened to sue the restaurant, Manuel had given Justin his walking papers.

Shayna called his name several times before rousing him. "Baby, I thought you had some interviews today. Why are you home so early?"

"Hey, baby. What time is it?"

"It's a few minutes after twelve."

"Midnight?"

A little irritated, Shayna answered, "Noon. Justin, would the sun be shining if it was midnight?"

Justin raised up a bit, peered toward the window and chuckled lightly as he said, "Oh, yeah."

Not finding her unemployed husband the least bit amusing, Shayna repeated, "I thought you had some interviews today."

Plopping his head back down onto the pillow, he said, "Yeah. I did."

"Well, what happened?"

"Shay, nobody's gon' hire me after what happened at the restaurant. Everybody knows about it. If they don't recall right away, as soon as they see my face they remember.

During the interview, they start acting a little fake. That's a sure sign they're not gon' hire me."

With her arms folded across her chest, Shayna stared down at him. "You don't know that. What about your interview today at one?" She checked her watch. "Don't you need to be leaving for it? And don't you have another one at four?"

"I cancelled 'em."

Shayna's eyes grew huge. "You what?"

"What's the point? I don't stand a chance."

Shayna's heart went out to Justin. He was losing his confidence, and it scared her beyond words. Sitting down on the side of the bed, she said, "Baby, you're giving up. You can't do that. It's only been a few days. You'll find a job, but you have to think positive."

As Justin pulled Shayna down so he could plant a kiss on her lips, she caught a whiff of alcohol in the air between them. "Have you been drinking?"

"I just had a couple o' beers. I swear. That's all."

Jumping up from the bed, Shayna screamed, "You promised me you wouldn't do this again!" When he'd come home intoxicated the day he'd been fired, she had let him know in no uncertain terms that she would not tolerate his drinking. "And of all times for you to be getting drunk, why now, when you need to be out looking for a job?"

"I'm not drunk. I'm trying to find a job. It's not my fault nobody'll hire me."

Suddenly, an intense wave of nausea struck Shayna. She made a dash for the bathroom and fell onto her knees in front of the toilet. As she threw up, Justin jumped off the bed and ran to her side.

Placing a cautious hand on his wife's back, he leaned forward and asked, "Baby, what's wrong?"

Not able to speak, Shayna attempted to push him away.

Justin sat on the side of the tub, staring at her, concern in his eyes. When she was done, she brushed her teeth, grabbed a washcloth and wiped her face with some cool water. She was beginning to feel a little better.

Justin stood and helped her to the bed. "Are you okay now?" he whispered.

"I'm fine," she answered as she sank onto the mattress.

"Why didn't you tell me you were ill?"

"I got sick at work and came home to lie down for a few minutes. I'm fine now, but I'm going to rest for a while. I have a client coming in at two, and I've got to get back to the office before then." But when Shayna bent over to take off her shoes, she was attacked by a dizzy spell.

Justin firmly stated, "Don't try to get up." He quickly went around to the other side of the bed and pulled back the covers. Then he returned to his wife's side, removed her shoes and helped her settle underneath the sheet.

Shayna had never felt as horrible as she did now. Her frustration over him cancelling his afternoon interviews having subsided, she was relieved that he was home to take care of her.

Chapter 14

The next couple of weeks, things were extremely tense between Estelle and Roger. Though they were civil to each other, it was obvious to them both that it was all a pretense. Estelle's anxiety regarding her marriage was causing her to eat more than usual, and she felt bigger than ever. She didn't care how huge she got. Roger wasn't attracted to her anyway.

Justine had noticed that her mother had not seemed at all like herself lately, and decided to ask her about it when she and Evan visited her parents after church one Sunday. Her father had taken Evan out for a ride on the boat, and the two women sat on the swing in the screened-in porch.

"Mama, are you all right?" Justine inquired.

Estelle's response was short and to the point. "Things aren't going too well between me and your daddy."

Justine let out a chuckle. "Oh, Mama, you always say that, but…"

Estelle looked into her daughter's eyes. "It's different this time. I don't know if we're gonna make it. I've tried, and I'm so tired."

The last time Justine had seen her mother look so serious was fifteen years ago, when she'd told her and Justin that they were leaving their father. Justine grew afraid for her parents. How could they have overcome something so horrific, only to end up years later in a similar situation?

"Are you saying you and Daddy are gonna separate again, or worse, divorce?"

"I don't know what's gonna happen. I just want you to be prepared."

"Have you told Justin?"

"Not yet. It's not the kind of thing I wanna tell him over the phone. I guess because you live so close and we see you all the time, I had to tell you."

Justine put her arm around her mother and leaned her head against her shoulder. "I'm sorry, Mama. I know you've been unhappy for a long time. I guess I just never thought it'd come to this—again."

"Neither did I, baby, but that's how it is sometimes."

As soon as Justine and Evan got home, Justine informed him that she was going to bed.

He grabbed her gently by the arm as she turned to walk away, and pulled her into his arms. "Are you okay? It's only eight-thirty. You were awfully quiet on the way home."

"I'm just tired." Justine felt she should share with her husband what her mother had told her. However, thinking about it was hard enough. Saying it out loud would probably make it too real.

Evan reminded her, "My appointment with the fertility

doctor is tomorrow. I wish you'd change your mind and at least come with me—you know, for moral support."

Justine couldn't deal with Evan's trip to the doctor on top of what her mother had just confided to her. As his wife, she knew she should be there. But how could she accompany him, all the while knowing why she'd hadn't become pregnant?

A thought occurred to her. If the doctor did find a problem with Evan, she could discontinue taking the birth control pills and be free of her guilty conscience. The very idea mortified her. Perhaps she would go. She owed Evan that much. It wouldn't pose a problem for her to simply call her supervisor in the morning and inform her that she and Evan had some personal business to tend to. Better yet, she could go ahead and place the call tonight before she went to bed.

Justine heard herself saying, "I'll go with you."

Evan tucked her hair behind her left ear. "I wish you'd reconsider and talk to him while we're there about you getting tested."

Gently wiggling free of her husband's embrace, Justine reminded him, "Evan, we already talked about this. I'll see my own doctor."

"I know. It's just that this one is a fertility specialist."

"I'd rather see my own doctor."

"Okay. Okay." Giving her one of his most flirtatious grins, Evan added, "Want me to tuck you in bed?"

Justine's usual response was a resounding *yes*. But not tonight. "That's okay." Planting a kiss on his cheek, she uttered a quick, "Good night," before turning to walk away.

Reaching for her arm again, Evan turned her around to face him. "What was that?"

"What?"

"Can't I at least get a more passionate kiss? I know you can do better than that. You're not my sister, you know."

Justine managed a smile. "You're crazy." Then she fell into her husband's arms, delivering a tempestuous kiss.

"Ah, now that was better," he said awhile later.

Justine grinned. "May I go now?"

"Sure. Good night. Love you."

"Good night. Love you, too."

Later that night, Evan awoke to what sounded like sobbing. He immediately rose up and turned toward Justine. "Honey, are you crying?"

As her body began to tremble, Evan tenderly said, "Come here," and drew Justine into his arms. "Baby, what's wrong?"

"Mama…and Daddy…may be separating…or divorcing."

"What? Who told you that?"

"Mama."

"When?"

"This afternoon while you and Daddy were out on the boat."

"Your dad didn't say anything to me about it. Are you sure that's what she meant?"

"That's what she said."

"Mom and Dad fuss all the time. Look how long they've been with each other. They'll always be together."

"Things happen in marriage that you don't expect, and they can make people change the way they feel about one another."

Justine considered telling Evan about the time her parents had separated when she and her brother were younger, but it was a road she had no desire to travel. Sometimes the only way to make the pain diminish was not to talk about the situation.

She wished she could control her mind and not ponder

over it. It didn't matter that she was now a grown woman. People were sadly mistaken, thinking that divorce only hurt young children. She was living proof that it was quite the opposite.

Justine sadly added, "Just as quickly as people can fall in love, they can fall out of love."

Placing his hand against her wet cheek, Evan said, "I don't believe that. When two people truly love each other, nothing will ever make them fall out of love."

"You're such an optimist. That's one of the things I love about you."

"Well, it's how I feel in my heart. You and I will never end up like that. I'll always love you no matter what, and I hope you feel the same way about me."

"I do." There was so much that Justine wanted to tell Evan, but some things were better left unsaid.

Shayna was so excited. She could hardly wait to share the news with Justin when he got home from his job interview. She had a good feeling about the restaurant where he was being interviewed today. This would be just what he needed to get back on his feet so they could get on with their lives, especially now that they had a baby on the way.

Feeling especially good today, Shayna prepared one of Justin's favorite dishes that he'd taught her to cook—chicken scaloppine with linguine Alfredo. She dimmed the lights in the dining room and lit the three huge lavender-scented candles of different heights that served as the table's center-piece. The sparkling red, nonalcoholic grape juice was chilling over ice.

When Justin hadn't arrived home by nine o'clock, Shayna dialed his cell phone number and left a brief message on his voice mail. When he still hadn't walked through the door at midnight, she put the food and wine away. She'd lost her appetite, so she went to bed without eating.

It was after two in the morning when Shayna felt Justin slipping into bed beside her.

His speech slurred, he asked, "Baby, you sle-sleep?"

Turning to face him, Shayna yelled, "Where have you been?"

"Baby, don't be ma-mad."

"Mad! I passed mad five hours ago. I'm psychotic, and if you don't get outta this bed right now, you're gon' see a side of me you ain't never seen and won't want to see again."

Despite his drunken state, Shayna's split personality caused Justin to stand up straight as a board. "Can I ju-just talk to you?"

"Didn't I just tell you…"

"Okay, baby, I'm go-going. Where you want me t-to go?"

Sitting up quickly in bed, Shayna shouted, "Where do I *want* you to go? Do you *really* want me to answer that?"

Justin answered, "No, I don' think so," and staggered out of the room.

The next morning, Shayna wrote a note to Justin before she left for work and taped it to the master bathroom mirror.

We need to have a serious talk when I get home this afternoon. So whatever you have planned for today, please stay sober because for what I have to say to you, I need you to have a clear head.
Shay.

Justin noticed that when she'd signed her name on the note, she'd left off the hearts she usually drew underneath her signature. He was a ball of nerves all day long. It had been a little over three weeks since he'd lost his job at

Southern Comfort, but it felt like three months. He still hadn't been able to secure another job as a chef. He was tired of going on interviews, only to have people turn their noses up at him. Was Shayna looking down on him, too, because he'd lost his job, even though it wasn't his fault? Did she want a divorce?

Despite his desire for a drink, Justin managed to grant his wife's wish of sobriety. He knew he was in the doghouse as far as Shayna was concerned. He appreciated her support and encouragement, but she had to understand that every now and then he needed something to help eradicate the stress he was under.

When Justin greeted Shayna later that afternoon as she walked through the door, all her hostile feelings for the man she'd married dissipated. The kind, funny gentleman she'd fallen in love with greeted her with a kiss and embrace that convinced her she meant the world to him.

As they sat down in the living room to talk, Justin said, "I found your note. I know I've been a jerk, and I'm sorry. I know you're upset that I haven't found a job."

"I'm not upset because you haven't found a job. I'm upset because you've giving up on yourself and us. I know how much you love being a chef. It's good to have a job that you enjoy, but until someone will give you a chance at what you take pleasure in, you're gonna have to start looking elsewhere and take what you can get, no matter what type of job it is."

"I know. You're right. I want to be a chef, but I'll start looking outside of culinary arts, too."

Now for the hard part. Shayna slowly shook her head. "I don't like you drinking the way you do—not to the point of intoxication. I'm asking you to stop. If you can't drink without getting drunk, then you have a problem, and I can't stay with you if it continues."

Justin hung his head. "Shay, I don't have a drinking problem. I admit I've overdone it a few times, but only because I've been under a lot of stress since I lost my job." He looked at her, his dazzling brown eyes begging for understanding. "You can understand that, can't you?"

"I understand you're stressed out, and I'm here to help you. I'll do what I can, but I can't do anything for you that you won't do for yourself. From now on, what you do doesn't affect just you and me. I found out yesterday I'm pregnant."

Justin's eyes lit up the entire room, and he moved closer to Shayna and put his arm around her. "Pregnant? For real?"

"For real. Our baby's due February tenth. That's why I've been so sick lately." Taking her husband's hand in hers, Shayna said seriously, "Justin, I need you to be here for me and our baby. Please don't let us down. I know you're going through a tough time right now, but you gotta stay strong for us—for our family."

"I know. Baby, you know you can count on me." Justin thought about his childish behavior as of late. "I'm sorry for the way I've been acting."

"I know you are." Shayna took a deep breath. "Just remember I need you to be here for me and our baby. I love you so much. I want us to always be together."

"Nothing's gonna break us apart. You have my word."

Chapter 15

"Roger, come 'ere!" Estelle yelled, covering the phone's mouthpiece with her hand. "Roger!"

Roger came rushing into the den, where his wife was sitting on the sofa. "Stelle, what are you yelling about? I bet the whole neighborhood can hear you. What is it?"

Still holding the phone in her hand, Estelle jumped up and threw her arms around her husband, almost wrapping the telephone cord around his neck. She grinned from ear to ear. "We're gonna be grandparents!"

Justine and Evan immediately came to Roger's mind, before Estelle added, "Justin and Shayna are having a baby in February. Ooh, I can't wait to hold my grandbaby in my arms."

Roger quickly corrected his wife. "What d'you mean, *your* grandbaby? It's mine, too. Let me talk to 'em. Are they still on the phone?" he asked, reaching for the receiver. He took the telephone and sat down on the sofa to speak to the parents-to-be.

Half an hour later, Estelle dialed Justine's number. When her daughter answered, she yelled, "Did you hear the news?"

Justine laughed. "Yes. I just got off the phone with the happy couple."

"Isn't it wonderful?"

"Yes, it is. I'm happy for them. So is Evan," Justine added. She winked at her husband, who was sitting nearby.

When Justine ended the call, Evan smiled and said, "Mom and Dad are excited, huh?"

"Yes. I can't believe I'm gonna be an aunt."

Evan walked over to her and wrapped his arms around her. "Just imagine how you'll feel when you're about to become a mother. I'm happy for Justin and Shayna, but I'll be so glad when our turn comes. It's amazing how things work out, isn't it?"

Just yesterday, Justine and Evan had gone to the fertility doctor and were now awaiting Evan's test results. Although she felt uneasy having this conversation, she asked, "What d'you mean?"

Evan looked into her eyes. "Well, we've been married for five years and have been trying for a year to get pregnant. Justin and Shayna just got married in April, and she's already expecting. Like I said, I'm happy for them, but it just seems kinda unfair. They probably weren't even trying to have a baby, and it's happening so quickly for them. Seems like the harder we try, the harder it gets."

Justine's jaws tightened as she listened to Evan pour out his feelings to her. She wanted to give him a baby, but she couldn't. Alcohol and families didn't mix. Evan never used to drink until he and Darryl had started hanging out with Jarrod and Ray. Some people didn't understand that what might not be a weakness for them could very well be for someone else.

No, she'd never seen Evan intoxicated, but she always feared the time would come. When it did, would her beloved husband change into someone she no longer knew, like her father had? Though what her dad had done to their family was a thing of the past, the emotional scars were still evident.

How could Justine come to terms with her fear of what might happen, and give her husband the child his heart desired?

The following Monday, Justine accompanied Evan to his follow-up appointment. The doctor informed them that all Evan's tests had come back positive, indicating there was no reason he couldn't help produce a child. The specialist tried to persuade Justine to allow him or one of the members of his team to test her, but again she refused, stating that she would go to her gynecologist.

While Justine was relieved that Evan was healthy, she grew more anxious about the predicament she'd gotten herself into regarding the true reason she'd not gotten pregnant.

As another week came and went, Evan pestered her every day regarding whether or not she'd made her appointment. Justine's excuse was that she'd been busy and it had slipped her mind. Evan told her he couldn't understand how she could forget something so important.

Finally, she reluctantly made an appointment for a consultation. However, her doctor was booked until the following month, which in Justine's eyes was a blessing. When the office called the next day to let her know they'd had a cancellation for that week, Justine gladly rejected their offer of an earlier appointment. She needed as much time as she could get to prepare for the unavoidable.

She desperately needed to talk with someone about her dilemma. At lunch the next day, she told Catina all the unpleasant details of her family's past.

Catina said, "So you're afraid that Evan's drinking will cause him to turn his back on you and your children, the way your father's drinking did?"

"Yes. I don't like feeling this way, Catina, but I can't help it."

"Justine, does he drink *that* much? I mean, does he drink constantly, day in and day out?"

"No. Just a little every now and then."

"Then what's the big deal? He takes a sip every once in a while. That doesn't mean he's gonna turn into an alcoholic."

"My father did."

"What are you saying? Your father just started drinking occasionally and then became a heavy drinker?"

"Yes. That's why I've never had a drink of alcohol in my life. I don't know whether or not I'd be able to handle it, especially since alcoholism seems to run in my family. We have other relatives, too—aunts, uncles and cousins—who drink heavily. But that doesn't affect me like my daddy's drinking did. We lived with it daily. It almost destroyed our family.

"Mama left Daddy and took me and Justin with her. We didn't see or talk to him for eight months. Our family suffered during that time, not only financially, but emotionally. People can get hooked from trying something just one time. That's the way it is with drugs, from what I've been told and what I've read. A person tries it once, and Wham! they're addicted. I never wanted to risk getting carried away, so I chose not to drink at all."

"Well, Justine, why don't you just explain to Evan how you feel and why you feel this way? I think he'll understand."

"He knows I don't like him drinking."

"Does he know *why?*"

Justine looked away and mumbled, "No."

"Well, why haven't you told him?"

"It's in my past, Cat. My family and I don't talk about it anymore. I wouldn't even have told you if it weren't for the fact that I needed someone to talk to, and you're the only one outside my family I trust."

"Justine, you need to tell Evan. Haven't you learned anything from what I've told you about my past relationships with guys lying to me and cheating behind my back? You and your husband have been trying for a year to have a baby. You're taking birth control pills behind his back. He just found out there's no reason he can't produce a child with you. You've set up a doctor's appointment that you have no plans to keep. Girl, I love you, but you're telling lies on top of lies, and they're gonna catch up with you sooner or later."

With tears in her eyes, Justine looked at her friend. "I'm scared."

Catina reached over and touched her hand. "I know." After a brief pause, she added, "I have a suggestion. I know of a group of people, men and women, who meet once a week. Have you ever heard of Al-Anon?"

The name sounded familiar. "What is it? Some kind of support group?"

"Yes. It's for families and friends of alcoholics."

Before Catina could go any further, Justine said, as she shook her head, "Are you telling me I should go talk to a bunch of strangers about my family's personal business?"

Catina patted her hand. "Justine, let me finish. From what you've told me, Evan's not an alcoholic, but your father once was. You're still living with the pain of it. Look at what you're doing to yourself with your web of lies. You need the support of people who understand what it is you're going through."

Justine was quick to ask, "How do you know about this group?"

"I attend the meetings."

Her eyes grew huge. "What? Why would you need to go?"

Without hesitation, Catina responded, "My baby sister—who's only twenty-one years old—is an alcoholic."

Justine's eyes doubled in size. "What? Cat, why didn't you ever tell me?"

"Like you said, it's not something you can talk to just anybody about. I didn't know you were dealing with issues of alcoholism until now. But the group gives me the support I need in trying to deal with my sister's problem. It's not a quick fix by any means. We just help each other to cope with it. At Al-Anon, we learn that the only person we can change is ourselves. Until you accept that fact, you'll continue to suffer. My meeting is on Monday nights at seven-thirty at the senior citizens' center. Please come with me to the next meeting."

Justine shook her head. "No. I'm not going to some meeting and talking to a bunch of strangers about my family."

"You don't have to talk if you don't want to. Just listen. Maybe you'll hear something that'll help you."

She shook her head again.

"Justine…"

"I said no. Please don't pressure me."

"Okay. I respect your decision. Let me know if you change your mind."

"I won't change my mind."

Justine blushed as Evan winked at her from across the room. She was conversing with her mother, who'd stopped by to visit on her way home from the shop.

It was Friday, and Evan had been flirting with her ever since he'd gotten home. They'd decided to stay in tonight instead of venturing out. Evan's recent good news from the fertility doctor had him feeling extremely virile. Although Justine was still due to be tested by her own doctor, he was in a romantic mood and hoped that somehow they'd conceive a child tonight. He couldn't wait for Estelle to leave so they could go to bed.

When Justine went to the kitchen to get her and her mother something to drink, Evan followed. She was pouring soda into glasses when he walked up behind her, wrapped his arms around her waist and kissed the back of her neck.

Justine giggled. Though not really wanting him to, she playfully ordered, "Evan, stop. Mama's in the next room. You don't want her to see us, do you?"

Evan whispered against the soft nape of her neck. "We're married. Mom knows what we do."

Justine giggled again as she swatted at him. "Stop!"

Evan spoke into her ear. "I love Mom, but I'm ready to go to bed. I'm not trying to be ugly, but can you get rid of her?"

"No, Evan, she's my mama. I can't ask her to leave."

"Don't ask her. Just throw some hints. Point her in the direction of the door, open it up and say good-night."

Justine swatted him again. "You're awful."

"Well, I'm going to bed. Mind if I pick out a cute little nightie for you to put on before you join me?"

"That's fine, baby. Go ahead. I'll be there shortly."

"Okay. Don't keep me waiting long."

"I won't."

Justine returned to the den with the drinks, and Evan went to retrieve his favorite teddy for Justine to put on later.

He smiled as he pulled out the flirty ivory-and-pink lace-and-chiffon nightie. As he started to close the drawer, he caught sight of a flat plastic, octagon-shaped container. He reached into the drawer, took the object out and stared at it. When he opened it, he felt his heart sink. Justine's birth control pills. What were they doing here? She'd stop taking them a year ago. Or had she? He looked at the date on the prescription. She'd just gotten it filled last month!

Grasping the container tightly in his hand, Evan went over to the bed and plopped down on it, dropping the nightie beside him. His head started spinning as the rage within him rose to the surface.

Chapter 16

It was almost nine o'clock, and Justine had been discreetly trying to get her mother to make her exit. Suddenly, she got the feeling that someone was watching her. Turning slightly, she caught sight of Evan standing in the hallway staring at her. She'd thought he was in bed.

This time, though, the look he gave her wasn't playful, as it had been earlier. His gaze was so intense she almost didn't recognize him.

Justine shrugged her shoulders and held her hand out slightly, as if to question what was going on. Evan just stood there, his glare boring holes in her, before turning on his heel and walking away.

Even Estelle had noticed the cold way Evan had been watching Justine. "Is Evan all right? He doesn't look good. He seemed okay awhile ago. Maybe I better leave so you can check on him."

She'd noticed how frisky and flirtatious he'd been with

Justine earlier. Just because Estelle didn't have a love life with her husband didn't make her dense. It didn't take a rocket scientist to tell that love was in the air. Standing, she gave Justine a hug and a peck on the cheek before leaving.

Justine's heart was palpitating as she made her way to the bedroom. Why had Evan's demeanor changed so swiftly? She had no idea what could be wrong until she saw her nightie on the bed and her lingerie drawer open. *Oh, my God!* The pills. When she'd told him he could pick out a nightie for her, she'd totally forgotten about them. Had he found them?

Almost afraid to look, she strolled over to the lingerie drawer and began rummaging through it. That's when she heard a baritone voice behind her say, "Looking for these?"

Forcing herself to turn around to face the man who had uttered the words with a bitter bite, Justine could only gaze at him.

After walking slowly toward her, Evan took her hand and placed the pills in her palm. That's when Justine noticed the suitcase on the floor, which his body had been obstructing before he moved toward her.

Pain seized Evan's chest. The part of him that had trusted Justine without hesitation was suddenly gasping for air. Without saying another word, he turned around, grabbed the bag and left the room.

Justine ran after him. "Evan, what're you doing?"

"Leaving," he replied curtly.

"Where're you going?"

"I don't know."

"Evan, please don't do this. Don't walk away like this."

Ignoring his wife, Evan went out the door to his car in the garage. He threw his luggage on the front seat and went around to the driver's side, with Justine following his every move. As he was about to climb in, she grabbed his arm.

"Evan, please don't throw our marriage away."

"You already did that yourself." The truth pushed the pain so deep that Evan could feel his heart breaking. His eyes were like piercing arrows when he glared back at the woman he loved with all his heart and soul.

"I was such a fool!" he declared. "You made me jump through hoops. I was the devoted husband, and you made a complete idiot out of me."

"I can explain."

"You can explain for the rest of your life, but it won't change what you did." Jerking his arm away, Evan got in his car and shut the door.

As he started the engine and began backing out of the driveway, he heard Justine yell, "Evan, please don't go. I love you."

Evan leaned forward, stared at the floor of Darryl's living room and shook his head. "I can't believe she did this."

Darryl didn't know what to say. All he could do was listen.

"We've been trying for a year to have a baby, and all along she was making me think neither one of us could produce a child. Then she went so far as to let me think the problem was with me. Went with me to the fertility doctor, sat beside me in a show of support when all along she was taking birth control pills." Evan jumped up from his seat and began pacing the floor. "Man, how could I have been so stupid? She played me for a straight-up fool." After a slight pause, he asked, "You mind if I crash here for a while?"

"'Course not, man. Stay as long as you need to." Before Darryl could say anything further, the telephone rang. He answered it. Holding the receiver out to Evan, he whispered, "It's Justine."

Shaking his head, Evan said, "I don't want to talk to her." Grabbing his suitcase, he walked in the direction of Darryl's spare bedroom.

Speaking into the receiver, Darryl said, "Justine, he can't come to the phone right now. Can I give him a message?"

Justine sounded sorrowful when she asked, "Darryl, what did he tell you?"

Darryl had no desire to get in the middle of their dispute. Both Justine and Evan were his friends. He'd always thought the world of Justine, for she made Evan happy—until now. His voice was a soft whisper when he answered, "He told me what happened."

Justine attempted to explain. "Darryl, I love him. I know what I did was wrong, but I never meant to hurt him. You believe me, don't you?"

Darryl didn't want to discuss the topic. "It doesn't matter what I believe. It's Evan you have to convince."

Justine let out a brief sigh before saying, "Yeah, you're right. Good night, Darryl."

"Good night."

It was almost ten o'clock. Justine decided to go to bed. Evan was upset with her and just needed a little cooling-off period. No matter how small or big a disagreement they had, after they took a slight breather from one another, they always returned to their affectionate state. She felt confident that when she woke up in the morning, she'd find him lying beside her as always.

As Catina stirred the peppermint tea she'd just made for her and Justine, she thought about the stew her friend had gotten herself into. She had known her deception would catch up with her sooner or later.

When Justine had frantically called her early this morning,

Catina had promised she'd stop by before going into the office. Picking up the wooden serving tray, she made her way into the living room and set the tray on the coffee table.

Offering Justine a cup, Catina said, "Here, sweetie. Drink it while it's still hot. It'll help you relax." Catina carefully lifted her own cup and sat back before taking a sip. Eyeing Justine, she asked, "You okay?"

Justine answered sadly, "No."

"Just give him some time. He's hurting right now."

"He didn't come home last night, Cat. I thought he just went to Darryl's to get away from me for a few minutes—to cool off, then come back home. I called over there this morning and got the answering machine. When I call his cell phone, he doesn't answer. I keep getting his voice mail. He wouldn't even talk to me last night when I called him at Darryl's. I just can't believe he left like that."

Catina wanted to ask Justine what she expected him to do considering what had happened, but held her tongue. "Are you coming to the office today?"

Justine placed her cup back on the tray. "No. I can't concentrate on work with all this going on. I've gotta talk to Evan."

"Honey, maybe you just need to leave him be for the moment. I think he'll talk to you once he gets over the initial shock."

"I need to talk to him."

"What're you gonna say to him? Are you gonna tell him why you did what you did?"

"Yes. I'll explain it to him. He'll understand."

"Justine, do you really believe it's gonna matter to him why you did it?" Catina couldn't stop herself from saying, "It's done. What he's wondering is *how* you could do what you did. It's not gonna matter why."

Justine stared at her friend. "Catina, why are you saying this to me?"

Irritated, Catina stated, "I told you to talk to him about your feelings before this happened, but you wouldn't listen. Did you ever consider how he'd react if he ever found out by any other means besides your telling him? How do you think he feels? How do you think *you'd* react? Don't you think you'd feel betrayed?"

With tears in her eyes, Justine confided, "I know in my heart what I did was wrong, but I couldn't help it."

Catina's gentle tone returned. "I know, but that's no excuse. You should've been honest."

Justine stared at her in silence. All she could think about was how badly she needed to talk to her husband.

Chapter 17

As Shayna strolled into the kitchen, she caught sight of Justin standing at the door to the patio, sipping his Saturday morning coffee. A gentle August breeze caused the café curtains at a nearby window to ripple.

He still seemed depressed, and she was worried about him. It had been almost three weeks since they'd found out she was pregnant, and had their heart-to-heart conversation about his job situation. He'd finally secured employment at a local car dealership, after seeing an advertisement in the newspaper. Although he had no experience in the field, the owner felt confident that Justin's sociable personality would make him a great salesman.

Shayna walked up beside him and placed her hand on his back. "Hey, why don't we go out tonight to celebrate your new job?"

Justin just kept staring out the window. "What's there to celebrate? It's just a stupid gig selling cars."

"Honey, you should be happy. It's a job. It's a lot more than what some folks have."

Justin turned abruptly and brushed past Shayna. She stared at him as he rinsed out his cup, then placed it in the dishwasher.

"Why are you so angry?" she asked in bewilderment.

Slamming the dishwasher door, Justin yelled, "I'm not angry!"

"Then why are you yelling?"

Justin threw up his hands. "Shayna, just drop it. Okay?" Then he walked away.

Shayna didn't understand her husband. They were going to be parents, and he'd finally found a much-needed job. Now they'd be able to take care of their child and each other. What more could he possibly want?

As Justine pulled her car into Darryl's driveway, her heart skipped a beat when she saw Evan's maroon Pathfinder parked there. She jumped out and ran as fast as she could to Darryl's front door, noting the shocked expression on his face when he opened it.

"Hey, Darryl. Can I speak to Evan?"

Stepping back to allow her entry, he responded, "Hey, Justine. S-sure. I'll let him know you're here."

"Okay. Thanks."

"Have a seat. I'll be right back."

Justine was too nervous to sit, and just paced between the sofa and the coffee table. She could hardly wait to speak to Evan so he would come back home. However, her hope faded when she spotted Darryl with a worse look on his face than when he'd opened the door.

She rushed over to him. "Can I go in and talk to him?"

Darryl hated being the bearer of bad news. "I'm sorry, Justine. He says he's not ready to talk to you."

Justine's jaw dropped. How long did Evan plan to punish her? He was never one to stay angry long. After he'd had a cooling-off period, he was fine. "What?"

"He won't come out."

Brushing past Darryl, Justine stated, "Well, I'll just go in and talk to him."

Darryl gently grasped her wrist. "I don't think that's a good idea."

Ignoring his warning, Justine shook off Darryl's hand and rushed through the house, opening and closing doors to every room she passed, with Darryl close behind her.

"Justine, don't do this. This isn't the way to get him back. Let him have his space till he's ready to talk."

Justine said nothing as she continued her search. Before she could open the next door, it opened briefly, then shut in her face.

Startled, Justine gasped, "Evan, I came to talk to you."

Evan replied through the closed door, "Didn't Darryl tell you I'm not ready to speak to you?"

"Ye-yes, he did, but we need to talk."

"No, we don't need to talk. You had your chance to talk a long time ago, but you didn't."

Justine sighed heavily. "Evan, can you just let me explain?" Turning toward Darryl, she asked, "Can we have a moment alone, please?"

When he turned to leave, Evan said, "Darryl, take Justine with you and show her out."

"Evan, I'm not leaving."

Darryl stopped in his tracks and turned around slowly. He hated being in this position.

"Justine, I came here because I needed to get away to clear my head," Evan called out, "and I can't talk to you right now. So will you just go? We've already got Darryl in the middle of our mess, and that's not fair. Why don't you just leave? I'll let you know if and when I'm ready to talk to you."

With tears welling in her eyes, Justine mumbled, "I'm sorry, Darryl," and ran to her car.

"Daddy, I need to talk to Mama." Justine's breathing was erratic as she spoke into her cellular phone.

"She left for the shop about fifteen minutes ago. What's wrong?" Roger asked.

Justine repeated, "I need to talk to Mama. I'll go by the shop. Bye." She ended the call before her father could say anything further.

As Justine drove to her mother's shop, she wondered how she could have let things get this far. When Evan had first found the pills, she'd had no desire to face him and admit what she'd done. Now she wanted to explain her actions, and he refused to talk with her. She'd never seen him as upset as he was now. The look of love he used to give her had been replaced with one of disgust. She'd messed up a good thing and would do whatever it took to get it back.

She pulled into the floral shop's lot, parked her car, jumped out and ran to the front entrance. When she pulled the handle to open the door, however, it wouldn't budge. Justine finally realized the shop wasn't open to the public yet, and she started banging on the door. By the time her mother let her in, Justine was frantic.

Locking the door behind her, Estelle said, "Justine, what's the matter?"

"Mama, I need to talk to you. I've made a terrible mistake."

Gently taking her daughter by the arm, Estelle escorted her to the office area. "Calm down. What'd you do? Have a seat."

She pulled up a chair for herself as Justine confessed her

betrayal of Evan. As Estelle listened, she couldn't believe that her daughter had done something so terrible to her husband.

"Okay, honey, calm down. You've gotta talk to Evan."

Justine cried, "He won't talk to me! I just left Darryl's house, where he's staying, and he still won't talk to me. Mama, I don't know what I'm gonna do. I love him. I don't want to lose him. I know I hurt him, but I was scared to tell him the truth. I didn't know how to tell him how I felt without making him feel bad. But now that he knows what I've been doing, I need to talk to him."

Estelle spoke slowly. "Justine, calm down. You've gotta give him time. Evan loves you as much as you love him. Right now, you've gotta give him the space he needs."

As Estelle listened to her daughter's sobs, she couldn't believe this was happening to Justine and Evan. Theirs was the last marriage she'd expected to get to the breaking point. She had long anticipated her own marriage dissolving, but not her daughter's.

Chapter 18

"Why don't you stay here tonight?" Roger asked as he handed his daughter the cup of hot lemon tea he'd made for her.

Justine sat back against the sofa and sipped the warm liquid, allowing it to trickle down her throat. "Thank you, Daddy, but I'll be okay. I need to get home. I have to be there when Evan comes."

Roger hadn't seen his daughter look this devastated in years. He didn't want to remember the last time he'd seen her in this state. When all the pain of years past flooded his mind, he felt a jolt to his heart unlike any he'd experienced in a long while.

Estelle interjected from across the room, "Your father's right. You should stay here tonight. As a matter of fact, you should stay here until you and Evan get things patched up."

"Mama, I just said I need to be home when Evan comes."

Estelle said, "Well, what if I stay with you at your house? I don't want you by yourself."

"I appreciate it, but I'll be fine. I'm just tired. I think I'm gonna go home and go to bed."

"Well, I don't want you driving by yourself. I'll drive you home in your car, and your father can come in ours so we can get back home."

Roger quickly interjected, "Yeah, we can do that."

Fifteen minutes later, they had dropped Justine off at her house. As they headed back home, Roger murmured, "How could Justine be so foolish? Lying to Evan like that."

His words immediately set the smoldering fire ablaze in Estelle's belly, one nothing could extinguish. "How could she be so foolish? Do you know *why* she lied to him?"

Roger looked at his wife. "She said she was scared to tell him she didn't want to have any children yet."

"Yeah, that's what she said," Estelle snapped, "but do you know *why* she didn't wanna have children?" A voice inside her head warned her to shut up. They'd managed to put that part of their lives behind them. But the fire inside her continued to blaze.

"What's wrong with you? Why're you bitin' my head off? All I know is she didn't want to have children, and she was scared to tell Evan."

Her husband was an insensitive jerk. "Well, I guess just like she was afraid to tell Evan the truth because she didn't wanna hurt him, she didn't wanna hurt you, either, by telling you she doesn't wanna have children 'cause she's scared Evan's drinking'll get outta hand like yours did, and her children'll suffer 'cause of it." There. Estelle had spoken the words at a very rapid pace, without stopping even once to catch her breath.

The air inside the car grew so quiet they could've heard

a pin drop. She suspected that her words had hurt Roger, since he offered no comment. Regardless, their daughter was still carrying around the pain of what his neglect had done to their family years earlier, and Estelle hadn't expected or appreciated his unsympathetic comments regarding Justine's dilemma.

The pain Roger felt stabbed at his heart. Estelle's words had hit him like a ton of bricks. When he'd least expected it, his past had come back to haunt him. He would give anything for his imprudence not to have happened at all.

The following Saturday after work, Catina took Justine out to eat in an effort to get her mind off her problems.

Catina eyed the portabello mushroom steak on her friend's plate as she gave Justine a smile. "You know, this restaurant ain't cheap. If I'd known you weren't gonna eat, I could've just taken you to McDonald's or Wendy's and got you a ninety-nine cent meal."

Justine's eyes were filled with sadness as she looked up at her friend. "I'm sorry, Cat. I just don't have much of an appetite. I'll take it home. I can eat it tomorrow."

Catina understood. "I know. I'm teasing you. I guess I'm just being selfish. I miss the old Justine."

Justine admitted, "I miss her, too." Quietly, she added, "I miss Evan, as well."

"I know you do."

"He still won't talk to me."

"Justine, can I ask you something?"

"Sure."

"Now, don't get mad. But you really need to think about what I'm going to ask."

"What is it?"

"If you and Evan get back to—"

"What d'you mean, *if?*"

Catina raised her hand. "Just let me finish. If you and Evan get back together, as long as he likes to hang out with his friends and drink, are you gonna change your mind about having children with him?"

Justine didn't understand why Catina was asking her such a ridiculous question. "What?"

"Evan wants to have children. If he doesn't stop drinking altogether, like you want him to, how are you gonna deal with the issue of the two of you having children? One or both of you have to change your views. What if he doesn't change his? How are you gonna handle it?"

"I don't know. All I know is I love him, and I want us to be together. But I'm still not willing to take a chance on having children and have them go through what my brother and I went through."

"So when you do talk to him, is that what you plan to tell him?"

"Yes, I've gotta be honest with him. I still think he'll see my point and stop drinking."

"What if he doesn't? What are you gonna do then?"

Justine began to rub her temples. Opening her purse, she pulled out a bottle of Tylenol and poured two tablets into her palm. Then she popped them into her mouth and washed them down with water, as Catina sat there glaring at her.

Frustrated, Justine asked, "What?"

"Are you gonna answer my question?"

"What was the question?"

"If Evan doesn't stop drinking like you hope, what are you gonna do?"

"Catina, I don't know. Why are you bombarding me with all these questions?"

"Because they're things you need to think about if you want your marriage to work." After a slight pause, she added, "I'm going to an Al-Anon meeting Monday night if you'd like to come."

Justine rolled her eyes. "Oh, here we go again with this. Catina, how is Al-Anon supposed to help my marriage?"

"You can meet with people just like yourself who are trying to deal with the issues of alcoholism. Your marriage is at the breaking point because you're still suffering from the pain of your father's alcoholism. You've been carrying it around with you all these years, to the point that you're afraid to live your life with your husband because of the fear that any children you might have may end up suffering like you and your brother did. The only people we can change are ourselves," she repeated. "Al-Anon will help you to not only see that but do it."

Justine didn't say anything. She felt lost without Evan. What if he didn't change his views about drinking?

She felt very strongly about her own opinions.

Could she possibly change after all these years? At this point, she was willing to try anything to get her husband back.

"Justine, I can't believe you're even considering this," Estelle stated with disdain. "How could you think about airing your dirty laundry in front of a bunch of strangers? Your father and I have our problems, but I don't go shouting them to the world. The only people I talk to are you and Gloria."

As Justine dried a plate, she asked, "Mama, why are you so mad? If it can help, why shouldn't I go?"

"It's indecent. Strangers sitting around talking to each other about personal matters."

Justine placed the plate in the cabinet. "Mama, maybe if

we'd talked about what happened to our family back then, we wouldn't be having some of the problems we're having now. Do you ever think about that?"

"Justine, everybody's got problems, but they don't go 'round telling 'em to every Tom, Dick and Harry they see."

"Mama, it won't be every Tom, Dick, and Harry. Catina says Al-Anon is a support group for families and friends of alcoholics, so everyone there will have something in common."

"Well, what if you run into someone you know? They may spread your business all over town."

"Well, Mama, if they go around telling people I was there, people will be wondering how *they* know I was there. Besides, Catina says the policy is they can tell whoever they want to that they attended, but can't mention the names of anyone else who went."

"Yeah. Like that's gon' keep somebody's mouth shut. Girl, do you know how many people are in trouble now for talking when they shouldn't have been? We see it every day on the news."

Justine thought of something funny. "Well, if that's what you're worried about, why don't you come and be my watchdog?"

Estelle gave Justine one of her serious looks. "Are you crazy? I'm not going."

"Why not? Are you still angry at Daddy for what happened? Things haven't been that great between y'all for a while."

Without any warning, Estelle whipped around to face her daughter. "Let me tell you something. What's between me and your daddy is between him and me and whoever else I tell it to, which as I already told you, is only you and Gloria. Don't be trying to get me involved in this mess."

Justine was flabbergasted. Her mother had never taken that tone with her, but she knew her mom well enough to let the matter rest.

Chapter 19

Justine nervously glanced around the room of the senior citizen's center, scanning the smiling, happy faces of the people who had come. The meeting began promptly at seven-thirty. Catina grabbed a book from her purse, opened it to the page for August 22, and handed it to Justine.

Different volunteers read passages from various Al-Anon publications, and everyone was given the opportunity to comment, if desired, on the material.

Justine had had no idea that so many people's lives had been affected by alcoholism. It had seemed to her that her family was the only one dealing with the awful "illness," as so many of the attendees kept referring to it. Over the years, she'd heard many people say that alcoholism was a disease, but she'd never agreed with that. In her mind, a person could will himself to stop drinking if he really wanted to. It was that simple. She couldn't listen to any more of this drivel. She raised her hand.

When called upon to speak, Justine said, "I have something to say. Y'all keep saying alcoholism is an illness. I disagree. If a person really wants to stop drinking, I think he can make up his mind that that's what he's gonna do and just do it."

A woman raised her hand. "I used to think that, too. But then I learned that an alcoholic can't control his drinking even though he—or she—may want to."

"It sounds to me like you're making excuses for 'em," Justine argued.

A male member of the group lifted his hand. When he was called upon, to speak, he said, "We're not making excuses for the alcoholic. Alcohol is an anesthetic. It dulls whatever pain the alcoholic is going through. It's his or her way of escaping pain. That's why they drink excessively, and this excessive drinking is what makes it an illness."

Justine shook her head in exasperation. "I still don't see how it's an illness."

The chairman of the meeting, a calm, professional-looking woman, offered Justine some reassurance. "It's okay that you don't see it that way," she said. "As mentioned earlier, many of us at one time felt the same way you do, because alcoholism affects not only the alcoholic but the family as well. That's why we have to concentrate on changing our *own* attitudes. Even if the alcoholic doesn't stop drinking, we can still become happier individuals."

As Catina drove Justine home after the meeting, she asked, "So what'd you think?"

Justine stared out her window. "It was all right. I still think all that talk about alcoholism being a disease is a bunch of mumbo jumbo."

Catina glanced at her friend. "Well, just keep in mind what was said about how a lot of us felt that way at one time."

Justine looked at Catina. "So how's your sister doing?"

"Better. She's in rehab. It's been hard on Mama. She's a single parent and always blaming herself, wondering where she went wrong. I remind her that she raised us both the same. Somewhere along the way, my sister got on the wrong track."

"It's sad. I hope she gets better."

Catina smiled. "Thank you. I appreciate it."

Justine was still perplexed. "If alcoholism is a disease and an alcoholic can't just will himself to stop drinking, why did my daddy stop suddenly?"

"Not everyone's the same. Just like with smoking. Some people do it cold turkey. Others do it gradually. Maybe that's something you should ask your father."

Justine shook her head. "Oh, no, I could never do that. My family and I never talk about that period in our lives. Mama got upset with me when I told her I was coming with you tonight. I asked her to come, but as you can see, she turned me down."

"Well, how about coming again next Monday?"

"I don't know. I'll think about it."

Justine wasn't quite sure what to think of the group's philosophy on alcoholism. Her mind drifted to her father. Had he been suffering something so painful that he'd needed to desensitize himself to it? Even though he didn't drink now, was he still agonizing over something injurious?

As Justine and her mother talked on the telephone later that evening, Justine shared details about the meeting.

Estelle said, "Justine, don't let those people fill your head with that nonsense about alcoholism being a disease. I hope you're not going back there."

"I don't know. I may go again next Monday."

"What for? So they can fill your head with more nonsense?"

"Mama, even though I don't agree with them, a lot of what they said made sense. Think about it. Daddy never drank until Grandmama died. He must have been hurting really bad from losing her."

"Justine, I know your daddy was hurting. It's only natural to feel that way when someone you love dies, especially your mother."

"I know, but remember how it happened? She went to the hospital to have surgery, suffered a stroke and never regained consciousness. She pulled through the operation with flying colors, complained of a headache, and the next thing we knew, she was dead. Imagine how Daddy must've felt to lose his mother so suddenly, without any warning. He had no time to prepare for it."

"Did they give y'all a psychology course while you were at that meeting?"

"What are you talking about?"

"You've been to one meeting, and you come back trying to analyze everybody."

"I'm not trying to analyze anybody, Mama. I'm just trying to understand what Daddy may have been going through—what he still may be going through." Justine remembered what Catina had told her. "Maybe I'll ask him."

"You don't need to ask your daddy nothing about that. It's in the past. We got enough to deal with as it is without you bringing up the past."

"Mama, I have to admit, being at that meeting tonight and hearing those people talk about what they're going through gave me a sense of relief. We never talked with each other about what our family went through. We just swept it under the rug as though it never happened. My marriage is in trouble because of it, and I need to get my feelings out in the open.

"The people at that meeting can relate to what I've been

through, and if my daddy is hurting, I need to know why. You're his wife. I can't believe you aren't curious, too, so you can try to help him. Maybe that's part of the reason he's the way he is. Maybe he's suppressing his true feelings about something. Have you ever sat down and asked him about it? I mean, tried to get him to open up his heart and share his feelings with you?"

Estelle didn't appreciate her daughter's accusations. "You hold it right there, young lady. You better remember who you're talking to. I'm the mama, not the other way around. I try to talk to your daddy plenty, but I don't have to answer to you."

"I'm sorry, Mama. I didn't mean any disrespect. For years, I've been suppressing my feelings. They've been bottled up for so long. That's why I couldn't talk to Evan about why I was afraid to have children. I love him so much, but I was too scared to tell him the truth, because I knew it would tear him apart to know that I felt he wouldn't be a good father because he drinks a little.

"So instead, I lied to him, and now I see that that's worse than just trying to talk to him about how I was feeling. I could talk to him about everything except that. I should have trusted him enough to know that he would've tried to understand so that we could've worked through it together. Now he doesn't want to see me or talk to me. I could lose him forever, all because I let fear rule my life." As she spoke, Justine started sobbing.

Estelle's heart went out to her daughter, and she felt bad for chastising her. "Justine. Baby, stop crying. Everything's gonna be okay."

"You don't know that, Mama, and neither do I."

Justine was right, but what was a mother to say? Should she give her child the cold, hard facts or give her some hope?

Justine asked, "Will you come with me and Catina to the meeting Monday? Please."

Estelle answered, "Justine, I'll do anything else you ask but not that."

Justine begged, "Please, Mama."

"I can't."

Wednesday afternoon, when Catina left the office, she decided to stop by the Super Wal-Mart. She was going to fix dinner for herself and Justine, and needed to pick up a few items. She was carefully examining the romaine lettuce when she heard a male voice call her name. When she turned toward the sound, she saw Darryl walking up to her.

Catina prayed he couldn't tell she was blushing. She really did like him and had regretted not going out with him when he'd invited her. Her eyes flashed with glee as she greeted him.

"Darryl, hi. How are you?"

"I'm fine. What about yourself?"

"I'm good."

"I see we both had to make the same pit stop."

"Oh, yeah." Before she realized it, Catina added, "I had to get a few things for dinner tonight. Justine's coming over."

Darryl awarded her a smile. "That's good. How is she?"

"She's hangin' in there. How's Evan?"

"Miserable."

Catina nodded. "I feel so bad for them."

"Yeah. Me, too."

Their encounter had suddenly become very awkward. Lamenting about their two friends had put a cloud over their otherwise enjoyable conversation.

Catina broke the silence as she gripped her shopping cart and started to push it. "Well, I guess I better be going."

It's now or never. The worst she can do is turn you down again.
"Hey, Catina."

She stopped and turned around. "Yes?"

Walking toward her, Darryl boldly stated, "I know I asked before, and at the risk of being rejected twice, I'm asking you again. Can we go somewhere Friday night? Maybe to eat or see a movie?"

Catina blushed once more, this time not caring whether or not Darryl noticed. "Sure, but I have to tell you, I don't watch R-rated movies. I'm even cautious about the PGs and PG-13s. Nothing with sex, violence, profanity or nudity."

Darryl replied, "Well, that pretty much limits the movies we can see."

He and Catina shared a laugh. She liked his sense of humor.

"Yeah, I know," she said. "Maybe we can find a decent G-rated movie to watch."

They laughed again.

"I'm sorry," Catina stated. "All kidding aside, I'd love to go out with you. But I must tell you, I'm an old-fashioned girl. I have morals and values that I plan to stick to. No inappropriate behavior." She bluntly stated, "So if you have a problem with that, now's your chance to renege."

Darryl responded in an equally serious tone, "No, I don't have a problem with that. My sentiments exactly."

They both broke out in broad grins.

Darryl continued, "I'll call you tomorrow. Then we can talk further about what we're gonna do and what time I'll pick you up. Is that okay?"

"Sure."

"Okay. Bye."

"Bye."

As they went their separate ways, they were both thinking about how the other seemed different, in so many good ways, than anyone they'd ever met.

Chapter 20

"Who's the guy?" Justine asked as she spread honey butter on her yeast roll.

Catina eyed her friend. She had not planned to mention her and Darryl's upcoming date, as Justine was suffering so much from her and Evan's separation. Although she was eager to share her joy, Catina felt compelled to keep quiet. Of course, it was now obvious that her broad grins all evening had aroused Justine's suspicions.

"What guy?"

Justine smiled as she sliced her fork through the succulent piece of fish her friend had prepared. "The one you're in love with."

Catina blushed. "I'm not in love."

"Then what is it? I know something's going on that you're not telling me. You're glowing like a neon sign."

Catina giggled. "No, I'm not."

"Yes, you are. Who is he?"

Catina took a bite of her Caesar salad, choosing not to respond to her friend's inquiry.

"Come on. Tell me. Who is he? Why are you being so secretive?" Justine's smile lit up the room. "It's Darryl, isn't it?"

Catina was bursting at the seams as she tried not to act like a giddy teenager. She rocked forward and yelled, "Yeah!"

Justine exclaimed, "Oh, I'm so happy for you guys."

Catina put up her hand. "Wait a minute now. It's not like we're engaged or getting married. We haven't even been out yet. We bumped into each other at Wal-Mart this afternoon. We talked a few minutes, and he asked me to go out with him Friday."

Justine screamed, "That's terrific! You've gotta let me help you get ready for your date."

"Well, Justine, it's not like I've never been on a date before."

Justine made a face and playfully eyed her friend. "I know, but you could use a little help in the what-to-wear department."

Catina playfully rolled her eyes, knowing quite well what Justine was implying. "I beg your pardon."

"You can beg my pardon all you want to. You know you dress old-fashioned. If I told you once, I've told you a million times to stop wearing those lil' grandma dresses down to your ankles. Show some leg, girl."

"You are *crazy*." Catina laughed harder as she recalled telling Darryl she was an old-fashioned girl. She supposed that compared to most, she was conservative, but she was extremely cautious about carrying herself like a respectable lady.

Justine broke into her thoughts. "Did Darryl say anything about Evan?"

Catina eyed her friend sympathetically. "Just that he's miserable."

Justine's mood suddenly turned despondent. "Oh."

Catina placed a piece of the broiled, seasoned tilapia in her mouth. "What's the matter?"

"Miserable means he's still hurting over what I did."

Catina touched Justine's hand tenderly. "Sweetie, it's gonna take time for him to get over it, but you guys love each other, and I believe you'll get through this."

"You really think so?"

"I do."

Justine prayed her friend was right. She missed Evan terribly and could hardly wait for them to be back together again.

"How do I look?" Catina asked Justine when she let her friend in Friday afternoon.

Justine disapprovingly eyed the plain black dress she wore. "Catina, I told you I was coming over to help you get ready. Why are you wearing black? You going to a funeral? Girl, you need to take that thing off and put on something bright and pretty. Mama always told me black'll catch everything but a man."

Catina burst into laughter. "I'm not trying to catch a man. Besides, I like this. What if I just throw a colorful scarf around my neck?"

"Why don't you just take that ugly thing off and throw it in the trash while I look through your closet and see if you've got anything decent in there to put on? I knew I shoulda brought you something from my closet. Girl, the only thing you gon' catch in that getup is a hard time."

Catina laughed as she followed Justine into her bedroom. "And I thought you were my friend."

"I am your friend. Only your worst enemy would let you leave here wearing that thing you've got on." Stepping into Catina's huge walk-in closet, Justine said, "Okay. Let's see what you have in here."

As she rummaged through the contents, she found various items that still had tags on them. "Catina, you've got some gorgeous clothes here. Some of 'em still have tags. Why don't you ever wear 'em? Did you just buy them?"

"No, I didn't buy those. Mama bought them for me. She's just like you—always telling me I need to quit dressing like an old woman. I can't help it if I don't like this kinda stuff. What's wrong with what I have on?"

Justine eyed her friend's attire again before answering, "Girl, I told you to take that ugly thing off." She pulled a dress off a hanger and handed it to Catina. "This is pretty. Try this one."

Catina was hesitant at first. However, when she saw her reflection in her floor-length mirror, she was beside herself. She liked the way the asymmetrical pink chiffon skirt flowed against her legs. The lightweight pink sweater was a perfect match.

Justine said, "Now if you just had some pink shoes, you'd be set."

Catina pointed to a shoe box on the closet shelf. "Get that box there. Mama bought those to go with this outfit."

When Justine returned with the box, Catina slipped her bare feet into a pair of pink, two-inch slides.

Justine exclaimed as she bobbed her head, "Looking good!"

Catina blushed and took off toward the bathroom.

"Where're you going?"

"Be back in a minute."

When Catina emerged again, she had a pink fabric flower

pinned in her hair behind her left ear, like a beautiful Hawaiian girl.

"You are gonna knock Darryl off his feet. You look gorgeous."

Catina blushed again. "Thanks. I really like it. Thanks for your help." She hugged her friend.

"Well, I better be going. Your date should be here in a few minutes. Have a wonderful time."

"Thanks. I'll tell you all about it."

"You better."

As Justine drove home, she felt happy for Catina and Darryl. The two were made for each other. Her thoughts drifted to Evan. She contemplated stopping by Darryl's to try to talk to him again, but quickly changed her mind. He'd told her he'd let her know when he was ready to talk. She had to respect his wishes. She'd already done enough damage.

Justine was asleep when her telephone rang a few minutes after midnight. She was tired and considered letting the answering machine pick up. However, when she turned on the bedside lamp and saw Catina's name and number on the caller ID, she quickly answered.

Catina was full of excitement as she told her friend about her evening. Darryl was such a gentleman. She'd never met a man like him. He possessed all the qualities she desired in a husband if she ever decided to get married. Of course, she wasn't saying that things would get that far. She just couldn't believe a man like him actually existed.

As Justine listened to her friend go on and on about her evening, her heart swelled with elation that the two were so compatible.

When the telephone rang early the next morning as she

was getting ready for work, and she saw Darryl's name and number on the caller ID unit, Justine's heart did cartwheels. She knew it was Evan.

"Evan?" Justine didn't care if she sounded desperate. He was her husband. She loved him, and she wanted him home.

"Hey." Evan's voice was subdued. His spirit sounded crushed. "Can we meet somewhere for lunch today when you get off work?"

Justine felt butterflies in her stomach, just as she had when she'd first fallen in love with him. "Sure. You know I get off at twelve. Any suggestions on the spot?"

They made plans before ending the call.

Twelve o'clock didn't come soon enough for Justine. She couldn't wait to see her husband and be back in his arms. When she pulled into the parking lot of the restaurant, her heart skipped a beat when she spotted Evan's vehicle. She entered the building and the hostess led her to the table where he was already seated.

As usual, he stood and pulled out her chair, then sat back down after he saw that she was situated. She was happy to see that he was still considerate of her despite what she'd done. That was a sure sign that he'd be coming back home with her today.

After their orders had been placed, Justine wasted no time in saying, "Baby, it's so good to see you. I've missed you. How are you?"

He was pale. It also appeared that he'd lost some weight. However, he still looked good.

Evan's tone was laced with sadness as he slowly said, "I'm hurt and confused. I don't understand what went wrong with us. Where did I go wrong? I tried to be a good husband to you. What happened?" His eyes were wet with unshed tears when he looked at her.

Justine reached over and grabbed his hand. "Baby, I'm so sorry. I never meant to hurt you. I don't know where to begin. I allowed something that happened in my family when I was a teenager to come between us, but I can't talk about it here in public. It's too personal. Can't we just eat and then go home and talk?"

Evan didn't respond, but simply stared at her.

Chapter 21

As Justine and Evan sat in their living room together, for the first time since they'd separated, she told him of her family's painful past.

When she was done, all Evan could say was, "Why didn't you just tell me instead of lying to me?"

"I should have. I know that now. I love you so much, and I didn't want to hurt you."

Evan let out a sigh. "You think this hurts any less?"

"No. I'm ready to try to deal with the past so you and I can get back together and get on with our lives."

He stared at her as though she had gone insane. "Well, you may be ready, but I'm not."

"What d'you mean?"

"Justine, I can't just put this behind me and act like it never happened."

Her heart was beating very rapidly. She didn't like where

this was going. "Evan, we can work through this. Please come back home."

He shook his head. "I can't."

Justine stared at him, her eyes huge with bewilderment. "What are you saying?"

"I'm not coming back. I don't know if we can work through this. You destroyed my trust. After what you did, how can I ever regain it?"

A heavy sigh escaped Justine's lips. "Evan, you can't be serious. I made a mistake. We can work this out."

"It's not that simple. Right now, I feel like two cents. You made me feel worthless. You must have a very low opinion of me to do what you did. I think we need some more time apart."

Tears began to stream down Justine's face. "We don't need more time apart. We need to be together. I need you. I need you like I need the air I breathe."

"There was a time when I needed you in that sense, too. But I don't need anybody who's gonna tear me apart and make me feel like I'm nothing."

"Evan, that's not what I meant to do."

"Well, it's what you did. I'm telling you how I feel, and I can't change my feelings just 'cause you want me to." Evan stood. "I need to get the rest of my stuff while I'm here. I can't keep imposing on Darryl, so I'm gonna start looking for an apartment."

At his last statement, Justine quickly rose from her seat and rushed over to him. This sounded like a permanent arrangement to her. "You don't have to get an apartment. Come back home. This house is big enough for the two of us. If you need your space, I'll give it to you."

Evan shook his head. "No, that won't work." He walked toward the master bedroom, with her close behind him.

Justine cried a river as she grilled Evan. "How can you just throw away our marriage? Is this how much it means to you? Why are you doing this? Are you trying to punish me for what I did? How many times do I have to tell you I'm sorry?"

Evan said nothing as he gathered up more of his clothes and some personal items.

Justine screamed at him, "Answer me!"

He continued to ignore her and proceeded down the hallway with his things. She followed.

"Evan, please don't go. I'll do anything." Justine didn't care how much begging she had to do to make him stay. She wasn't concerned about how low she had to sink in order to get him back.

She followed Evan out to his car and shed more tears as he put the items in his vehicle. Before he could climb inside, Justine threw her arms around him and hung on tight as she buried her face in his back. It felt so good to be this close to him again. She had no desire to let go.

"I love you," she cried. "Please don't go. Please don't leave me."

Evan managed to get out of Justine's grip. He turned around, took her by her hands and walked her away from his vehicle. "I can't stay here. Now you need to get yourself together 'cause I'm not staying."

Justine knew he meant it. Somehow, when he walked back to his vehicle and climbed in, she managed to remain where he'd taken her. As soon as he pulled out of the driveway, though, she crumpled to the ground in a heap and cried harder.

On Monday morning, Shayna hummed baby tunes as she cooked breakfast and got ready for work. She felt happy again. Today was the beginning of Justin's third week of working at the car dealership, and in six months, they would be parents. She'd known if her husband put his mind to it, he could find a job.

Now that she was pregnant, Shayna seemed to want to eat everything in sight. She hadn't been able to wait until she'd finished cooking before she began eating, taking mouthfuls here and there of grits, sausage, eggs and toast. She'd eaten so much that by the time breakfast was ready, she was full. She did, however, leave enough for Justin.

"Honey," Shayna called out, as she neared the bed, "it's almost eight o'clock. You need to get up. I left your breakfast in the microwave. Hurry and eat so you can get ready for work."

When Justin didn't budge, she moved closer and shook him. "Justin, come on, sleepyhead. Time to get up."

He sleepily mumbled from underneath the covers, "I'm not going in today."

"What? Why not? Are you sick?"

No, he wasn't sick, but he could pretend to be so as not to have to listen to Shayna's complaints. "Yeah."

Shayna sat down on the edge of the bed. "What's wrong?"

"I just don't feel good."

"Well, is it a headache, a stomachache or what?"

Annoyed, Justin answered, "Shay, I told you I just don't feel good. Will you leave me alone?"

Shayna felt as if she would burst into tears. While she got ready for work, every now and then her lips trembled as she contemplated how Justin had snapped at her. She didn't understand what was wrong with him. He'd finally found a job, but he still didn't seem happy. Keeping her tears at bay, she uttered a silent prayer that their lives would soon return to normal.

★ ★ ★

Justine was quiet as Catina drove them to the senior citizen's center. She hadn't wanted to go to the meeting tonight, but she'd let Catina talk her into it.

Justine felt numb. She couldn't believe that Evan was not coming back home. Her mother had spent all weekend trying to console her. The one thing Estelle still refused to do was accompany her daughter to the Al-Anon meeting.

Justine hadn't been herself at work, either. She was usually very spunky and cheerful with her clients. Today, she had been there in body but not in spirit.

Catina talked all the way to the center but got nothing from Justine. Once the meeting began, the discussion got under way.

It wasn't long before Justine heard herself saying, "My husband left me recently because he found out I'd lied to him about something. He isn't an alcoholic, but my father was many years ago. I've been carrying around with me all these years the pain of what my father did to our family. Alcoholism wasn't discussed then like it is now, at least not in our family. We just tried to live with it as best we could.

"I allowed my fear of what my father did to affect how I dealt with my husband. Even though my dad is the one who had the drinking problem, sometimes I feel like I'm the one who has a problem. How could something he did affect me this way? I don't understand it."

A female attendee raised her hand. Her tone was empathetic. "You feel sick, too, because for years you've been suffering in silence from the effects of your father's drinking. But you can overcome it one day at a time."

After the meeting, Catina tried to get Justine to spend the night at her house. As much as she hated being alone, Justine felt the need to be in her own home. Although Evan was gone, she could still feel his presence among some of the items he had left behind.

She opened his closet door and stared at a few pieces of clothing that still hung there, then slid a jersey knit shirt from a hanger. The reddish hue, almost the color of chili powder, looked so good against his medium brown complexion. As she caressed her face with the shirt, her nostrils took in the soft aroma of the musk cologne he was so fond of wearing.

While tears spilled down her cheeks, Justine whispered, "I've gotta get him back, Lord. I know I was wrong, and I don't deserve him. Please help me to change."

Chapter 22

The next day, Justin seemed to be in a much better mood. He got up before Shayna and cooked breakfast. They kissed before heading out the door to start their day.

Shayna decided to surprise Justin. He'd been acting so despondent lately. Even though he seemed better today, she thought it was the perfect opportunity to stop by the dealership and take him to lunch if he wasn't with a customer.

When she didn't see him at his desk, she asked one of his coworkers nearby if she knew where he was. The peculiar look the woman gave her caused Shayna's heart to race.

The lady replied, "Justin doesn't work here anymore."

That's when Shayna realized his nameplate was no longer on his desk. She imagined he'd gotten fired again, but why? Was it because he hadn't come to work yesterday? He'd only missed one day.

The woman added, "He quit yesterday."

Without saying a word, Shayna left the building. Back in

her car, she tried to imagine where he might be. If she found him, she would wring his neck. Here they were, about to have a baby, and he'd just up and quit his job, without even sharing the news with her. What was he thinking?

Shayna quickly dialed his cell phone number. When she got his voice mail, it made her so angry she ended the call without leaving a message. She wanted to talk to him face-to-face.

Instead of going back to her office, she obeyed a voice inside her head that told her to go home. When Shayna saw Justin's vehicle as she pulled into the driveway, her temper grew even hotter. Stomping through the house, she looked for him, and finally found him in the master bedroom, lying across the bed on his stomach, fast asleep. His clothes were disheveled, and he looked a mess.

Without saying a word, Shayna pounced on top of Justin like a tiger aiming for its prey. Straddling him, she pounded his head and back with her fists. He came to and managed to flip her off him onto the bed.

"What the— Shay, what's wrong with you?"

Shayna dived back on top of him and started pounding him again. "You quit a job after two weeks, and here I am, pregnant. Are you crazy?"

Justin managed to get away from her and stood, his clothes more disheveled than ever.

Shayna jumped off the bed like a cat on the prowl. She yelled, "Get your things and get outta here now."

His eyes looked as though they were about to pop out of their sockets. "Baby—"

"Don't *baby* me. I said get your things and get out." Shayna pointed toward the door as fire blazed in her eyes.

Justin took a chance on taking a step toward his wife, and

reached out to her. "Baby, I know you're upset that I quit my job, but I'm a chef, not a car salesman."

Shayna pushed his hands away from her. "You're whatever you need to be to help take care of your family. I don't care if it's scrubbing toilets. If you think you gon' lay 'round here drunk and not work while I foot all the bills, you got another think coming."

Justin begged, "Baby, please just give me a little more time. I know I can find another chef's job. I just need some time. This has been hard on me, and you, too. I know it has. But I love you, and I love our baby. Just please give me another chance." He was now on the floor on his knees, clinging to her.

Suddenly, all her anger dissipated. Shayna leaned down and kissed the top of Justin's head before falling on her knees and wrapping her arms around him. She couldn't give up on him or them. It was like he said—he just needed a little more time.

On Saturday, Evan drove by the house. When he didn't see Justine's car, he decided to stop and pick up some more of his stuff. He was making his third trip out the door when he bumped into her coming home.

It tore Justine up to see his hauling more of his things away. "Hey," she said sadly, in greeting.

"Hey. I just thought I'd come and get some more of my stuff. I'll be outta your way in a minute."

"You're not in my way," she said mournfully.

Evan didn't respond but made his way to his vehicle and loaded in his things, then went back into the house one last time.

He was worried about Justine. She looked tired. He hated seeing her this way, but he couldn't just act as though nothing had happened between them. He loved her still. Perhaps that's why it hurt him so much to see her hurting. He didn't know if things would ever be the same between them. She had destroyed his trust.

"Do you need anything?" he asked.

She didn't have to think twice before answering dejectedly, "I need you to come home."

Evan wasn't about to go there. Disregarding her request, he took out his wallet, removed three hundred-dollar bills and offered them to her.

Justine just stared at him. Although he had ignored her heartfelt plea, she had no regrets about stating that she was in need of him. "I don't want your money. I want you."

Evan placed the money on the kitchen table and left before she could say anything else.

Estelle eyed Roger as he read the Sunday paper.

"I was thinking that since tomorrow's a holiday, and we don't have to work, maybe we could invite Justine and Gloria and Donald over for a barbecue or something. You know, just a little get-together since we're all off work. What d'you think?"

Her husband continued reading.

"Roger, did you hear me?"

He looked at her. "What?"

Estelle was so mad that she came close to blowing up at him. Instead, she repeated what she'd just said.

"Do whatever you want."

"What d'you mean, do whatever *I* want? I'm talking about the two of us—you and me—having our daughter and our friends over. Why can't you get involved sometimes? Why is that so hard for you to do? Here our daughter is going through one of the worst times of her life, and you

don't even want to be there for her. You are so selfish. Sometimes I wonder why I married you."

She'd done it again. Every time she tried to talk nicely to
Roger, she ended up getting angry and saying something
rash. She tried to heed Gloria's advice, but it just wasn't
working.

Roger cut into Estelle's thoughts. "Well, maybe I wonder
sometimes, too, why I married *you*. Do you ever think about
that?" Throwing his paper aside, he got up and walked away.

Roger's words had cut Estelle like a knife. Most of the
time, he just walked away when she started rattling off at
the mouth. Lately, though, he'd been coming back at her. If
his words hurt *her*, how did *he* feel when she tore into him?
Whether she was nice to him or harsh, she just couldn't seem
to get through to him.

Chapter 23

The Labor Day holiday allowed Justine some time with her parents and the Edmonds, and it also took her mind off Evan for a brief period.

As Estelle watched Justine and Roger team up in the back yard against Gloria and Donald for a game of badminton, she thought back to a time when the children were younger, before things had changed. They had been a close-knit family who spent time together in family and spiritual activities.

The next thing Estelle knew she was crying uncontrollably. Her contemplation of the way she and Roger used to be had tugged at her heart. She quickly dried her face with a paper towel and went about rinsing the tomatoes for the salad she was preparing.

Everyone was having a great time. They ate and played more badminton. Then Roger made a surprising move, offering to take them all out on the boat for a ride. Estelle was excited because Roger had never taken her out on the boat. He always acted as though he didn't want to be around her.

The boat ride was exhilarating. Roger seemed like a different person out on the rippling water. No wonder he liked it so much. Estelle just wished he would share this part of himself with her. This was the Roger she remembered of old. Out here, he opened up and showed more of himself to others, including her.

When they got back home, and everyone else left, Estelle said warmly, "I had a really nice time today."

Much to her surprise, Roger declared, "Yeah, it was nice."

"I think it did Justine a world of good."

"Yeah."

Now that they were home and it was just the two of them, Roger had shut down again. Estelle would give anything for them to express their love for each other the way they used to.

Evan had invited the guys over to his apartment complex on Saturday to go for a swim in the pool. Afterward, they went back to his apartment and sat around talking while the steaks cooked on the grill.

Although his heart was still breaking, Evan tried to be his usual jovial self around his friends, but it wasn't easy. Darryl joined him for a moment on the deck when he went out to check the steaks.

"Man, how's it going?" Darryl could see the unshed tears in his friend's eyes. He'd never seen Evan like this.

Evan flipped over the steaks with a two-pronged fork. "I'm hanging in there." He didn't want to talk about him and Justine. "How're you and Catina doing?"

Darryl grinned like a teenager in love. "Great. I really like her. She's not like any other woman I've ever known. She's got morals. She's a strong woman who stands up for what she believes in. She's the kind of woman I always prayed for."

Evan let out a bogus chuckle.

Darryl raised his eyebrows halfway up his forehead. "You're laughing, but I'm serious."

Evan sucked in a deep breath and held it a moment before releasing it through his nose. "Naw, it's not that. What you just said about Catina being a strong woman who stands up for what she believes in made me think of Justine." He paused before adding, "Be careful what you pray for 'cause you just might get it."

Darryl gave his friend's shoulder two quick pats. "I know it's hard on you. What you and Justine are going through. I've never been married, but I don't imagine it's always a bed of roses. Y'all had a good thing. She made a mistake. I know you're hurting, but from what you've told me, she wants the two of you to get back together. I'd give anything to have somebody in my life as special as she's been to you. That's how I feel when I'm with Catina. She makes me feel whole."

Evan wiped a hand underneath his eyes as he playfully sniffed.

Darryl grew concerned as he thought his heartfelt sentiments regarding him and Catina were causing his friend more heartache over his marriage. Placing his hand on Evan's shoulder, he gazed into his face and asked, "What's wrong?"

"Nothing," Evan said, grinning. Looking Darryl square in the eye, he added, "It's just that my little boy's growing up."

Darryl let out a loud laugh as he spun around. "Man, you're crazy."

Evan continued wiping away pretend tears. "I'm just so happy for you." Then he walked over, grabbed Darryl and threw his arms around him. "I love you, man."

Darryl laughed as he hugged his friend, then quickly pulled away, straightening his shirt. "Okay, that's enough of that. If Ray and Jarrod see us, they'll think we've gone crazy."

Finally, the steaks were done, and the fellows sat down to enjoy them, along with baked potatoes, grilled corn on the cob and yeast rolls. They were almost done eating when the telephone rang. When Evan got off the phone and returned with his car keys in his hand, Darryl asked where he was going.

"That was Justine on the phone. She's got a plumbing problem and needs me to come take a look at it. You guys can stay here. I'll be back as soon as I'm done."

Jarrod let out a yelp. "Man, you're crazy. I can't believe you gon' run over there after the way she played you. She was always looking down her nose at me and Ray, and all along, she was treating you like yesterday's trash. She got exactly what she deserves. Kicked to the curb, and if you got a lick o' sense, that's where you'll leave her. You're crazier than I thought if you go help that broad after what she did to you. Tell her to call a plumber."

Darryl and Ray knew that Jarrod had overstepped the bonds of friendship with his repugnant comments, especially at a time when Evan was feeling so low and dejected. The whole while Jarrod was talking, no one else said a word or cracked a smile. The next thing they knew, Evan had yanked Jarrod up by his shirt and had him plastered against the dining room wall like a fly that had met its demise with a flyswatter.

Evan said through clenched teeth, "I've heard enough of your mouth to last me a lifetime. It's none of your business what I do. She's not a broad. She's my wife. And if you ever disrespect her like that again or say anything negative about her, I will beat the crap outta you."

Jarrod looked scared to death at having Evan's hand pressing into his chest, holding his body against the wall. Hardly able to breathe, he yelped, "Man, I was just playing. Let me go."

Evan slowly released his grip, and Jarrod straightened his shirt.

"I'm all for joking and playing, but I have my limits. From now on, you don't joke about my wife. Remember that, and don't let it happen again." With that said, Evan strode out the door.

As soon as Evan was gone, Ray looked at Jarrod and slowly shook his head. "See what you did? You know he's stressed out about his marriage, and you just had to go there. Even *I* had sense enough not to say all that."

Jarrod said, "Y'all saw what he did to me. He's *crazy*. He threatened me."

Darryl and Ray simply shook their heads and dived back into their food.

Shayna became more and more frustrated with Justin as she sat at the kitchen table paying bills. She was trying to be a loving, supportive wife, but he had to hurry up and get a job to help with their expenses. She didn't know how much more she could take of him being jobless, but that wasn't the worst part. He was drinking more than usual. Every time she attempted to discuss it with him, he got upset and started complaining about how stressed out he was from not having a job. Well, he'd finally found one. Even though it wasn't what he wanted, he should have kept it.

She didn't know what else to do. Sometimes she thought about picking up the telephone and calling his parents or hers. She didn't think she could continue carrying the burden alone. However, when she thought about how everyone had cautioned her that she was too young to get married and how she and Justin should get to know each other better, she changed her mind. She hated for them to know they were right. She was feeling stressed herself, and it couldn't be good for the baby.

Justin popped into the kitchen and sat down. "Let's go out to eat tonight."

Trying to hide her irritation, Shayna replied, "We barely have enough money to pay bills, let alone go out to eat. We have food here. We'll eat at home."

Justin didn't appreciate her sarcastic response. He leaped out of his chair, picked it up and slammed it back down on the floor. "What're you trying to say, Shay? You saying I don't deserve to go out and eat?"

The crazed look in his eyes frightened her. She wondered if he'd been drinking again. She tried to choose her words carefully, as she didn't want to tick him off further. "That's not what I'm saying. We can't afford to go out to eat. We need to pinch our pennies, especially with the baby on the way."

Justin yelled, "You think I don't know that? I'm tired of you trying to make me feel guilty 'cause I lost my job. It wasn't my fault. You know that."

Shayna didn't want to argue with him, so she stood to walk away. Before she realized what was happening, Justin grabbed her by her arm and spun her back around. The hold he had on her arm was tight.

"Justin, let me go." When she looked down at her arm, she saw him ball his other hand into a tight fist. "That's it! You get your things and get outta here right now." Shayna managed to pull from his grasp and bolted away.

Justin followed her into the bedroom, where he saw her snatching his clothes out of drawers and the closet and throwing them on the floor.

"Shay, what're you doing?"

Shayna kept removing clothes as she spoke. "I saw you ball up your fist at me. You think you're gonna start hitting me? I tell you what you can hit. You can *hit* the *road*."

Justin walked over to her. "Shay. Baby, you know I'd never hit you. I was just trying to scare you."

"Well, mission accomplished. But you just scared your butt out on the streets, too, 'cause you not staying here. Get your stuff and get out."

"Shay, I know you're not serious."

Shayna turned toward him, the fury within her irritating her insides. "Do I look like I'm joking? Get your stuff and get out. If you don't leave right now, I'm calling the police. Either way you go, it's your choice, but you're leaving here."

Chapter 24

Sunday morning, when Estelle awoke, Roger was already up. Her heart dropped when she saw that he was about to go out. She had hoped to try to persuade him to do something with her today. Going out on the boat Labor Day and seeing how he had livened up had given her hope that they might spend a little time together. It had rekindled her resolve to try to make their marriage work.

When she saw him with his fishing pole, she knew he was going out on the boat. She'd never been fishing. She'd never had the desire to do so, but she would love it if Roger would teach her.

She had an idea. Maybe if she asked nicely this time instead of demanding, he'd take her with him.

"Hey, why don't I go fishing with you?"

"Stelle, you've never been fishing. You don't even know how."

"You could teach me. Can't we just spend one day doing something together for a change?"

"Fishing relaxes me. I'm not gon' be relaxed if I'm trying to teach you in the process. I'll take you another time."

Suddenly, Estelle's demeanor changed. She was tired of him making excuses for not spending time with her. "No, you won't."

Roger just looked at her.

"Don't you stand there and lie to me. I'm not some child you can tell what you think I wanna hear just to pacify me. Go on your lil' stinking fishing trip. I don't wanna go now, anyway."

Estelle called Justine when she thought she'd gotten home from church, and invited her to the mall and a movie. They were two lonely women, but had a good time while they were out.

When Estelle reached home later in the afternoon, she saw that Roger had returned. When she saw the boat, a feeling of exasperation raced through her. She climbed out of her vehicle and walked toward the vessel. For a moment, she just stood there staring at it. She hated it. All Roger wanted to do was take it out on the water and spend time on it. He petted and pampered it, spending more time with it than he did with her. She was tired of being at the bottom of his list of priorities.

Estelle felt as if she was in a trance when she went inside the garage, grabbed a two-by-four and went back to the boat. The rage within her exploded, so much so she wanted to smash it to pieces. This was his pride and joy, not her. This was his wife, the one he spent all his time with. She also imagined that if he *was* cheating on her, he probably took whoever it was with him on the boat. They got to enjoy it, not her.

Hit it! Don't hold back! Smash it to pieces! The next thing Estelle knew, she was pounding the two-by-four into the boat, leaving dents everywhere. She was so into her mission that she didn't see or hear Roger come rushing out the door, yelling at her.

Grabbing her, he screamed, "Stelle, what're you doing? Are you crazy?"

"Yeah, I'm crazy, and you better let go of me before I take this piece of wood and pound you over the head with it."

Roger managed to wrestle her to the ground and take the plank from her. He stood, not bothering to help her up. When he saw what she'd done to his boat, he felt like crying. "Look what you did! You're gonna pay for this!"

"I'm not paying for anything," Estelle roared as she made her way toward the house. Yelling back over her shoulder, she added, "Let your insurance pay for it. I'm sick of playing second fiddle to that thing and everything else you put ahead of me." She proudly walked away, feeling triumphant over a battle won.

Inside the house again, Roger began moving his clothes from the master bedroom closet to Justin's old bedroom.

Estelle yelled, "You think you're hurting me by moving out of the bedroom? We never did anything, anyway. How's a person gonna miss something they haven't had in years? You know what? I'm fed up with you and this sham of a marriage. I want a divorce."

An hour later, there was a knock on the door. When Estelle answered it, she was surprised and happy to see her son. However, she was getting some very bad vibes.

As she led him into the living room, she inquired, "Where's Shayna? Why didn't she come with you?"

Purposely ignoring his mother's inquiry, Justin asked, "Where's Dad?"

Estelle was glad it was dark outside. Perhaps Justin hadn't noticed the smashed boat.

"When'd he get the boat?"

"Back in the spring. Sit down."

Justin repeated, "Where's Dad?"

"I'll get him."

Estelle returned a few minutes later with Roger in tow.

Roger grabbed his son in a bear hug. "Hey, Justin. How you doing? It's good to see you. Where's Shayna?"

They sat down.

Estelle asked, "Justin, what's wrong?"

"Shay told me to leave."

Estelle's mouth fell open. "Why?"

Justin told his parents about how he'd lost his job at the restaurant. He left out the part about his drinking and quitting the job at the dealership.

Estelle was confused. "I didn't think Shayna was the type of woman who'd do something like this. It's not your fault you lost your job and haven't been able to find another one. She *is* pregnant. Maybe it's just hormonal. She'll change her mind. When I was pregnant with you and Justine, I used to get mad at your daddy all the time." A voice inside her head said, *You're not pregnant now, and you're madder than ever.*

"Well, until she does, can I stay with you guys?"

Estelle answered, "Of course you can." She had no idea how she and Roger were going to keep their marital problems a secret from their son, especially with Roger's things in the room that used to be his. Justin was bound to get suspicious when they put him in Justine's old room. Maybe they should just tell him. "You'll have to sleep in Justine's room, though."

"That's fine. But what's wrong with my room?"

Roger quietly responded, "I'm sleeping in it," before getting up and leaving the room.

Justin looked at his mother. "Mama, what's wrong? Did I come at a bad time? Why is Dad sleeping in a separate room?"

This wasn't the kind of thing a mother wished to discuss with her children, especially her son, but Justin was a grown man. "Me and your daddy had an argument this afternoon. I got mad and busted up his boat, and he moved to another bedroom."

Justin's eyes grew huge. "You did what?"

Estelle had to be honest with him. "Justin, a lot has happened over the last several months that you don't know about. Your daddy and I haven't been happy with each other for a long time, and I'm at the point where I want a divorce."

Justin couldn't believe what he was hearing. His parents' marriage had survived something that most marriages wouldn't have. "Are you serious?"

"Yes. That's how I feel." Estelle wondered if Justin knew about his sister and Evan. "Have you talked to Justine lately?"

"No. Why?"

"Well, she and Evan are separated."

Justin jumped up from his seat. "What? Why?"

"It's a long story, honey. I only told you 'cause I thought you should know before you talk to her. I'll let her tell you herself."

Justin couldn't believe that all three of their marriages were on the rocks.

The next afternoon when Justine answered the ringing of her doorbell, she couldn't believe her eyes.

"Justin!" she squealed as her brother threw his arms

around her and lifted her up in the air. "Wshen did you get here?"

"Last night."

"Where's Shayna?"

It seemed that lately those were the two million-dollar questions. As they entered the living room, Justin answered, "She's at home. I'm by myself."

"She and the baby doing okay?"

"Yeah, they're fine."

"Well, tell her I said hello when you get back. How long are you gonna be here?"

Justin hung his head as he quietly responded, "Indefinitely."

"What d'you mean?"

Again, Justin relayed the story about how he had lost his job. He explained that Shayna was upset with him and had evicted him from the house, but left out the other details.

"Oh, Justin, that's horrible. I'm so sorry. I know being a chef means the world to you. You'll find another job. Shayna'll come around."

Justin looked pitifully at his sister. "Do you think Evan'll come around, too?"

Justine stared at her brother. "How do you know about Evan and me?"

"Mama told me last night, but said it was a long story and she'd let you tell me yourself. Justine, what happened? I mean, I know how much you and Evan love each other. I never expected anything like this."

Justine honestly responded, "I did something foolish. I lied to him about our having children. He was ready to start a family. I wasn't, because of what you and I went through when Daddy was drinking, but I was afraid to tell him. He didn't know I was still taking birth control pills, and found them one night. That's when he packed his things and left. He said he's not coming home. He's got an apartment now."

"Are you guys gonna get a divorce?"

Justine immediately shook her head. "No. I want to make my marriage work. I don't want a divorce. 'Course, right now, I don't know how I'm gonna get him back. He's still hurting over what I did. I've been going to Al-Anon with a friend."

Justin looked puzzled. "What's Al-Anon?"

"It's a group of family and friends of alcoholics who meet weekly and share their problems and experiences with each other. The meetings increase their knowledge and understanding of themselves and the alcoholic."

"I don't understand. Evan's not an alcoholic, is he?"

"No, but the effect alcoholism in our family had on me is what caused me to do what I did. The problem goes back a lot further than when I started lying to Evan. My fear had me paralyzed to the point where I allowed it to make me behave irrationally. Although at the time, it didn't seem irrational to me. It made sense to do what I did to try to prevent the same thing we went through from happening to my children. Do you understand?" Justine looked at her brother, a questioning light in her eyes.

"Unfortunately, yeah." Justin wondered if his sister knew about their parents' situation, but chose not to mention it.

Chapter 25

The next afternoon, Estelle was alone in the shop when one of her best customers came in, smiling from ear to ear.

"Hello, Mr. Lewis. How are you doing today?"

"Wonderful," answered the beaming gentleman, who was in his seventies. "How are you?"

Despite her heartache over her unhappy marriage, Estelle put on her happy work face and answered cheerily, "I'm fine. What can I do for you this afternoon?"

The man placed both hands on the counter. "Well, me and the Mrs. will be celebrating our fortieth wedding anniversary this weekend, and I want to order one of your best bouquets of flowers and have them delivered to the house Friday. I've got a special evening planned, and I want her to get the flowers before we go out."

As Estelle listened to the man carry on about his wife and the celebration he'd planned especially for her, the distress she was experiencing from her own failing marriage ripped at her heart. Suddenly, she burst into tears.

The poor man didn't know what to do. "Estelle, what's the matter?" he asked.

She dashed from behind the counter and ran to the bathroom. Placing one hand on the sink and the other on her knee, she leaned over as her sobs came more loudly and frequently. She was so embarrassed. She'd lost it in front of a customer. She'd just run off and left him standing there.

Even a couple in their seventies had more romance in their lives than she and Roger. Here was a man and wife about to celebrate forty years of marriage. She and Roger weren't even going to make it to their thirty-eighth year. They had made it through one of the worse storms of their lives, only to hit another one and crash, with no signs of survival.

Estelle raised herself up and stared at her reflection in the mirror, praying silently. *Lord, what happened? What happened to my marriage? Is this your punishment for me turning my back on you—a loveless marriage? 'Cause if it is, you win. It's tearing me apart. I don't know what to do. Please help me.*

She took a few pieces of toilet tissue and blew her nose. Then she wet some paper towels and patted her face before returning to her customer, who was waiting at the counter with a frantic look on his face.

When he saw her, he rushed to her. "Are you okay?"

Estelle could only answer what her heart was feeling. "No." Fearful that she'd frighten him more, she added, "But I'll be all right."

"Well, is there anything I can do for you? Call your family or something? You look terrible."

Estelle stepped behind the counter. "No, that's okay, Mr. Lewis. Thank you, though. I'm sorry I rushed away like that.

I didn't mean to scare you." Grabbing her pad and pen, she said, "I was about to take your order."

Estelle wrote as the man gave her a description of the flowers he wanted delivered to his wife. When they were done, she even managed to smile at him briefly. As soon as he was gone, she closed up the shop, even though she had another hour before quitting time. She needed to talk to someone. She went by Gloria's house, but no one was home. She hated to bother Justine at work, but she needed a shoulder to cry on.

When Estelle stopped by the travel agency, Justine could tell from the look on her face that it meant bad news. When she inquired if something was wrong, Estelle broke into tears. Justine informed her supervisor that she had a family emergency and needed to leave for the remainder of the day. She and her mother walked across the street to the town square and sat on one of the benches. Justine assessed Estelle as she waited for her to speak.

Estelle cried, "Your daddy and I are getting a divorce."

Justine's eyes grew large. "A divorce? Mama, you're not serious."

"I am. I can't stay with him any longer. I'm tired of trying to make it work. It's hopeless."

Justine argued, "No, it's not hopeless. I can't believe you're gonna give up on your marriage just like that. Look at what you and Daddy have been through. You can make it through this, too."

"It's not *just like that*. Justine, you know your daddy and I have been having problems for years. For some reason, they've just now come to a head. Maybe it's because I'm older and tired. I'm physically, mentally and emotionally exhausted, and I have nothing else to give him. He says all

I do is nag. Well, if he'd get up off his rump and show me some affection sometimes, I wouldn't nag him. Gloria tells me to be nice to him. I do that, and I still get nothing. He acts like I don't exist."

"Mama, how does Daddy feel about all this? Does he want a divorce, too?"

Estelle shook her head in frustration and irritation. "Justine, I don't know how he feels about anything. You know I can't get him to open up and discuss things with me. I told him Sunday night that I want a divorce, but he was just worried about his precious boat."

Justine raised her eyebrows. "What's his boat got to do with this?"

Estelle still had no regrets about destroying the thing, so she didn't hesitate to tell her daughter, "I banged it up Sunday."

Justine's mouth fell open. "Mama, you what?"

Estelle explained about her rampage two days before.

"Mama, please don't do this. Can't you and Daddy talk about it?"

Estelle hit her fist on her leg. "Justine, how many times do I have to remind you there's no talking to the man? I'm tired of talking."

"What if I talk to him? Try to explain to him how you feel."

"He knows how I feel. I've told him a thousand times. It doesn't matter to him."

"I think it does matter. He just doesn't know how to show it. I think something's causing him pain, and he's just not telling us. Why else would he change? Mama, think about it. You remember how outgoing Daddy used to be. After Grandmama died, he changed."

"Justine, are you gonna start that again? You're just like Gloria. Always trying to make excuses for him."

"I'm not trying to make excuses for him. I'm just trying to figure out what's eating away at him. Daddy started drinking heavily after Grandmama died. You took me and Justin and left. The only way he could get you to come back home was to promise to stop drinking. To this day, I've never seen Daddy drink. And neither have you. You told me yourself.

"All Daddy wants to do is spend his time fishing and hunting. He's trying to escape something. It's like his hobbies have replaced the drinking. I learned at Al-Anon that the alcoholic drinks excessively in order to relieve himself from things that cause him unpleasantness, tension and anxiety. It dulls the pain."

Estelle jumped up. "Justine, I already told you I don't wanna hear this stuff. You go to a few meetings, and you think you're the expert on alcoholism. Stop trying to analyze your daddy. The only one who can tell you why he's like he is is him. If you wanna ask him, go ahead. I'm sick and tired of begging him to talk to me."

When Roger got home from work, he was greeted by his entire family in the living room. He didn't like the looks on their faces.

"What's going on?"

Justine got up and walked over to her father. "Daddy, we want to talk to you. I know you just got home and you're tired, but this is important."

It seemed strange having the children at home in the same room with him and Estelle for no apparent reason. Roger reluctantly sat down. "What is it?"

As their spokesperson, Justine said, "Daddy, do you want to divorce Mama?"

Roger immediately replied, "Your mama is the one who

told me *she* wants a divorce. I didn't bring it up. She did. So why're you asking me this?"

"Because I want to know how *you* feel. Is that what you want?"

Roger responded with earnest sincerity. "I don't care what we do. It doesn't matter."

At his words, Estelle felt her heart drop into the pit of her stomach. Well, she didn't need to hear any more. She stood up to leave.

Justine stopped her. "Mama, don't go."

Estelle halted, but asked, "Why should I stay? You heard what he said. Our marriage doesn't mean anything to him."

Justine turned to her father. "Daddy, tell Mama how you feel. About her. About your life. What the two of you have been through."

Roger stood in turn. "Justine, I don't know what you're trying to do, but I don't want any part of it."

Roger's antagonistic response moved Justin to speak. "Dad, all Justine's trying to do is get you to talk to Mama about your feelings—how you feel about her. It's important that she know."

Roger's eyes flashed with outrage. "You know, it seems to me that you and Justine have forgotten who's the parent and who's the child. I raised y'all. I know I made some mistakes, but you're here."

Turning to his son, Roger added, "And Justin, I don't think you're in any position to be counseling me. You're here because your wife put you out 'cause you lost your job. Once your Mama and I married, I never had to run back home to my parents. So if I was you, I'd watch what I say."

Without uttering another word, Justin stormed out of the house.

Chapter 26

Justine glared angrily at her father. "Daddy, why'd you have to say those things to him? He was only trying to help, just like me."

His eyes still flashing anger, Roger looked at his daughter. "Well, you'd do well to check yourself, too. Your husband walked out on you."

Justine was beginning to feel a loathing for her father. She had never felt this way until now. She was about to tell him so when her mother spoke up.

"Roger, our children love us. They're only trying to help. Don't you dare talk to them like that."

Roger glared at Estelle. "I suggest you back off. I've had enough of your big mouth to last me a lifetime."

Estelle felt like cursing him out. Something—she didn't know what—held her back. It was as though her mouth had been clamped shut. She and Justine just stood there as Roger walked away.

Justine frowned as she looked at her mother. "What is wrong with him? He sounds so bitter."

Estelle didn't say anything.

"Mama, something's obviously going on with Daddy. Why don't you come with me Monday to the Al-Anon meeting?"

Estelle was finally able to speak and snapped, "He's the one with the problem. Why do I have to go?"

"Alcoholism is a family disease," Justine answered. "I know Daddy doesn't drink anymore, but our problems began years ago when he started. We never talked about it. We just got back together and never discussed it, as though it never happened. I guess it was so painful that we didn't want to relive it, but look at where not talking about it has gotten us."

"Justine, I'm only gonna tell you this one more time. I'm not going."

The next morning about two o'clock, Estelle got up to see if Justin was home. He still had not returned when she'd gone to bed at eleven, and she was worried about him.

He wasn't in bed. She went to get a glass of water. As she placed the pitcher back in the refrigerator, she heard a key in the door. She knew it was Justin. Even though he and Justine were married and on their own, they still had keys to the house. What she wasn't expecting when he came through the door was the unsightly creature who resembled her son.

"Justin, where've you been?"

"H-hey, Ma-ma." He reeked of alcohol.

Estelle threw her hand over her mouth. "Are you drunk?"

"Ye-yeah," Justin giggled.

Estelle tried not to lose her temper. "I don't appreciate you coming home like this. You need to go to bed. I'll talk to you in the morning."

As she helped Justin to his room, her heart raced. She couldn't believe her child, the son who'd developed as she carried him in her womb, was intoxicated. She didn't even know he drank. Immediately, bells started going off in her head.

When Estelle hung up the telephone, she was still in a state of shock. On her way home from the shop, she stopped by Justine's.

Justine shook her head. "I don't believe it."

Estelle appeared depressed. "Neither did I till I called Shayna and talked to her. When he came home drunk this morning, something went off in my head and told me there was more to his story than what he told us." She shook her head as tears flowed down her cheeks. "I can't believe my child is an alcoholic."

"Mama, I admit he has a problem, but from what you told me Shayna said, it doesn't sound to me like he's an alcoholic."

"He came home drunk, didn't he?"

"Yes, but one of the symptoms of alcoholism is an uncontrollable desire for alcohol. Justin's gotten drunk on some occasions, but that doesn't mean he's addicted."

"Well, alcoholic, drunk—I don't care. Either way, it's wrong."

"I'm not saying it's not. I'm just saying maybe it's not as serious as we think."

"I don't know what to think anymore. I can't believe any of this is happening to our family. On top of everything else, all three of our marriages are falling apart."

Justine quickly stood up for her own. "My marriage isn't falling apart. I intend to make it work."

Estelle wished she could have the kind of confidence her

daughter had. She admired Justine. "I think I'll go with you to your meeting Monday night."

Justine couldn't believe it. She smiled broadly. "You mean it, Mama?"

"Yes. Seeing your brother this morning scared me. I'll go, but I'm not gonna make any promises about doing it on an ongoing basis."

"That's good enough for me."

Chapter 27

Estelle decided not to mention to Roger or Justin what Shayna had told her. She figured the reason Justin had gone out drinking was to blot out the hurtful words his father had hurled at him. Perhaps Justine was correct in her thinking. As much as Estelle despised Roger, she wouldn't accuse him of being at fault for their son's unacceptable behavior. She'd already blamed him for what Justine had done to Evan.

On Monday, Estelle and Justin accompanied Justine and Catina to the Al-Anon meeting. Estelle had tried to persuade Roger to go, but he refused.

Justin seemed to be okay, but Estelle was feeling extremely uncomfortable in her new environment. Another thing she didn't like was the cheerful attitude of the participants who spoke about their situations.

When she could take no more, Estelle blurted out, "I don't understand why y'all are laughing. Alcoholism is no laughing matter. It almost destroyed my family years ago. I came tonight because my family is still struggling with the effects of it, but I see now I made a mistake."

Members of the group tried to explain that they weren't laughing at alcoholism, but were happy because they were dealing with it in better ways than they previously had. As a result of attending meetings and talking with others who shared their plight, they had been able to change *their* attitudes, and now lived happier, more peaceful, lives.

Estelle didn't care to hear any more. She went outside to wait until the meeting was over. Justine tried to get her to come back in, but when Estelle refused, she returned to the meeting.

On the ride home, Justine attempted to explain further. "Mama, I can understand why you're upset, but no one was laughing at alcoholism. Most of the people in the group have been coming for years, and they're finally at a point where they've regained control of their lives despite the painful effects of alcoholism."

"I don't care how long they've been going. It's not funny. And don't ask me to go back."

No one said anything. They all thought it best to just leave the matter alone for now.

Justin had learned a lot at the meeting. Although his family had suffered due to his father's insobriety, he'd never thought of alcoholism as a family disease until tonight. Of course, that made sense because it did affect the entire family, not just the alcoholic. He vowed to call Shayna.

When Evan opened the door of his apartment, he was shocked to see Justine standing there.

She admired how nice he looked in a crisp, light blue button-down shirt with a gold silk paisley tie and navy pants.

She wondered where he was going. Surely not on a date. After all, they were still married. Jealousy joined the host of emotions wreaking havoc on her insides.

"I'm sorry. Looks like I caught you at a bad time." Justine refused to hide her curiosity. She turned up the corners of her mouth in a wee smile when she boldly said, "You look nice. Where are you going all dressed up?"

Evan said, "Thank you," without returning her smile. "Coke's annual conference."

Oh, yeah. The one he and I used to go to, Justine thought sadly. "Who's going with you?" She didn't care if he knew she was worried that he might be seeing someone else.

"What d'you mean, who's going with me?" Evan's voice was laced with irritation. He didn't like this little game Justine seemed to be playing. More than that, he didn't appreciate her low opinion of him, to suspect him of dating while they were married.

"Justine, is that how little you think of me? To suspect I'd go out with someone else while we're still married? I'd never do that. Whatever you came to say, say it, but don't start this nonsense. I've gotta leave in a few minutes, so I don't have much time."

Justine suddenly looked embarrassed. "I'm sorry. I know that's not the type of person you are, and I don't think little of you." She breathed an inward sigh of relief as he led the way to the living room, where she sat on the love seat and he on the matching recliner.

"I won't stay long. I just wanted to see you. You doing okay?"

"I'm all right. You?"

"Missing you still."

Evan felt uneasy. "You want something to drink?"

Justine was disappointed that instead of sharing her sentiment, he'd changed the subject. But then again, what more should she have expected? "No, thank you."

When she saw him check his watch, Justine said, "Evan, I came to tell you that I'm not giving up on our marriage. I know I hurt you, and I know the pain will be with you awhile. But I still love you, and I don't want to lose you. Please come home. How can we make things better with us living apart?"

Evan grabbed at the thoughts floating through his mind and ordered them to sit still long enough for him to express them. However, when he spoke, he only said, "It's not that easy. Maybe it is for you, but not for me."

Justine studied his face and swallowed hard. "Well, what're we gonna do? To work things out, I mean. Do you want to go to counseling?"

"I don't want people messing about in my business."

"I have an idea."

Evan held Justine's gaze.

"Do you have plans for tomorrow night?"

"No. Why?"

"Let's go out. On a date like we did before we got married."

A small snicker escaped Evan's lips, but Justine heard it. Her heart skipped a beat, for it was the first time in a while she'd heard or seen any hint of life in him. She had been hungering for his laughter. She missed everything about him.

"You're asking me on a date? I suppose I should be flattered." Evan's merriment faded as quickly as it had come.

"Yes. I'd do anything for you. I love you."

Evan hoped Justine didn't expect him to say the words back to her, because he couldn't. It wasn't that he didn't love her. The sorrow in his heart just wouldn't let him express it. His eyes darkened with regret. It was quite obvious that Justine deeply desired for them to make amends, but her deceit had drained his confidence in her.

"I don't know. Let me think about it."

Justine wanted an answer now. However, she responded, "Okay. Can you let me know by tomorrow morning?"

"Yeah."

After Justine had gone, Evan wondered if he would ever be able to trust her again.

Much to Justine's surprise, Evan agreed to go out with her. He treated her to dinner and a movie. Although she'd insisted on paying, he wouldn't let her. As they strode across the parking lot to Evan's vehicle afterward, Justine thought back to happier times when they would walk hand in hand. It was funny how you didn't miss the little things until they were gone.

Justine tried to find happy things they could talk about on the way home. "Catina and Darryl really like each other."

"Yeah. I don't think I've ever seen him as serious about anyone as he is about her."

"Hey, maybe we can double-date sometime."

Evan didn't respond. He didn't want Justine to think that they were going to make a habit of this. He still didn't know what to do about them. Her appearance tonight was intoxicating. She had pinned up her hair and left short curly strands of it on both sides of her face, just the way he liked. The style really complimented her round face.

He truly missed her. One part of him wanted a reconciliation, but another felt like going his own separate way for good. He didn't want to hurt her, yet he couldn't overlook the broken pieces of his life.

"Justine, tonight was nice, but I don't think we need to keep this up."

She shot him a look tinged with desperation. "Why not? What's wrong?"

"Because I'm not sure I want us to get back together."

Justine turned in her seat. "Evan, how can you say that? You're my husband. We married for better or worse."

"I know, but what you did… I just don't think it can ever be the way it was." Evan's tone sounded just as hopeless as his words.

With tears in her eyes, Justine spoke above the pounding of her heart. "You're right. It won't be like it was, but we can at least try to get there—make it the best we can. Evan, don't you even want to try?"

"Justine, you took away a huge part of me when you lied to me. I know you said you were fearful because of what you and your family suffered when you were younger, but that doesn't make it any better. It's like you ripped out my heart and stomped all over it."

Justine cried, "I know, and I'm so sorry. Evan, I love you. Have you stopped loving me?"

"No, but it's not like it used to be."

His words stung her soul. "I'll accept what I can get till you're ready to give more."

"That's just it. I don't know if I'll ever be ready to give more."

"Evan, what are you saying?"

"I want a divorce."

Chapter 28

A lot had happened since September. Shayna had finally allowed Justin to return home after he agreed to continue his Al-Anon meetings in Savannah. He'd secured another job, this time as an insurance agent. It wasn't what he wanted to do, but at this point, he'd do whatever it took to keep his family together.

He and Shayna had been going together to the Al-Anon meetings since he'd come back home two months ago. It wasn't until Shayna heard him open up at one of the meetings that she became aware of his father's past problem with alcoholism and the bad effects it had on their family.

At the same time, the meetings were extremely educational. Although overdrinking was never an issue in her immediate family, Shayna had a few relatives who liked to "take a swig every now and then," as they put it, and some of them did drink a little too much. Perhaps more families than not were suffering from this problem.

Estelle filed for divorce from Roger and reluctantly moved in with Justine. Estelle desired to get her own place, especially since she didn't want to be in the way in case Evan changed his mind and came home. Justine was trying to accept the fact that her marriage was over, and told her mother she didn't think Evan would have a change of heart.

Justine continued going to the Al-Anon meetings with Catina. She felt much more mature than she had when she first started attending. She still loved Evan with all her heart, and if he changed his mind about the divorce, she'd take him back in a heartbeat. However, she was learning to live her life without him, and no longer spent her days agonizing over their breakup. Despite the fact that her marriage would soon be over, she was beginning to feel an inner calm that she hadn't felt in a very long time.

Estelle had noticed the changes in her daughter and liked what she saw. A month ago, one day out of the blue, she had decided to accompany Justine to a meeting again. Once there, Estelle opened up about how she was still angry at Roger for the pain he had caused their family all those years ago.

Every time he refused to show her affection or just sit down and talk with her, all those feelings resurfaced, causing her to become the witch she so often turned into. She hated being that way. She and Roger used to bring out the best in each other. All they'd seen for the last several years was the worst. She didn't like the person she had become. For the first time ever, she could see why Roger didn't like her— and didn't love her.

Estelle saw the need to make adjustments in her attitude, thinking and actions. She hadn't reached the level Justine had, and suffered a couple of relapses from the Estelle she wanted to be. However, she was still willing to put forth the needed effort to make the necessary changes.

Thanksgiving had come and gone, but the holiday just wasn't the same anymore, since their families were torn apart. At least Justin and Shayna were back together.

On Saturday, Estelle decided to take Roger a plate of leftovers from the Thanksgiving dinner she and Justine had prepared just for the two of them. She didn't think he'd be home, and had planned to simply leave the dish in the refrigerator with a note. She was surprised to see him outside when she pulled up. They greeted one another when she got out of her vehicle.

Estelle appeared embarrassed as she looked at the boat. "I see you got it fixed." She set the plate on top of her car.

"Yeah," Roger said, as he began pulling the cover over the vessel. To his surprise, Estelle grabbed the opposite side and helped him. "Just got her back today."

When they were done, she looked at him regretfully and said, "I'm sorry for damaging the boat. I shouldn't have done what I did. No matter how angry or hurt I was, I was wrong."

Roger responded with a straight face. "Don't worry about it. It's in the past."

Estelle kindly offered, "I'll pay you back for fixing it."

"It's okay." Roger's eyes told her he meant it. "Insurance took care of it."

Estelle nodded sadly. She walked back to her car and grabbed the plate. Handing it to him, she said, "I brought you some food. Leftovers from the Thanksgiving dinner Justine and I cooked."

Roger missed her cooking. He reached for the plate. "Thanks. I appreciate it."

Estelle cast him a smile. How he missed that enchanting expression of hers, especially her grin.

He was still mesmerized by it when Estelle said, "Once you heat it up in the microwave, it'll taste just as good as the day we cooked it. Well, I better go."

"Okay."

Roger watched Estelle as she strode away. He liked the way her hips moved when she walked. He was pleased with her size. Had loved having something to hold on to before things had gotten so bad between them.

Later in the day, Gloria stopped by to see Estelle.

"I still can't believe you and Roger are getting a divorce. It's so sad." She grabbed one of the oatmeal-raisin cookies from the tray that Estelle had set on the kitchen table, and took a bite before sipping her milk.

Estelle concurred. "Yes, it is, but life goes on. It was good up to a point. Things weren't getting any better, and I'm tired. I feel like I've been dragged through the mud and back again. You know, a person can only take so much."

Gloria licked her lips. "Do you think that if you and Roger hadn't gone through what you did that you would've been able to make it through this?"

Estelle looked at her friend. "I don't know. Maybe we put so much energy into fixing what went wrong then that we're too wiped out to try to fix anything else. You know, tests are supposed to make us stronger for the next ones that are sure to come along, but I feel like this one completely wiped me out."

"Maybe it would help if you and Roger went to see a marriage counselor. Or better yet, some spiritual counseling."

"Gloria, I know what you're getting at, and maybe you're right. Maybe we do need some counseling. Roger won't even go to Al-Anon. He just doesn't open up like he used to. Justine thinks he's suffering from some kind of emotional pain that he's trying to block out. She thinks that's what led to his overdrinking in the first place."

"Well, she may have a point. I mean, after all, he did start drinking after his mother died."

"Yes, I realize that it's traumatic to lose a loved one in death, especially a child, spouse or parent, but it's been over fifteen years now. Shouldn't he be over it by now?"

"Depends on the person."

Estelle considered what Gloria had said. Maybe Justine was right. Perhaps there was more to Roger's attitude than met the eye.

As they headed to their cars after leaving the office, Justine asked Catina, "What're you doing the rest of the day?"

"Nothing much. Darryl and I are going out later."

Justine's face lit up. "That's nice. Where are you going?"

"There's a new restaurant that just opened up in Birmingham. We'll probably go there and eat. Do you want to come?"

Justine let out a snort. "Girl, are you serious? I don't want to be a third wheel. I'd rather stay home with Mama."

Catina giggled. "I won't tell your mama you said that."

Justine countered, "You know what I mean. I didn't mean it in a bad way."

"I know. How are your parents?"

"Okay, I guess. Sometimes it's hard to tell." Justine had no desire to talk about her parents' breakup so she quickly changed the subject. "Has Darryl said anything lately about Evan?"

"Anything like what?"

"How he's doing."

"He's okay."

Justine's expression was one of concern.

"What's wrong?" Catina asked.

"I just worry about him. I hurt him so badly. I wished I'd listened to you. I wish I could turn back the clock. Every time I think about what I did, I..." Justine started to weep.

Catina took her friend in her arms.

"Every time I think about what I did to him, I just want to die."

"Justine, don't torture yourself. Sometimes we have to experience things in order to get past a painful period in our life. You held your fear inside for years. It caused you to make a bad decision, but it'll pass. Look how much you've grown since you started going to the meetings."

"If I've grown so much, why am I standing here blubbering like a big baby?"

"Because you're human. And because you love your husband."

Justine gave Catina a grateful squeeze before they broke apart.

"I think I'll call Darryl and cancel our date for tonight."

Justine's eyes grew huge. "Why?"

"So I can spend some time with my best friend."

Justine grinned. "Who? Me?"

"No, that lady standing across the street over there whom I have no earthly idea who she is."

Justine giggled.

"So what d'you want to do?"

Justine felt as if she was having a relapse and needed a shoulder to lean on; therefore, she didn't try to talk her friend out of breaking her date with Darryl as she would have done under different circumstances.

"Have a nice quiet evening at your house just talking, maybe do our nails."

"Sounds good. We'll order a pizza. Why don't we invite your mama? I'm sure she could use some cheering up, too."

"Yeah. I think she'd like that."

Chapter 29

"What time does your morning service start?" Estelle asked Justine the next morning as they ate breakfast.

Justine almost choked as she sipped her hot cocoa. She must have been hallucinating. Had her mother just inquired about what time worship service began? In a voice filled with hope, she said, "I'm sorry, Mama. What did you say?"

"Your morning service. What time does it start?"

"Nine-thirty."

"Okay." Estelle rose. "You go ahead and start getting ready. I'll clean up the kitchen."

Justine's heart dropped. She'd thought her mother had asked so that she could join her for worship this morning. Disappointed, she got up from her seat and went to get ready. When she came out of her room forty-five minutes later, she thought she would jump out of her skin when she came upon Estelle dressed in a black-and-white pin-striped suit with a hot-pink stretch-lace top.

"Wow! Mama, you look *hot*." Justine's slip of the tongue forced her to put her hand to her mouth. She blushed. "'Scuse me. Good. I mean you look good."

Estelle's laughter filled the room. Justine hadn't seen her mother really laugh in a long time. Her heart was turning somersaults at the mere sight.

"It's okay." Estelle teased, "You can say your mama looks hot."

Justine heartily chuckled. "Mama, where are you going?"

Estelle smoothed her hands over her skirt. "I'm going with you. You ready?"

"Yes, I'm ready."

Justine grabbed her purse and keys. She and her mother laughed and talked as they made their way to the car.

As Estelle listened to the gospel message in church, something within her stirred. The topic was centered around having a happy family life.

The minister was saying, "The family should be a haven of safety and security. However, remember that there will be problems. Today's family is under stress. Satan doesn't want families to be happy, but God does. After all, God is the one who instituted the family arrangement. He performed the very first marriage back in the Garden of Eden, when he brought Adam and Eve together as husband and wife. But what happened? Satan used a serpent to bring ruin to them and all their offspring, which includes all of us."

Estelle thought about her own marriage, which would soon be brought to a conclusion. Thirty-seven years ago, when she and Roger had tied the knot, she'd never imagined they'd end up here.

The sermon continued. "There are two keys to a lasting marriage. The first is love. The second is respect. Today, we're going to discuss these and see how they can make our family lives happy."

The preacher had both Estelle's and Justine's undivided attention, for this was something they both desperately needed to hear. Mother and daughter grinned at each other as they both pulled out pens and pads from their purses so they could take notes. Estelle felt a flutter within her chest. It did her heart good to see that the spiritual routine her daughter had been brought up with was still ongoing.

From the platform, the minister went on. "The Bible identifies different kinds of love. There's the warm, personal affection that exists between close friends. There's the type of love that develops among family members. A third kind of love is the romantic love that one has for someone of the opposite sex. Of course, our lives will be much happier if all three of these are cultivated by both the husband and wife.

"But did you know that there is a love that is more important than these three? The word for this fourth kind of love, in the original language of the Christian Greek scriptures, is *agape*. First John 4:8 tells us "God is love." And how is it that we come to love? First John 4:19 says we love God because he first loved us.

"Agape love is governed by the right principles found in God's word. It moves us to have an unselfish concern to do to others what is right in *God's* eyes, whether or not they appear to deserve it."

Estelle mentally repeated, *an unselfish concern to do to others what is right in God's eyes, whether or not they appear to deserve it*. She'd been cruel to Roger for years because of his unloving attitude toward her. She had felt justified in her treatment of him, but now, she saw that she was wrong in her thinking.

"It means letting God's word guide us in all we do just as Psalm 119:105 says. Turn with me there, please, and let's read it together."

The rustle of turning pages filled the auditorium. After the verse was read, the minister said, "So, friends, we want to do like it says here and let God's word light our path. It doesn't mean we won't have problems, for none of us are free from sin. But when we cultivate this love of God and each other, our marriage will be lasting and happy, because as Proverbs 10:12 states, 'Love covers all sins.' Now we're going to talk about how respect leads to a happy family life."

Estelle felt a stirring within her soul. For the first time in years, she felt God's holy spirit enveloping her. Perhaps he'd listened to her brief, infrequent prayers regarding her marriage, after all.

"Did you hear what he said about agape love?" Estelle asked Justine. "How it's an unselfish concern to do to others what's right in God's eyes?"

Her notes still in her hand as she and Justine rode home, Estelle glanced down at them and added, "Whether they *appear* to deserve it or not."

Justine broke into a huge grin. She hadn't seen her mother this excited in quite a while. "Yes, I really appreciated that part. I also appreciated what he said about respect being a key element to a lasting marriage." Her tone grew sad. "I guess I was showing a lack of it when I lied to Evan. Now our marriage is ending because of it."

Estelle threw a serious glance Justine's way. "Talk to him."

Justine continued gazing straight ahead at the road. "I have, Mama, but he wants a divorce. Even when I call to see how he's doing, he never answers the phone. It's obvious he's trying to avoid me. He used to *want* to be with me. Not anymore."

"Do you remember what you told me when all this happened?"

"What?"

"You said you wanted your marriage to work."

"I do, Mama. But I can't force myself on Evan. He has to want it to work, too. And what about your own marriage? You're divorcing Daddy." Justine's emotions had gotten the best of her. She stole a peek at her mother. "I'm sorry. I shouldn't have said that."

Estelle nodded as she agreed wholeheartedly. "You're absolutely right. And after hearing that sermon today, I've made up my mind that I wanna give my marriage one more try. 'Course, I don't know how your daddy'll feel about it. I realized something about myself today that I hadn't even thought about. I haven't been showing your father the proper respect he deserves as my husband.

"Yeah, I get angry at him 'cause he ignores me, but maybe my actions have played a part in the way he treats me. You know, Al-Anon says we can only change ourselves, not other people. So maybe it's high time I started working a little harder on trying to change myself. And girl, you know your mama. That's gonna be a full-time job itself."

The two women burst into hearty laughter.

"Mama, I can't believe I'm hearing this from you. My mama's growing up. I'm so proud of you."

Estelle felt like a nervous teenager on her very first date with the guy of her dreams. For the first time in years, she seemed to have Roger's undivided attention as they sat in their living room with the television off.

Estelle's words were flowing easily. "I don't want a divorce. I wanna try to make our marriage work. I realize now that I've contributed greatly to our marriage's downfall. I just didn't know how to get your attention. My ranting and raving was my way of releasing my feelings of frustration and loneliness. I *need* for you to *show* me that you love me. I need you to spend time with me and talk with me. I understand that you need your space sometimes. So do I. But we also need to take time out to be together. Do you understand what I'm saying?"

As much as Estelle argued when she was around, Roger had missed her presence. Her vivacious spirit had kept their home environment alive. With her gone, the place seemed lifeless. Now she was actually talking to him in a tone that denoted tenderness. It was nice.

Shame filled Roger's soul. Not once had he stopped to consider how his dear wife might be suffering. He nodded. "Yeah, I do."

"I go with Justine and Catina every Monday night to Al-Anon. Do you wanna come with us tomorrow?"

Roger immediately shook his head. "No, I'm not getting involved in that."

Hopelessness washed over Estelle. How could they mend their marriage if Roger wasn't going to cooperate? A huge part of her wanted to put up a hard fight to get him to change his mind. However, she replied, "Okay. Can I ask you a question?"

"Yeah. As long as it doesn't have anything to do with that group."

Her eyes wet with tears, Estelle asked, "Do you still love me?"

Roger felt the rapid beat of his heart beneath his shirt. "Yes," he honestly answered, "I love you."

Estelle felt her heart do a flip, and a warm current radiated throughout her body. She couldn't recall the last time she'd heard those three simple words from Roger. Something in the way he said them assured her that he meant it. Time would surely tell.

"Do you wanna give our marriage another try?"

Roger's voice was filled with relief when he answered, "I do."

Chapter 30

Justine had taken her mother's advice to heart. Evan hadn't answered the telephone when she called; therefore, she'd just have to make a surprise visit. She prayed she'd catch him at home. Her heart leaped for joy when she saw his vehicle in the parking lot of his apartment complex.

Justine's heart was racing when Evan opened the door. He looked good in a pair of black jeans and a red turtle-neck shirt.

As they made their way to the living room, Justine apologized, "I'm sorry to just barge in, but I wanted to talk to you." She gently added, "You never answer the phone when I call."

A pang of self-pity tore into her when Evan failed to respond to her last statement. As they sat on the sofa, their eyes locked. Evan propped his elbow on the back of the seat and pressed his hand against the side of his face as he stared at her.

Justine asked, "Are you okay? How've you been?"

"I'm fine. You?"

Justine could still sense the pain she had caused Evan. His zest for life seemed to be drained from him. It tore her up inside. She had come over all poised for her conversation with him, but now felt herself coming apart at the seams.

As the tears began to flow, she said, "I know I hurt you terribly, and I'm so sorry. I love you, and I don't want a divorce. I messed up, and I'll regret it for the rest of my life. I know you don't have a drinking problem, but all I could concentrate on was what my family and I went through when my daddy started drinking. All I could picture was our children going through the same thing. What I did showed a lack of respect for you, and I'm sorry. I'm going to Al-Anon now, and I'm learning to deal with my past. Maybe if I'd done it sooner, I wouldn't have done what I did."

Justine felt the walls caving in on her, and she buried her face in her hands as she wept bitterly. "I know I don't deserve you or your love." Jumping up, she headed for the door and tried to open it. "I'm sorry. I shouldn't have come."

The door wouldn't open. After frantically twisting the doorknob, she gave up and pressed her face to the panel, still sobbing.

Suddenly, Justine felt herself being pulled into Evan's arms. As they held each other, they both cried.

January came in full force with cold, blustery conditions. However, the warmth in her heart and Evan by her side were all that Justine needed to keep her glowing. After an early afternoon movie, she, Evan, Catina and Darryl browsed through the mall, catching a few of the stores' after-Christmas sales.

When the two women excused themselves and ducked

into the nearest women's restroom, Catina happily inquired, "So how's everything going with you and Evan? Good?"

Justine smiled. "Things are fine. Better than I expected. I still sense his hurt. I think it's gonna be awhile before he can fully trust me again," she stated sadly. "But I understand. I'm just glad he's home. So how are things with you and Darryl? Do I hear wedding bells in your future?"

Catina smiled as she shook her head. "Don't go rushing things now. We haven't gotten that far. *Yet.*"

Justine grinned broadly as she swatted Catina's arm. "I knew it. I told you he was a great guy."

"He is. I never knew anyone like him existed. Sometimes I feel like I'm dreaming. Then I pray, if I am, Lord, please don't wake me up."

Justine swatted Catina again. "Girl, you're crazy."

When they emerged from the ladies' room, Evan and Darryl were waiting patiently nearby.

Evan joked, "What took you so long? I thought we were gonna have to send security in after you."

Justine and Catina both blushed.

They went to a local restaurant for dinner and enjoyed each other's company as they ate.

Later that night, after Justine and Evan had gone to bed, she whispered in his ear, "I want to have a baby."

Evan remained speechless.

"Did you hear me, Evan?"

As he lay there in the dark, staring up at the ceiling, he said, "Yes, I heard you."

Justine propped herself up on one elbow and stared at him. "What's the matter? Why don't you say something?"

"What d'you want me to say?" Evan's demeanor had suddenly turned apathetic.

"Well, I thought you'd be happy."

"Why? Because now *you* suddenly decide we should have a baby?"

"Evan, I'm sorry. I'm not trying to decide anything for us. I just wanted you to know that I'm ready if you still are."

Without uttering another word, Evan turned and hopped out of bed. Justine immediately followed suit. As he walked toward the bedroom door, she placed her hand on his back and reached for his hand. When he stopped, she stood in front of him, looking up into his face.

"I know that just because we're back together doesn't mean things'll be easy, but I hope you'll hang in there with me so we can work it out. I'm sorry. I won't say anything else about having a baby till you're ready to talk about it."

Evan simply walked away.

As Roger made up the bed, he stole quick glances at Estelle as she prepared for morning service. She was indeed the most beautiful woman he'd ever laid eyes on. However, now she seemed more lovely to him than she ever had. He had begun to feel a deep desire for her welling up inside of him, a yearning he hadn't experienced in quite some time. He had often wondered what was wrong with him. After all, he was a man. Why did he no longer have any sexual feelings?

Estelle had accused him on many occasions of being unfaithful. At least once, she'd even point-blank asked him if he was on the down low. When she'd yelled those incriminating words at him, he'd felt as if his soul had been torn to shreds. Yet he'd allowed her to think such terrible things about him instead of sharing his deepest emotions with her.

For years, Roger had been trying to hide from the things that caused him pain. It was the only way he could cope. To talk about them, even think about them, only made him hurt more.

Estelle looked exquisite in a mulberry-colored pleated skirt set. When she caught him eyeing her, he quickly looked away.

"What is it?" she asked.

Roger plumped up the pillow shams. "What?"

"You were staring at me. What's wrong?"

"Nothing." He placed the pillows on the bed. "You look nice. Very pretty."

When she smiled, it took his breath away. That beautiful smile draped him like a warm cloak.

"Thank you." Estelle's heart swelled with elation. For so long, she'd felt totally unattractive to Roger. To know that she was still beautiful in his eyes did her heart good. "Since you're in such a good mood today, maybe you wanna come with me."

Roger straightened his back. "Don't push it."

Estelle couldn't help but laugh as he walked past her out of the room.

After church, Estelle pondered the idea of her and Roger doing something together. "Hey, why don't we go on a picnic?"

Roger looked at his wife and shook his head in a playful way that let her know her whimsy was ludicrous. "Stelle, it's January. It's cold outside."

"It's not that cold, you big baby. It's in the fifties. I can put the chicken, potato salad and rolls in the picnic basket. We could bundle up and go to the park and eat."

She was forgetting one food item she had prepared that he really loved. "What about the greens?"

"What about 'em?"

"Well, you know how much I love your greens. You didn't mention 'em."

"You want greens? We'll take some with us."

"They'll be cold."

"I'll heat 'em up for you in the microwave. They'll still be warm when we get there, and you can dig in before they get cold. How's that?"

"Okay, I guess."

"Well, let's do it."

Roger couldn't believe he and Estelle were going on a picnic in the cold. Suddenly, he didn't care what the temperature was outside. The warmth he was feeling in his heart would more than compensate for it.

Chapter 31

As Justin stood in front of the bathroom mirror, staring at his reflection, it took every fiber of his being not to remove the bottle of liquor from his secret spot in the linen closet. He hadn't had a sip of alcohol since he'd returned home. The pressure of having to work at a job he hated was building up, and he didn't know how much longer it would be before he went for the bottle. However, he knew if he gave in to his craving, it would be over for him and Shayna.

She was a very supportive wife, but he knew she would not take any grief from him. The baby was due next month, and Justin wanted to do nothing to mess up his family life. Since he'd come back home, he'd also been fighting the idea of joining Alcoholics Anonymous. It would be too embarrassing to admit that he had a problem, so he had vowed to try to handle the situation on his own. Attending Al-Anon meetings with Shayna wasn't bad, because there he only focused on his father's past drinking and not his own. However, he could run no longer.

Suddenly, Justin heard a knock on the door.

"Justin, are you okay?" Shayna asked.

"I'm fine," he managed to answer. "I'll be out in a minute."

Removing the bottle from its hiding place, Justin poured the bronze-colored liquid in the toilet and flushed it down. When he opened the door to come out, Shayna was standing there.

When she saw the empty bottle in his hand, she went into a frenzy. "Have you been in there drinking? I told you I'm not putting up with this mess. You may as well just pack up—"

"Shay! Shay!" He had to yell her name to get her to hear him over her ranting. "I haven't been drinking. I poured it down the toilet."

"You had to have been drinking at some point to even have it in the house. Pack your stuff and leave."

All Justin could think to say was, "I'm not going anywhere."

Shayna's eyes were huge as she stared at him. "Excuse me?"

"Let me explain. I need to talk to you."

"You can talk all you want while you pack. As soon as you're through packing, the talking stops. I told you I'm not putting up with you drinking."

"Shay, will you just be quiet and listen a minute?" Gently grasping her arm, Justin led her into the living room, where they sat down. "I have a problem, and I need you to hear me out. Don't say anything till I'm finished. Okay?"

With her arms folded across her chest, Shayna gruffly responded, "Okay."

"I'm not an alcoholic, but I'm going through some things right now that may lead me to drink. And I don't want that to happen 'cause I love you and our baby. And I want us to be happy. I *hate* my job. I'm not a life insurance agent. I'm a chef. But I know it's what I have to do in order to help take care of you and our baby till something else comes along.

"I admit I came close to taking a sip while ago, but I thought about you and how much I love you. I thought I could fight these urges by myself, but I don't think I can. I'm gonna join Alcoholics Anonymous. I can go to the meetings the same night we've been going to Al-Anon. While you're at Al-Anon, I'll be in the next room at AA. I need you, and I don't want to lose you. Can I count on your support?"

Shayna moved closer and threw her arms around her husband as her tears wet her cheeks. "You know you can."

Estelle had noticed during their picnic the looks Roger had been giving her, and they hadn't stopped even when they'd gotten home.

As they put away their picnic items, she stated, "You've been staring at me all day."

"Can't a man look at his wife? You complaining?"

"No. Just curious."

When they were done in the kitchen, they went to the den to watch television.

When a commercial came on the screen, Estelle said, "You mind if I ask you a question while this ad is on?"

"No. What is it?" Roger looked at her as she spoke.

"I need your opinion on something. I'm helping a bride-to-be pick out flowers for her wedding and reception. What d'you think would be pretty?"

Immediately, Roger responded with interest, "What about those pointy flowers on the long stems like the ones we have in the flower bed every year? You know, the red, yellow and purple ones. What're they called?"

Estelle raised her head as she smiled. "Calla lilies. You're right. Those would be perfect. Her main color is fuchsia. I think a soft pink and white would look nice. What d'you think?"

"I think they'll look good."

Estelle smiled as their television program came back on.

Later that night, after they'd gone to bed, she felt Roger turn over. When he put his arm around her, chills went up and down her spine. Was she ready for this moment? She'd been mentally complaining for a long time that he no longer found her attractive. As though she were a virgin, she grew nervous and timid. In a way, it would be like doing it for the first time, it had been so long.

Without saying a word, Estelle turned around to face Roger and fell into the warmth of his arms. When he kissed her, she felt fireworks. What came afterward was the grand finale.

The next afternoon, Gloria stopped by the shop on her way home from a hard day of work at the local high school, where she taught.

She jovially exclaimed, "Girl, you are glowing. What happened to you?"

Estelle blushed.

Gloria burst into laughter. "Oh, I should've known. You and Roger got your groove back."

Estelle laughed as she made a fist and playfully punched her friend's arm. "Gloria, you should be ashamed of yourself."

"Why? All I'm saying is you and Roger are back in your settled routine. What's wrong with that? You're husband and wife. Don't act all embarrassed. Remember some of the things you said to me when you were mad at him. Now that everything is lovey-dovey, you want to try and act all timid. I'm happy for the two of you. Well, now that everything's okay between you, I guess Donald and I won't be seeing that much of you anymore."

Estelle burst out laughing. "You need to stop."

Chapter 32

"Stelle!" Roger yelled from the kitchen. "We're gonna be late. Didn't you say the movie starts at five?"

"Something like that," Estelle called back. "I don't remember. Look on that piece of paper where I wrote it down. It's on the kitchen counter."

Grabbing up the slip of paper, Roger read it and stalked up the hallway to the bedroom. "Stelle, what is this? I told you I wasn't looking at no kid's movie. Isn't this that animated thing we've been seeing the previews of on TV?"

Estelle fastened her necklace around her neck. "Yes. I know you did. I thought it'd be fun."

"Two grown people sitting in a movie theater watching a cartoon. I don't think so."

"Roger, that's not fair. When we went to the movies last month, I saw that science fiction thing you wanted to see. You know I don't like that stuff, but I compromised. Now it's your turn. It won't kill you, you know, to watch something I wanna see sometimes."

She was right. "Okay. Okay. Are you ready yet?"

"Yes. I'm coming."

Estelle got the biggest thrill watching Roger try not to laugh during the movie. Several times, however, he couldn't keep in his chuckles. After the seventh or eighth time, he stopped trying to be discreet and hung loose.

Afterward, as they walked to their car holding hands, Estelle asked, "Now wasn't that fun?"

Roger tried to look serious. "It was aw-right."

Estelle laughed as she laid her head against his shoulder.

The next morning, while she was getting ready for worship service, Roger stepped out of the bathroom wearing a gray pin-striped suit with a cobalt-blue shirt and red striped tie. She'd never seen him look so handsome.

"Wow! You look good."

Roger grinned from ear to ear. "Thank you."

"Where are you going?"

"With you. Is that okay?"

Estelle smiled. "Sure." She couldn't believe this was happening. When Roger stepped back into the bathroom, she raised her face toward heaven and whispered, "Thank you, Lord."

The next day, it was almost lunchtime when one of their regular customers came into the shop.

"Mrs. Brickman," Lidia said, "Ms. Adams is out front. She wants to ask you a question about some flowers."

Estelle looked at her assistant and smiled. "All right, Lidia. I'll be right there." She finished entering the data she'd been inputting into the computer before getting up and going to greet the woman.

The two of them embraced.

"Mildred, it's so nice to see you. How are you doing?"

She smiled. "I'm fine, Estelle. And yourself?"

"Oh, I'm wonderful. It's a beautiful day, and spring is in the air." Although it was still January, with February just two days away, they were having mild weather. "What can I help you with? Lidia said you had a question about some flowers."

"Yes. Well, as you mentioned, it feels like spring already. My daffodils are in full bloom. I cut some Friday when I went home for lunch. Now they look horrible. They were so vibrant when I cut them. What happened?"

"Well, Mildred, I think I know what your problem is. If I remember correctly, it was a pretty sunny day Friday. You should never pick your flowers in the middle of the day when the sun is at its hottest."

"Oh, really? Why not?"

"The sun's heat lowers the water content in the flower stems, and the blooms won't last long."

"Oh, I see."

"Always pick your flowers in the morning or late evening. The best time is early morning, because that's when the stems are filled with water after the cool night air."

The woman grinned. "Now I never would've known that if I hadn't asked you. Thank you so much. I'll remember that."

As Estelle walked Mildred to the door, she said, "You're welcome. No problem. Have a good day."

Estelle returned to her office. When the private line on her telephone rang, she cheerily answered it. "Good afternoon. Stop And Smell The Flowers."

The deep baritone voice caught her by surprise. "Good afternoon. I would *love* to smell your flowers."

"Who is…?" Estelle heard a familiar laugh. "Roger, is that you?"

When the laughter on the other end grew louder, she got her answer.

Roger said, "Hey, baby."

The sound of his voice sent Estelle's heart reeling. "It's the middle of the day. What're you doing calling?" He never phoned her at work.

"Can't a man call his wife and see how her day is going?"

"Yes, he can. I—I just wasn't expecting you to call. How sweet."

"So how's your day going so far?"

"Wonderful. I just gave a customer some tips on what time of day to pick her flowers so they last longer."

"You did? Oh, that's important stuff. Everybody needs to know that," Roger teased.

Estelle laughed. "Will you stop? People love flowers. They cheer them up when they're feeling blue. Even if they're not sad, they make them even happier."

Roger laughed.

Estelle asked, "Well, how's your day going?"

"It's going. Not as exciting as yours. All I do is mess with electricity all day. You know, the stuff that helps keep your business going so you can sell your pretty flowers to everyone."

Both of them let out hearty laughs.

Roger said, "Well, I'm on my lunch. I better go. I'll see you when I get home. I love you."

"I love you, too."

Estelle was still smiling when she hung up the telephone. She could hardly believe how much better things had gotten between her and Roger in just a short while. She felt as though she was falling in love with him all over again. Her entire body shook from the happiness simmering inside her.

★ ★ ★

Catina bit into a plump red grape tomato at her and Justine's favorite pizza joint during lunch. She savored the delicious fruit as it burst inside her mouth. "Ooh, I love these little tomatoes. They're so sweet and juicy. They just make me want to scream, they're so good."

Justine didn't respond. Catina had noticed lately that, considering Evan was home, her friend didn't seem too happy.

"What's the matter?"

"Hmm?"

"You're so quiet. What's wrong?"

Justine shifted in her seat, a puzzled expression on her face. She took a sip of blackberry lemonade. "I don't know, Cat. It's Evan. He seems so distant since he's come home. He's not the same person. I mean, I know I hurt him. I don't expect everything to be exactly like it was, but I didn't expect this, either." She smiled briefly as she let out a fake chuckle. "You know, there used to be a time when he couldn't keep his hands off me. Now, I practically have to beg him for affection."

Catina eyed her friend. "He's still hurting, Justine. It's gonna take some time."

Justine blinked back her tears. "I know. It's just that this is a lot harder than I imagined it would be. Maybe a part of me expected things to just go back to normal once he came home. I know that's naive thinking. But I was hoping."

"Well, have you tried talking to him about it?"

"No. He's so touchy now I'm afraid I'll upset him. Recently, when I told him I wanted to have a baby, he got mad at me. He asked me if he's supposed to want a baby now 'cause I feel the time is right. I don't know what to say to him. It's like I'm walking on eggshells. I'm afraid if I say the wrong thing, he'll leave again, and I don't want that."

"I know you don't, but you have to talk to him. Things aren't gonna get better if you don't. Try to be tactful when you talk to him."

Later that night, when Justine and Evan were eating supper, she asked, "How was your day?"

He answered without looking up from his plate. "Fine. Yours?"

"Okay. I've had a lot on my mind lately."

Evan said nothing.

"Can we talk?"

"Sure."

Justine could feel her underarms perspiring as she struggled to find the right words. "Honey, I don't mean to upset you, but I've noticed how distant you've been toward me since you came home. I just thought maybe we could talk about it. I know you're still hurting over what I did. I wish I could erase that part of our lives. I know it's gonna take some time for you to be able to trust me again, but I'll wait as long as I have to."

Evan continued eating his food and said not a word.

Justine pleaded, "Evan, please speak to me. How can we work things out if we don't talk?"

He stared into her eyes. When he spoke, his words were like a slap in the face. "There's nothing to talk about. I'm home. That's what you wanted."

Justine blinked back tears. "Isn't it what you wanted, too? Didn't you want to come home?"

"If I didn't, I wouldn't be here, would I?"

That was not the answer she wanted to hear, but for now, Justine decided to leave the matter alone.

Chapter 33

Chase Matthew Brickman was born a week early. Justine, her parents, and Evan drove down to Savannah the morning of his birth to welcome him into the world and personally congratulate his parents.

In the waiting room, Roger teased Justin, asking where they'd gotten the baby's name. He said "Chase" made it sound as if the baby needed to be running somewhere. Justin Roger Brickman III would have sounded much better, in Roger's opinion.

Justin explained that he and Shayna wanted their son to have his own identity, and they thought a different name was a great start.

Justin was pleased to see his parents getting along, a much different scenario from when he'd been home a few months ago. However, he noticed that his sister and Evan seemed a little distant toward one another.

Later that night, after they'd all returned from the hospital, they sat in Justin's and Shayna's living room talking and reminiscing.

Roger was saying to Justin, "And just wait till you have to change Chase's diaper. If his poop is anything like yours was, you're gon' need an oxygen mask to keep from passing out."

Everybody burst out laughing, including Estelle, who elbowed her husband and playfully reprimanded him. "Roger, I can't believe you said that."

"Well, it's true," he insisted. "You know it is."

Justin shook his head. "I'm glad Shay's not around to hear all this. Dad, you're embarrassing me."

Estelle added, "Oh, and just wait till he gets a little older and you start reading him bedtime stories. You'll be like your daddy. Whenever he'd read you a story when you went to bed, I'd peek in on the two of you. You'd be up, running all over the bedroom, and he'd be sprawled out on your bed, snoring up a storm."

Laughter filled the room again.

Roger playfully protested, "No, I wasn't."

Estelle said, "Yes, you were. You know you were. Don't be denying it."

When Evan exited the room, everybody was still chuckling. He went to the kitchen and out onto the patio. The crisp, cool breeze of the February night swept across his face as he sat down at the table and stared up at the stars.

Suddenly, he heard someone say, "Hey, man. You okay?"

Evan turned slightly to see Justin standing behind him. "Yeah, I'm fine."

"Mind if I join you?" Justin asked as he pulled out a chair.

"Naw. Go ahead."

He took his seat. "I'm glad you and Justine are back together. Is everything okay?"

When Evan wasn't quick to respond, Justin added, "I'm not trying to be nosy or anything. I just sense a little tension between you two."

Evan didn't know quite how to respond. He didn't want to say anything negative about Justin's sister, yet he couldn't pretend everything was back to normal. "It's gonna take some time for things to get back the way they were, if they ever do."

Justin didn't like his brother-in-law's last statement. It sounded as if Evan had doubts about his marriage. "Man, Justine loves you. Everybody knows that. I know what she did was wrong, but you guys can make it through this."

Evan shook his head sadly. "I don't know, man. When trust is gone, what else do you have?"

"Love," Justin answered.

"Is love enough?"

"Yeah. It can help you trust again."

"I want to trust her again, but I don't know if I can. I love her. I've never loved anybody like I love Justine. That's what makes it so hard. She took what we had and threw it away. If you love somebody, how can you do that?"

Justin shook his head in dismay. "We're all imperfect. We make mistakes."

"That's not an excuse."

"I'm not saying it's an excuse. I'm saying it's the reason we mess up sometimes. Why we do stupid things and wonder later why we did them."

Justin felt the need to share something personal with Evan. "You're the first person I've told this to, but when I came home to Alabama a few months ago, it wasn't just because I'd lost my job. I let Mama, Dad and Justine think Shay put me out just 'cause I didn't have a job. The truth is, Shay told me to leave 'cause I quit a job I was finally able to get as a car salesman. I did it without talking to her about it.

"The day she found out, she had gone to my workplace to take me out to lunch. Someone there told her I'd quit. She came home and found me passed out drunk on the bed. She was upset, and rightfully so. When I made a fist to try to scare her, that's when she told me to pack my things and leave. I wasn't gonna hit her. I'd never hit my wife. But she didn't know that at the time. I told her I was only trying to frighten her, and she said, 'Mission accomplished.' I'll never forget those words.

"Way before that happened, though, I'd been having drinking binges. It all started one night when I went out with some friends. We got to drinking, and I stayed out till sometime the next morning. Shay told me it better not happen again. I stayed straight for a while and eventually started back.

"Losing my job killed me, especially since I know I'm not guilty of what I was accused of. Then when we found out Shay was pregnant, I was happy, but even more stressed 'cause it wasn't gonna be just me and Shay anymore. I was gonna have another person to take care of.

"Recently, I had to do one of the hardest things I've ever had to do. I had to admit to my wife that I have a drinking problem. But she's been so supportive. On Monday nights, she goes to Al-Anon meetings, and I go to AA, in the same building, right next door to each other.

"Justine doesn't have the same problem I do—drinking. I drank so I couldn't feel the pain of what I was going through. Justine dealt with her fears in another way. You have every right to be mad. Shay has every right to be upset with me for what I put her through. It's not easy to forgive, and it's even harder to forget."

★ ★ ★

Shayna's family arrived the next day. Evan didn't feel like socializing, so he stayed at the hotel. His day was spent at the indoor pool, then walking around the city, taking in the sights.

Later that evening, as he and Justine were riding the elevator to the first floor to go to dinner in the hotel restaurant, a beautiful young woman spoke to Evan by name when she entered the elevator on the fifth floor. He greeted her and quickly introduced her to Justine.

As soon as they were out of the elevator, Justine turned on Evan. "How d'you know her?"

"Who?"

"Lil' Miss Priss," Justine said, frowning and nodding her head toward the attractive beauty, who was walking several feet in front of them.

"We met this afternoon at the pool."

"Oh, really?"

"Yeah."

Evan continued toward the restaurant. However, Justine had stopped in her tracks, her arms folded across her chest.

When he noticed she wasn't keeping up with him, Evan halted and turned around. "You coming?" Justine just stood there, shooting daggers at him with her eyes. "What?" he asked, walking toward her. "Are you coming?"

"Not till you tell me what's going on with you."

"Justine," Evan whispered discreetly, "this isn't the time or place for this. Come on," he said, gently grabbing her arm.

Justine snatched her arm free and snapped, "Don't be pulling on me."

Evan said, "I wasn't pulling on you. Are you coming?"

"No, I'm *not* coming. I'm not going anywhere with you till you talk to me. Ever since you came home, you've been acting like a spoiled child. You act like you don't want to be with me, but I see you didn't waste any time meeting someone else."

"Meeting someone else. Justine, what're you talking about? I haven't met anybody."

"What about lil' Miss Priss back there? I guess you'd rather be with her than me."

"Justine, I just met that lady today, and I hadn't even thought about her till we saw her on the elevator a minute ago. Can we go eat now?"

"No, I don't want to eat with you. Go by yourself, or find lil' Miss Priss to eat with you. I'm sure you'll be happier with her than you are with me."

People were starting to stare at them.

"You're making a fool of yourself."

"Yeah, I'm a fool all right. A fool for wanting you to come back home."

Evan found Justine in their room, lying across the bed crying. Sitting on the bed and clasping his fingers together, he looked at her heaving back.

"Justine, we need to talk."

She suddenly sat up and yelled, "I've been trying to get you to talk to me since you came back home. What do you want to tell me? You're gon' leave me for that lil' heifer back there?"

"Justine, that's crazy. I told you I just met her today at the pool. I'm not interested in her."

"Well, you're not interested in me. What's wrong? Why did you come back home? Was it 'cause you felt sorry for me the day I came to your apartment to talk? Or was it 'cause you really love me and wanted to try to make our marriage work? If you came back out of pity for me, you may as well leave, because it won't work. There was a time right after you left that I felt sorry for myself and wanted you to feel sorry for me, too. But not anymore. I've changed."

Although her episode this afternoon concerning the girl was her biggest relapse so far, Justine still felt good about how far she'd come. "I'm sorry. I didn't mean to behave like a crazed, jealous woman. It's just that you act like you don't want to be with me anymore, sexually or otherwise. For the first time, I think I know how my mama must have felt all those years she complained about Daddy not showing her he loved her.

"I thought we could get through this, but now I don't know if we can. Maybe you should've gone ahead with the divorce. I've messed up our lives forever. I can't change what I did. I wish I could, but I can't. I've never loved anyone the way I love you. To not have you in my life would be like not having the air I need in order to breathe. I'm lost without you, but I'll have to learn to go on, with or without you."

Evan met Justine's gaze. "I didn't know it would be this hard. I try not to think about what you did, but it keeps coming back. And I guess us being here, in Savannah, and seeing Justin and Shayna and the baby, has just made it harder. I'm happy for them, but I envy them, too. I wish I could just act like nothing ever happened, but I can't. Maybe we need a little more time apart."

Justine began to cry. "Oh, Evan, I know I messed up. I don't deserve your love."

He put his arms around her and pulled her close to him. As she lay her head on his shoulder, he spoke in a tender tone. "Don't ever say you don't deserve my love or anybody else's. Everyone deserves to be loved. No matter what you did, you deserve to be loved. I'll always love you, no matter what."

Savannah—this was their city. The city of love. Where they'd honeymooned, then come back to almost a year ago for Justin's wedding. Now they'd returned for the birth of Justin's son. But it was also the end of a marriage.

Chapter 34

Estelle whispered as she sat in Justine's cubicle, "You can't let on to your daddy about this trip now."

Justine grinned. She was very happy for her parents and excited about the surprise belated honeymoon cruise to the Bahamas that her mother was planning for their thirty-eighth wedding anniversary next month.

Justine murmured, "I won't," playfully mocking her mother. "You don't have to whisper. He's not here. He won't hear you."

Estelle laughed. "I know. I'm just trying to get in the habit of keeping a low profile. You know how loud I can get sometimes."

"Yes, I know."

Estelle did a double take as she eyed her daughter. "Okay, now. You weren't supposed to agree with that." Her heart went out to Justine. Ever since they'd all returned home five days ago and Evan had moved out again, Estelle had been worried about her. Although Justine seemed to be all right, she couldn't help but express her concern. "Are you okay? You look like you've lost weight. You're not eating, are you?"

Much to her surprise, Justine had finally accepted the fact that she and Evan might never get back together. Their parting was a peaceful one. The Al-Anon meetings and her spiritual routine were helping her to stay grounded.

"I'm fine, Mama." She attempted to change the subject. "Are you excited about your fishing trip with Daddy tomorrow?"

Estelle grinned widely. "Honey, yes. I can't *wait* to get out on that boat."

Justine frowned. "I still don't understand why y'all want to go fishing in February in forty-degree weather."

"Well, your daddy said we can light the kerosene heater and wear our coats and gloves. Besides, there's a full moon tonight. He said the fish'll really be biting tomorrow."

Justine grinned at how her mother was clinging to her father's every word as though it was gospel. Justine was extremely happy that her parents had gotten back together and, for the first time in years, seemed to really be getting along. Her mother's glow had returned. Even her father had found his smile and seemed more cheerful and pleasant. "You still planning to make it an all-day thing?"

"Yep."

"Well, I hope you have a wonderful time. I know you've been looking forward to this for quite a while."

"Yeah, I can't wait."

Later that afternoon, when Justine got home from work, her father called to go over the vow renewal details. Although Estelle wasn't home yet, Roger whispered into the telephone receiver as he sat in the den. "She doesn't know anything, does she?"

"No, Daddy. Not to my knowledge, she doesn't. If she does, she hasn't let on. Did you get the invitations ordered yet?"

"Yeah. They should be back in a couple of weeks. In plenty of time for me to address 'em and mail 'em out."

"You sure you don't want me to help you with them?" Justine admired her father's heartfelt desire and determination to take care of every detail of the surprise ceremony himself.

"I got it. You just keep your mama's nose off my trail."

Estelle couldn't believe she was out on a boat on a lake at nine o'clock on a Saturday morning in forty-degree weather. As she sat waiting for Roger to teach her his favorite sport, all she could think about was her nice, warm bed at home.

He handed her a pole. "Okay, the first thing you have to do is bait your hook."

Estelle frowned as she took the pole. "Bait my hook? We're not gonna use live bait, are we?"

"Yep. That's the best kind."

"Don't they make artificial bait—those lil' plastic things?"

"Yeah, but I told you we're using live bait."

"I hope we're not using worms. I'm not touching those slimy things."

"You don't have to worry 'bout that. Here," Roger said, holding something out to her, "have a cricket."

Estelle shrieked, "Ooh! That's just as bad. I'm not touching that thing."

"If you want to catch anything, you've got to. I'm not gon' do it for you. You wanted to learn. Now here's your chance. So come on. Take it and put it on."

Estelle attempted to grasp the small black insect between her fingers. It felt cold and squishy. As soon as she touched it she screamed and dropped it in the boat. "Aww! I can't do it."

"Stelle, you're a florist. You love gardening. You run across these things all the time in the yard when you're planting flowers."

"Yeah, but when I see 'em, I squish the life out of 'em. I don't pick 'em up. I can't touch those things. Put it on for me, please."

Roger took the pole from his wife, teasingly chastising her as he baited her line. "You're always giving me a hard time about something, and the first time you see a cricket, you go screaming." He gave the pole back to her.

Estelle took it. "You can talk about me all you want. I'm still not touching those things."

"Okay. Now you gotta cast out your line. Always swing the pole behind your head and flick out with your wrist. Let the reliever go when you get ready to throw the line."

Roger stood off to the side while she attempted to follow his instructions. The first time she tried, the line landed in a tree. He was able to retrieve it, and she got it in the water on the second try.

"Okay. Now you have to pull the line toward you to take the slack out of it." As Estelle tugged on it, Roger murmured, "Good. A little more. Little bit more. There you go."

Estelle was beaming that she'd finally done something else right. She was enjoying this.

"Now when you see your line moving, and your float goes underwater, that means a fish bit your hook. You'll need to pull back on the line real quick and start reeling it in. If the fish starts fighting, just let it fight till it gets tired. Pull the line a little bit, then give it some slack. Pull a little more and give some slack. Keep doing that and pull him in."

After several minutes of waiting, Estelle felt a bite on her line. Roger cheered her on as she reeled in her catch.

"Hey, you got a pretty good-size one for your first time. Now you gotta take him off the hook."

"Roger, I can't do that. I don't wanna touch it."

"Stelle, how come you want to go fishin' but don't want to touch the bait or the fish? You shoulda stayed home," Roger snickered. "At least try."

To her surprise, she managed to remove the hook from the fish's mouth. However, as soon as it was free, it wiggled in her hand and jumped back into the water.

Estelle screamed, "Oh!"

Roger playfully complained, "Now we're gon' have to catch that one all over again."

"I couldn't help it. It started wiggling and just jumped out before I knew it."

"Yeah, yeah."

They fished until noon. Then Roger told her they could stop and eat the lunch they'd brought.

Estelle looked around the lake, asking, "Where do we wash our hands?"

He laughed heartily. "All this water out here and you wonder where to wash your hands? Just dip 'em in the lake and rinse 'em off."

Estelle's eyes grew huge. "Are you crazy? I'm not sticking my hands in there. There's no telling what all's in there."

"Well, suit yourself."

After a brief contemplation, Estelle imitated Roger and rinsed her hands in the lake.

They returned to their fishing after they ate. Another boat soon drifted by.

A man aboard yelled, "Fish biting here?"

Before Roger could respond in the negative, Estelle blurted, "Yes, they sure are. We've caught a bunch."

As the boat anchored nearby, Roger said, "Stelle, don't *ever* tell anybody the fish are biting."

She wrinkled her brow. "Why not?"

"We don't want them catching all the fish. Next time somebody asks you that, tell 'em no."

Estelle sighed. "Well, Roger, I can't lie to people."

"You don't have to. Just be quiet, and I'll tell 'em."

They fished some more until Estelle said, "I've gotta go to the bathroom."

"Well, give me a minute. I'll steer the boat over to those trees, and you can go behind the bushes."

Estelle cocked her head and gave him a crazed look. "Have you lost your mind? I'm not going to the bathroom out here. I need a *real* bathroom."

"Stelle, nobody'll see you. That's what people do out here."

"Well, it may be what everybody else does, but not me. You're gonna have to take me back where we parked the truck so I can use one of those Porta Potties. I'm not pulling my clothes down out here for every Tom, Dick and Harry to see my big behind."

Roger sighed. "Well, we're almost done anyway. We'll just call it a day and head back."

Relieved, Estelle said, "Thank you."

It would be a very long time before she asked Roger to take her fishing again. To her, it wasn't all it was cracked up to be. She couldn't wait to get back on dry land.

Chapter 35

Catina was on the telephone with a client when she saw Justine breeze by her cubicle like a streak of lightning.

When Justine returned, Catina asked, "Girl, are you okay? You came flying by here awhile ago. I didn't know you could move that fast. Where were you going?"

Justine plopped down onto one of the chairs in Catina's office. "I had to go the restroom. That sausage-egg-and-cheese biscuit made me sick. I took one bite and had to go throw up."

Catina eyed Justine mysteriously.

"What?"

"You're pregnant."

Justine's eyes looked as though they would pop out of her head. "I am not."

"Yes, you are."

"Why is it every time a woman gets sick or throws up, everybody thinks she's pregnant?"

Catina chuckled. " 'Cause that's usually what it is."

Justine covered her mouth with her hand. "Oh, no. You think I am?"

"I could be wrong. What d'you think?"

"Evan and I hardly did anything when he came back home. We only made love once. He was acting so strange."

"Girl, if I had a nickel for every baby conceived the first time his parents had sex, I'd be rich. I wouldn't be working here."

Justine suddenly put her hand to mouth and said, "Oh, no."

"What's wrong?"

"Now that you mention it, I think you may be right. I was so stressed about Evan that I forgot to take my pills a few times. It never occurred to me that I might get pregnant."

"Have you had any other symptoms?"

"I'm tired. A little light-headed. But that could be anything."

"Well, you know what to do to find out."

"A home pregnancy test."

"Yeah. Unless you can wait until you can get an appointment and see your doctor. Are you still taking the pills?"

"No, not since Evan left this last time."

When she got off work, Justine stopped by the store and bought a pregnancy test. When she got home, she read the instructions, took the test and waited the required amount of time to check the results.

Positive. Justine couldn't believe her eyes. She was pregnant. She and Evan were having a baby.

Evan. She couldn't tell him. He'd come home for sure if he knew. He had to return of his own free will. If he knew she was expecting, he'd come back out of obligation. That wasn't the way she wanted them reunited, if they ever did get back together.

What would she do if they didn't work things out before she started showing? What if they did settle their situation, though, and it ended in divorce? Then she'd be a single parent. That wasn't what she wanted for her child. What would she do?

"Hey, honey!" Estelle yelled to her husband. "Justine's here."

Despite her apathy, Justine smiled at the endearment her mother now used when speaking to her father. Sometimes she'd hear him call her mother "baby." Justine was happy that they seemed to have fallen in love all over again.

Roger appeared. His face lit up when he spotted his daughter. "Hey, honey. How ya doing?"

"I'm fine, Daddy," Justine answered as she stood on tiptoe to peck him on the cheek.

Estelle observed her daughter meticulously. "You look tired." Glancing at Roger, she added, "Doesn't she look tired?"

"A little, but she said she's fine."

"Well, I don't believe her. I'm her mother, and a mother knows these things." Taking Justine by the arm, Estelle led her into the den. "Come and sit down. Are you hungry? You still look a little thin. You want me to fix you something to eat?"

Justine held up her hand. "No, Mama. I'm fine. I've already eaten."

"What did you eat? Probably had a bag of popcorn and called it supper."

"Stelle, she said she's fine. Leave her alone."

Estelle gave her husband one of her stern motherly looks. "Roger, I know my children. She's not fine. That's what she wants us to believe, but I know better."

"Mama, I'm *okay,* but I do have something to tell you and Daddy."

Estelle faced Roger again and playfully stuck her tongue out at him. "I knew it." Turning back to Justine, she asked, "What is it, baby?"

Justine knew of no way to tell her parents the news except to be forthright. "I'm pregnant."

Estelle almost hit the ceiling when she jumped up. "You are?"

Justine nodded as anxiety flooded her heart. Estelle sat down beside her and wrapped her arms around her. "Oh, baby, that's wonderful."

Roger stood and joined them on the sofa. He and Justine embraced. "Congratulations. Evan must be excited."

Justine's eyes fell to the floor. "He doesn't know."

Estelle asked, "Well, you're gonna tell him, aren't you?"

"No, not right away."

Estelle wrinkled her brow. "Why not? He's the father. He has a right to know. You know how much he's been wanting the two of you to have a baby."

"Mama, that was before everything got so complicated. If I tell him now, he'll come home."

"Well, isn't that what you want?"

"Yes, but not under these circumstances. I want him to come back because he *wants* to. When he moved back the last time, I think it was because he felt sorry for me. I went to his apartment and got all upset trying to talk to him. And you see what happened. I can't go through that again. My heart can't take it. Neither one of you can tell him. Promise me you won't say a word to him. You've got to let me handle this my way."

Estelle hung her head and shook it from side to side. "I don't know, Justine. Don't take this the wrong way, but not being honest with Evan in the first place is why things are the way they are now."

Justine immediately replied, "This is different. I misled Evan when I let him think I was off the pill. This time, I'm not trying to deceive him. I forgot to take my pills a few times after he came back home 'cause I was stressed that things weren't going as well between us as I'd hoped they would. I'm pregnant, but I didn't plan it. I mentioned to him one time after he came back that I wanted us to have a baby. He got upset, and I didn't say anything else about it. Please promise me you won't tell him."

Estelle and Roger looked at one another before responding in unison, "We promise."

The next morning, Roger grinned as he informed Estelle, "I'm going fishing. Want to come?"

Estelle smiled as she waved him off. "No, that's okay. You go and have fun. Gloria and I are spending the afternoon with Justine."

Roger laughed. "Stelle, you beat all I've ever seen. You pitch a hissy fit about me going fishing and tell me you're gonna come. You go one time, and now I can't get you to go back. What's up with that?"

Estelle grinned. "You know what's up with that. I admit I bit off a lil' more than I could chew, and I'm just not interested anymore. I've learned it's good for us to do things together, but we should also have individual interests. So you can keep fishing to yourself."

Roger let out a hearty chuckle. "I love you," he said as he kissed her forehead.

Estelle frowned as she wiped her brow. "Your lips are wet."

Roger grinned. "Yeah, I know. I just got through drinking some water."

"Next time, wipe your mouth. You know I don't like that."

"Yes, you do. You love it, and you know it. You just don't want to admit it."

Estelle hiked her head in the air as she turned to leave. "Oh, get outta here." Whirling around, she added, "Smoochies," as she puckered her lips for a kiss.

Chapter 36

The ladies were treating themselves to a four-hour serenity spa, which included lunch. For Justine, it was just what the doctor ordered. The stress she'd felt earlier had been washed away. She bit into a sweet, succulent chunk of pineapple and savored the juiciness.

Gloria cheerily declared, "Ooh, ladies, I feel fantastic. We should do this more often."

"I know," Estelle said. "Girl, if I did this as much as I'd like to, we'd have to take out a second mortgage on the house."

"Don't I know it," Gloria agreed.

When they were finished at the spa, they went shopping at the mall. As they browsed through the stores, Justine eyed the baby clothes and furniture, trying her best not pick up anything and buy it. She was getting really excited about the baby. She just wished Evan were around to share it with her.

At the end of their evening together, she went home and climbed into bed early.

Justine woke up the next morning feeling extremely nauseated. She hated to miss worship service, but got some crackers and water, climbed back into bed and nibbled on the saltines. She was soon fast asleep, dreaming about herself, Evan and the baby. They were together and happy. They had a little boy who looked just like Evan. When she awakened and realized she'd been dreaming, sadness flooded her heart. She prayed for strength to endure whatever resulted.

The following Saturday, the guys played cards at Darryl's house.

"Evan," Darryl called out, while Jarrod and Ray stared at him, waiting for him to throw down his card.

Evan looked at Darryl. "Hmm?"

"It's your turn."

"Oh." He placed his card on the table.

"Man," Ray said, "you been sitting there for ten minutes just staring at the cards. Why don't you go talk to her instead of sitting here looking like a lovesick puppy?"

"Yeah, man," Jarrod agreed. "It's obvious your mind ain't here. I haven't seen you look this pitiful since I whipped you at basketball a few weeks ago."

Evan placed his elbow on the table and rubbed his left temple.

Darryl said, "They're right, man. Why don't you call her or go over there or something?"

Without saying a word, Evan stood, grabbed his jacket from the back of his chair and left.

Justine wasn't expecting company. She wondered who was at the door. When she asked who it was and heard Evan's voice, her heart skipped a beat. Suddenly, she felt nervous.

"Hey," Evan said. "Can I come in?"

Justine opened the door for him to enter. "Sure."

He followed her to the living room, where they sat down.

When Justine offered him something to drink, a voice inside her head said, *He isn't a guest. He's still your husband. This is his house, too, even though he doesn't live here. Let him get his own drink.*

It didn't matter. He'd declined her offer.

Evan looked sad. "I'm sorry for coming by unannounced. I just wanted to talk to you."

Justine simply stared at him, not really knowing what to say, if anything.

Evan's heart was filled with sorrow as he struggled to find his voice. "I've really missed you." With his hands clasped together in front of him, he said, "I've missed *us.* I know I didn't make things any easier when I came back, but I was so angry at you. I told myself a thousand times that I didn't want to stay with you, but my heart kept telling me something different. I tried to run away, but I'm tired of running. I need to come home. Can I move back?" He looked at Justine with tears in his eyes. "I'll try to make it work this time. I'll even go with you to your Al-Anon meetings if it'll help me understand how living with alcoholism can affect people. I love you. I can't lose you. Can I come home?"

This time when Justine spoke, she shed no tears. It wasn't that she had no compassion for her husband. It was just that for the first time in a long while, she felt at peace about the changes in her life and how far she'd come to get where she was emotionally. Yes, she still loved Evan with all her heart and had a deep desire for him to come back, but this time, he would do it of his own accord.

Justine surprised herself when she swallowed back the sadness in her voice. "I want our marriage to work. I've always wanted it to work, even when I messed things up. You can come home. That's where I've always wanted you, but I know now that it's not gonna work if it's not where you want to be."

Evan looked at her longingly. This was a different Justine than the one he'd left behind. This one seemed much stronger. "It's where I want to be. With you is always where I want to be."

Justine said, "I have something to tell you, and I don't know how you'll feel about it, or if you'll still want to come home after I do tell you. Your feelings on the subject have changed since I destroyed your trust, but I have to share this. Then you can decide if you still want to move back."

Evan's heart was racing as fear about what Justine might tell him rose inside him. "What is it?"

Her tone was serious when she replied, "We're having a baby."

Evan looked at her with deep adoration and smiled through his tears. "We are?"

She nodded. "Yes. How does that make you feel?"

He got up and joined her on the sofa. Taking her hand in his, he said, "It makes me very happy."

Though he had given the answer she wanted to hear, Justine was trembling inside. "So you're not angry?"

Evan wrinkled his brow. "No. Why would I be angry?"

She looked deep into his eyes. "When you came back home, you got upset with me when I said I wanted to have a baby. I was stressed because things between us weren't going as well as I expected. A few times, I forgot to take my pills. I don't want you to think I got pregnant intentionally to try to lure you back home. I—"

Evan tenderly placed his index finger on her lips. "Shh. I don't think that. Besides, I'd already asked to come back when you told me."

Good point, Justine thought, feeling much better.

Evan continued, "All that matters is that we're back together. I love you."

Rays of happiness began to shine brilliantly throughout Justine's soul. "I love you, too."

When she and Evan kissed, she felt as though the love they shared would last forever.

As Justine and Evan lay in bed the next morning, he happily declared, "We were so busy making up last night I forgot to ask when's our baby due."

She giggled. "September twenty-third."

"Wow. I can't believe it. We're actually gonna have a baby. I hope it's a girl and she looks just like you."

"Well, I hope it's a boy and he looks just like you."

"Maybe it'll be twins."

Justine laughed. "Whoa. Don't wish that on us. One at a time will be enough."

"What did Mom and Dad say?"

"They're tickled to death."

"Man, I can't wait to tell Darryl and Jarrod and Ray. I'm gonna be a daddy. I feel like shouting it to the world."

Justine laughed.

"How are your parents? Is everything still okay with them? I remember how lovey-dovey they were when we went to Savannah to see the baby."

"They're great. Guess what?"

"What?"

"Their thirty-eighth wedding anniversary is next month. Daddy's planning a surprise vow renewal for them, and Mama's booked a surprise belated honeymoon cruise for the two of them. Neither one knows what the other is planning, so don't spill the beans."

"I won't. That's really amazing. A year ago, they were

fighting like dogs and cats. Now they're acting like two lovebirds." Evan's tone took on a serious note. "I think it just goes to show how life is. I mean, I never expected us to go through any of the things we've gone through. Despite all that's happened, we're together again. Right here in your arms is where I always want to be."

Justine smiled. "Well, in seven months, you'll have to make room for little Evan or Justine."

"That's fine. I think there'll be enough room for both of us."

Chapter 37

Roger was quiet on the drive home from the service. Estelle commented on his demeanor.

"I was just thinking about the sermon. What the minister said about how sometimes we make decisions in life and later start to second-guess them—even though we prayed about them beforehand—when we start having problems."

Estelle sensed that her husband was trying to tell her something. She looked at him and asked, "Have you ever second-guessed any of your decisions?" Disappointment rang in her voice. She thought back to the day he'd expressed his regret about marrying her. His words had hurt her terribly. Then she remembered that initially, it was she who had voiced her negative feelings about him.

She'd asked him the question about second-guessing his decisions to get him to open up to her. Things were so much better between them, but sometimes she still found it difficult to get him to talk to her about certain things. She didn't want to hear anything negative about herself. Just thinking about her harsh treatment of him made her heart ache. Why hadn't she just kept her mouth shut? She mentally chastised herself for talking too much.

"Yeah. Have you?" Sadly, Roger already knew the answer. Hopefully, Estelle no longer wished she hadn't married him since things were better between them.

"Yes" was her honest reply.

Roger hated bringing up the past, but asked anyway, "Like the time you said you wished you'd married somebody else instead of me?"

Estelle felt consumed with guilt. "Roger, why'd you have to bring that up? At the time I said it, I was angry. Things are better between us now. I used to feel that way, but I don't anymore." Irritated, she added, "We were having a nice conversation, and you spoiled it. That's what I get for trying to talk to you." She pouted as she looked out her window.

Roger's voice was filled with warmth when he stated, "I'm sorry. I didn't mean to upset you. I see that's a painful subject for you to talk about, so I won't bring it up again."

Estelle came to her senses and looked at him. "No, you shouldn't have to suppress your feelings for me. I'm sorry." She suddenly realized that it actually felt good to apologize to him. He'd just done the same to her. She thought back to times in the past when neither one of them would put their pride aside and beg the other's pardon.

She continued, "I know we don't talk about the past, and Justine seems to think that's part of our family's problems. She believes your mother's death caused you so much pain that you had to find something to numb it, so you started drinking. Is that what happened?" Estelle looked at Roger and grew still, uncharacteristically silent with the weight of the moment.

Roger let out a heavy sigh and tightened his grip on the steering wheel. He didn't want to hurt her any more than he already had, but the truth had to come out sooner or later.

When he said, "She's partially right," Estelle thought she would fall out of her seat. Actually hearing him admit it sent a shiver down her spine.

Guilt ground against Estelle's soul like an object brushing across sandpaper. The few times after his mother's death that she had attempted to get Roger to talk about his feelings, he'd become aggravated at her, telling her he didn't need to talk. Should she have been more persistent in trying to get him to open up to her?

Roger continued, "Mama was just going to the hospital for routine surgery on her gall bladder. Do you remember me telling you she got scared and changed her mind at the last minute and decided not to go through with it?"

Estelle slowly nodded her head as she looked at her husband, curious about where this conversation was headed. "Yes."

Roger relived the painful events. "I felt she needed to have the surgery, and you agreed with me. So I talked her into going ahead with it even though I wasn't sure I'd made the right decision. She came through the actual operation fine, but went into the coma afterward and never regained consciousness."

The memory of that tragic day flooded Estelle's mind.

Roger added, "She wouldn't have died when she did if I'd just respected *her* decision. It was my fault Mama died. I blamed myself."

Estelle's heart sank another notch as she listened to her husband share feelings that he'd kept buried in his soul for years. She was about to tell him that he wasn't to blame when his next words sent her reeling.

He confessed, "I blamed you, too."

Estelle turned in her seat and gave him a puzzled look. "Me? Why?"

Roger sensed that his declaration was distressing to his wife. He couldn't bear to look at her, for if he did, he would see clear to her wounded soul.

He answered, "Because you assured me I was making the right decision by convincing Mama to have the surgery. I was mad at you because you were always the smart one in our marriage and always knew the right thing to do. I felt like you steered me wrong. That you should have tried to talk me out of getting her to go through with it. I know it sounds crazy, but that's how I felt.

"It was hard trying to deal with all those negative feelings. One day when you and the kids had gone somewhere, I went to the store and bought a bottle of wine. Before I knew it, I'd drunk the whole bottle without even realizing it. That's when I noticed that the pain I was feeling wasn't so bad under the influence of the alcohol. So I kept drinking."

When Roger said, "I never meant to hurt you, Stelle, or our kids," Estelle observed a lone tear rolling down his cheek. "And I never cheated on you. I've made a lot of bad decisions in my life, but I've never been unfaithful to you."

It was such a relief to Estelle to hear that her husband had not defiled their marriage in such a way.

He tenderly added, "I've always loved you." He looked at her directly. "Even though I stopped acting like it, I always have." He turned again to face the road. "When you left with the kids, I didn't understand how you could leave me in my time of need. That made me even angrier. That's when the feelings of resentment started building up inside me. And even though I still loved you, it became so hard for me to show it."

Estelle said quietly, "Roger, pull the car over, honey. Do it slowly. Take your time."

He managed to maneuver the vehicle onto the side of the highway. After he'd shifted to Park, Estelle slid over and took him in her arms. They held each other for a long moment. Then she released him, raised her hands and wiped his face.

"It's okay," she whispered. "I know you didn't mean to hurt us. It's in the past."

When Roger leaned his head back against his seat and closed his eyes, Estelle stared at his face and placed a gentle hand on his chest. "Are you okay?"

He was all right. He'd just needed to close his eyes long enough to collect his thoughts. He drew in a sharp breath of air and quickly released it prior to lowering his head so that they were at eye level. "If you hadn't given me an ultimatum, I probably would've drunk myself to an early grave, or even worse, hurt you and the kids more than I did. You told me if I ever took another drink, you'd leave for good. I believed you. That's why I stopped, but I also knew if I ever drank again, I wouldn't have been able to control it 'cause I was so weak.

"The only way I could do it was to just quit cold turkey. But to keep from going back to the bottle, I had to occupy myself and my mind with something else other than you. So I started fishing, and that's all I wanted to do. It probably sounds crazy, but it kept me from drinking. It was my escape. But in the meantime, I allowed it to destroy what you and I had together. I hated myself for what I was putting you through. All those years, I could've tried to make you happy, but instead, I was making you miserable."

Roger had just laid a lot on her. His heartfelt apologies for the way he'd treated her touched her soul. Yet Estelle realized that she, too, had played a part in the near demise of their marriage. She was quick to remind him of that, for him bearing the burden alone was a heavy load to carry and totally unfair to him.

"Baby, it wasn't all your fault. Yes, I was lonely and hurting, too, but I didn't exactly go about it in a nice way when trying to express my feelings to you. I was so angry at you, and I never knew of your pain. Why didn't you tell me?"

"Sometimes, Stelle, it hurts too much to talk about things that cause us pain. Like how Justine handled the situation with Evan wanting a baby. Sometimes we use keeping things in as a defense mechanism, but in the long run, the pain catches up with us."

Estelle couldn't believe that it had taken them fifteen long years to start working on getting over the pains of the past. Yet as hard as everything had been, she still believed she had done the right thing when she'd left Roger all those years ago.

On Monday evening, as Justine and Evan drove home after the Al-Anon meeting, she asked, "So what'd you think about tonight?"

Evan nodded his head slightly as he drove. "It was very enlightening. I learned a lot. I'm glad I came."

Justine looked at him and smiled. "Thank you for coming."

When he glanced at her, he cast a smile her way. "You're welcome. Do you think your dad'll ever come?"

"I don't know. Daddy's changed a lot, but he's still set in some of his ways. Even though he finally confessed to Mama why he started drinking, that may be as far as he takes it. But at least he's talking about it now. I think that alone will help. Some people don't like talking about their private life in a group setting. I guess as long as they're talking, whatever works for them is okay."

"Yeah." Evan looked at Justine and noticed that she looked pale. "Are you okay?"

She propped her elbow on the car door and nodded her head. Suddenly, she'd begun to feel weak. "I'm fine. Just a little tired."

Evan glanced at her again. "You sure? Do you need to go to the emergency room?"

Justine shook her head. "No. I'm fine. I think when we get home, I'm going to bed."

He'd noticed lately that she didn't seem to be eating like she should. "You know, you really should eat better."

Justine countered, "I can't eat like I normally do because of the nausea."

"What did the doctor say about it?"

"Well, nausea's a common symptom of being pregnant. She said as long as the baby and I are both gaining weight, we should be fine."

Guilt consumed Evan. "I should've been with you when you went to the doctor. I'm sorry I wasn't. When's your next appointment?"

"In about three and a half weeks. March twenty-fourth." Justine didn't want him worrying about something he'd not known at the time. "Don't feel bad about missing the appointment. You didn't know."

They were quiet for a moment.

Evan suggested, "Maybe we should call the doctor and just tell her how you're feeling and see what she says."

Justine looked at him and remembered to smile because she wanted to prove to him that she was all right. "Baby, please stop worrying. I told you I'm fine. I'm just pregnant is all. It's how I'm supposed to feel."

Evan eyed Justine again. "I just want you and our baby to be okay."

"I know. I'm fine."

Despite Justine's reassurances, Evan still felt a little apprehensive. They had been waiting for this child for a long time, and he wanted nothing to go wrong. He decided not to press the issue of Justine getting medical attention, and vowed to keep an eye on her.

On Saturday, Justine and her mother went shopping.

"Justine," Estelle said, as they browsed through the plussize women's lingerie, "you got to be out of your mind if you think I'm gon' wear something like this."

Justine held up the blue floral chiffon baby doll set. "Mama, this would look gorgeous on you. It'll be a nice surprise for Daddy when you go on your cruise." She grinned and batted her eyes at her mother.

"Are you crazy? There's no way I'd let your daddy see me in that. I'm way too big to wear such a thing."

"No, you're not. Why d'you think they have it in your size? Here, go try it on. You want me to come with you?"

"Girl, no. I'm not gonna be embarrassed in front of my own child with this thing on. Only me and God'll see me in it."

Justine giggled. "And Daddy when you wear it on your surprise honeymoon cruise."

Estelle playfully swatted her daughter's hand. "Girl, you need to stop."

Justine smiled as her mother strode to the dressing room. When Estelle returned, she was wearing a grin so sparkling that it cast a glow over the entire store.

"That smile on your face tells me all I need to know."

Estelle simply blushed.

"See? I told you, didn't I?"

Estelle swatted her hand again. "Oh, hush."

As they made their way to the checkout counter, Justine said, "And thanks to Daddy giving you some money to buy yourself something nice to wear on your anniversary, you've got enough to buy your dress *and* your nightie."

Later, Justine talked to her father while her mother put her purchases away.

"What'd she get?" Roger asked.

Justine playfully elbowed him as she whispered, "Back off, Daddy. I can't tell you. If I do, she'll kill me. Your anniversary's almost two weeks away, and you're celebrating on the eighteenth, exactly two weeks from today. You'll just have to be patient."

"Well, can you at least tell me if it goes with the charcoal-gray suit I bought?"

Justine teasingly rolled her eyes. "Yes, Daddy, it matches your suit. It's pink, and that's all I'm telling you. She'd probably kill me if she knew I even told you that. Now stop asking me so many questions."

Roger grinned. "Well, you know, your mama's an attractive woman. She'll look good in anything she wears. I just want everything to be nice. She deserves it."

"I know. You both do. You've been through so much, and look at where you are now. I'm so happy for you and Mama and so glad you worked things out."

"Me, too. I love that woman with all my heart. Sometimes she still makes me mad, but I love her."

"I know, Daddy. She loves you, too."

Estelle had been on her way to join her husband and daughter when she overheard Roger expressing his feelings for her. And when he said she was attractive, he sent her heart reeling. He oftentimes expressed to her how good she looked, but hearing him rave about her to their daughter filled Estelle with an indescribable joy.

Chapter 38

The next day, Justine, Evan, Catina and Darryl decided to spend their Sunday afternoon at a jazz festival in the park. The women had packed a picnic basket full of goodies and spread a cloth out on the lawn. The weather was a pleasant sixty-eight degrees. Lots of people had come out to enjoy the music; however, it was not uncomfortably crowded.

Justine nibbled on a piece of fried chicken as she leaned against Evan and listened to the harmonics that danced on the gentle breeze. It was the first time during her pregnancy that she'd been able to keep a little something down. She didn't want to overdo it, so she was careful not to eat too much.

Evan asked, "Do you think the baby likes the music?"

Justine grinned as she tilted her head back to look up at her husband. "I think so. It's very soothing."

Evan leaned down and kissed her forehead. "Maybe she'll be a jazz musician."

"Or maybe *he'll* be a jazz musician."

Evan quickly countered, "Or maybe both *he and she* will be jazz musicians."

Justine laughed. "I told you don't be wishing twins on us."

Darryl asked, "Are you two arguing again over what sex the baby is and if it's one or two?"

"No, we're not arguing," Justine answered.

"Just voicing our opinions," Evan added.

Catina asked, "Have you felt him move yet?"

Justine shook her head. "No, it's too early."

"When will you be able to feel her move?" Evan asked curiously.

Justine decided not to debate the baby's sex with him this time. "Probably another six to eight weeks."

He placed his hand tenderly on her stomach. "It's hard to believe there's a little Evan or Justine in there—or both."

"Yeah, I know," Justine concurred before catching on to the last part of what he'd said. She quickly added, "I told you about that."

Evan chuckled. His laughter caused Justine's heart to swell with elation. He seemed to be finding his old self. He hadn't totally unearthed him, but Justine understood that it would take time. At least his sense of humor had returned, as he was mischievously revealing this afternoon.

Catina said, "I'm so happy for you guys."

"Me, too," Darryl added. "Hey, man, are you gonna be in the delivery room?"

"You know it," Evan said with enthusiasm. "I'm gon' be taking pictures and videotaping it all."

Justine almost fell over trying to sit up so she could see if he was serious. "Now, honey, I don't know 'bout all that. I don't want people in my business."

"It's not like we're gon' invite people over and show them

home movies. It'll be for the baby. When she gets older, we can let her see her birth."

Justine was still doubtful. "I don't know. Anyway, how're you gon' be by my side and help me relax if you're snapping pictures and videotaping like you were shooting a movie?"

Evan felt confident. "I can do both."

"Well, like I said, I don't know 'bout all that. This requires further discussion."

Evan joked, "We can discuss it all you want to, but when you're sedated, how're you gon' stop me?"

Justine laughed as she rocked her head from side to side. "I won't be sedated forever. Besides, I might just have the baby naturally."

Evan said, "I think that's a good idea."

Justine playfully rolled her eyes. "Yeah, *you* would think that. I'll be the one lying there in pain."

"Yeah, but I'll be by your side the whole time."

"Too bad I won't be able to switch places with you."

Catina and Darryl laughed, and Catina said, "Y'all are crazy." They enjoyed the rest of their food and the music.

"Honey, you don't look too good," Estelle told her daughter when she and Roger stopped by for a visit later that evening. "Are you sure you're okay?"

Justine sat back against the sofa, clutching one of the big plush throw pillows in her lap. "I'm fine, Mama. We went to a concert this afternoon. I'm just a little tired."

Ignoring her comment, Estelle asked, "Are you still feeling nauseated?"

"Yes, but I'm pregnant. Remember? All pregnant women feel nauseated."

"I know, but you need to be able to eat and keep your food down. When are you going back to the doctor?"

"The twenty-fourth of this month."

"That's almost three weeks away."

"Mama, I said I'm fine." Justine's tone was a little stern and her voice rose a notch.

"Okay, Miss Hardhead. Miss Can't Nobody Tell You Nothing. If you weren't pregnant, I'd put you over my knees and give you a good spanking."

"Mmm-hmm."

"Don't be mmm-hmming me."

Justine let out a deep sigh.

"Okay. I won't say another word about it." Looking around, Estelle inquired, "Where'd your daddy and Evan go?"

"I think they're outside playing basketball."

"In the dark?"

"We have lights outside, Mama. I think it's wonderful that Daddy's finally socializing more."

"Oh, I'm not complaining. I think it is, too. You know, it seems like he and I are totally different from the way we used to be. It's like we've rediscovered each other."

Justine was proud of the way her mother's face lit up when speaking about her father.

Estelle was still chattering away. "Like we only met for the first time recently and fell in love. I get butterflies every time I think about him. I never thought I'd feel this way again. I came really close to divorcing him. I'm glad now I didn't."

Justine smiled. "I'm glad, too. Marriage isn't easy. It takes a lot of hard work and commitment. But most of all, it takes God in your marriage to help you make it work."

Estelle wholeheartedly concurred. "I believe that. Do you remember the day I first went to church with you?"

Justine nodded.

"The sermon was about having a happy family life. The

Lord knew how unhappy I was, and I think he moved me to go with you that day. 'Cause if I hadn't, your daddy and I would probably be divorced by now. That's not really what I wanted, but I was so miserable that I felt it was the only way I could get any relief."

"I believe God moved you to go, too, Mama. He saw your heart was breaking, and he sent you to get the help you needed. But I also think he used Al-Anon to help us, too. I don't think either of us would be where we are without God's holy spirit and the group. I used to believe that if I trusted in him I shouldn't need any outside help, but sometimes he helps us through other people."

Estelle nodded at her daughter's wisdom. It just showed that a person was never too old to learn, not even from her children.

On Friday, Estelle and Roger decided to catch a movie. Since she had to stay on at the shop a few minutes to do some paperwork, they'd arranged that he would stop by and pick her up after he'd gone home to shower and change.

A few minutes before closing, someone entered the store. Estelle thought the man looked familiar, but she couldn't place his face at the moment.

She smiled as she greeted him, as she did with all her customers. "Hello. How are you?"

The gentleman returned her smile. "Hi. I'm fine and you?"

"Wonderful. How may I help you?"

After a brief hesitation, he said, "You don't remember me, do you?"

Estelle studied his face again. "No…but you look familiar. Have we met? I remember faces but not names."

"Yes, we met at Alabama Power's Memorial Day cookout

last year." Extending his hand, he said, "John Sinclair. I came over to where you were sitting, and we talked briefly."

Shaking his hand, Estelle's recollected their meeting. "Oh, yes, Mr. Sinclair. I'm sorry. I thought I recognized you from somewhere. It's good to see you again."

He stole a quick glance at her left hand, which rested on the counter. She still wore her wedding ring. His heart flipped over in his chest and did a nosedive to the pit of his stomach. He wondered how things were at home. The day they'd met at the picnic, he had sensed that she was depressed about something.

"It's good to see you, too. And please call me John. 'Mr. Sinclair' makes me feel like an ol' man."

"Oh, I'm sorry. I certainly wasn't implying…"

They released each other's hands. He cast her a gentle smile. "I know. It's okay."

"Well, what can I do for you today? Are you looking to send some flowers to that special someone?" As soon as the words were out of Estelle's mouth, she felt like crawling under a rock. She didn't want to give him the impression that she was interested in his availability. She didn't know what ideas, if any, she'd given him that day at the picnic. None, she hoped. She felt embarrassed when she quickly recalled the nice compliment he'd given her when they'd met. At a time when she had been feeling low, he'd made her feel ten feet tall.

"Oh, no." Realizing he'd probably insulted her, he said, "I mean, your flowers are very beautiful, but that's not why I stopped. I drive by here all the time. I saw you come in here one day this week. I didn't know you worked here."

Estelle wasn't offended by his assumption. She smiled. "Well, I kinda have to work here. I'm the owner."

John grinned. "Well, looks like I put my foot in my mouth

again. I am so sorry. I hope my comment didn't make me sound like a male chauvinist."

Estelle held up her hand. "No, I never thought that for a moment. It's okay."

John looked around admiringly. "You have a beautiful store."

"Thank you."

When she turned her beautiful smile on him, his heart skipped a beat. Well, she was still married, so he couldn't pursue her. He had no intention of coming between another man and his wife, but he was glad he'd stopped by to see her.

The door chime sounded. John turned around quickly to see a tall man with black-and-gray hair, mustache and sideburns enter the store. He nodded at John.

Estelle said, "John, this is my husband, Roger Brickman." To Roger, she said, "Honey, this is John Sinclair."

The two men shook hands.

"Well," John said, "I guess I better be going." He was careful to keep his tone natural, as he didn't want Estelle's husband getting any wrong ideas. "Goodbye, Mrs. Brickman." Nodding at Roger, he added, "And Mr. Brickman. It was nice to meet you, sir."

Roger quietly responded, "Nice to meet you, too."

Estelle said goodbye.

When the door had closed, Roger turned on Estelle. "He a customer?"

She grew nervous. Why, she didn't know. She hadn't done anything wrong. "No, he just came in to say hello."

Roger raised his eyebrows. "So you know him?"

"Not really."

Roger looked at her curiously. "Stelle, what d'you mean, not really? Either you know the man or you don't. He just stopped to say hello to a perfect stranger?"

"We only met once."

"Where?"

Roger's eyes seemed to be piercing straight through her. Estelle felt intimidated by all the questions he was hurling at her. "Roger, why are you asking me all this?"

He glared at her. "Why are you getting all defensive?"

"I'm not getting defensive. I just don't like your attitude."

"I'm just asking you some simple questions. Why're you getting all upset? You're acting like you've got something to hide."

"I don't appreciate your tone or your insinuation."

"You still haven't answered my question."

Estelle stalled in an effort to come up with a reply that would be pleasing to him. She was sure, though, that no matter what she told Roger, he'd take it the wrong way. "What question?"

"Where'd you meet him?"

In an effort not to appear as though she had anything to hide, which she didn't, Estelle blurted, "At the company picnic last year." She was quick to add, "That I went to with Gloria and Donald. The one you didn't wanna go to, remember?"

Roger felt something unpleasant brewing in his gut—suspicion and jealousy. "Oh, so because I didn't want to go, you met somebody while you were there and got all buddy-buddy with him?"

"No, I didn't get all buddy-buddy with him."

Roger folded his arms. "Well, what'd you do?"

Estelle glared at him from behind the counter. "You know what? This conversation is over." She rushed around past him and headed toward her office. "I'm not gon' stand here and argue with you over something silly. I think you better go, 'cause I'm not liking you right now." She stormed into her office and slammed the door.

Chapter 39

As soon as Estelle walked in the door, Roger started again. "So is he your boyfriend? Is that who you ran to when things were bad between us?"

Estelle turned on him. "If I'd had someone to run to, do you think I would've gotten so upset at you for constantly ignoring me? I'd never cheat on you. As lonely as I was, I never once considered it. And I'm not gon' stand here and be accused of it. After all I've put up with in this marriage, I deserve better than to be treated like this."

"If you haven't done anything, why'd you look so guilty when I asked you about him?"

"'Cause I knew you'd take whatever I said the wrong way, and I didn't wanna have to deal with this."

"All I know is I come to the shop to pick you up to take you out, and I catch you talking to another man."

"*Catch* me?" Estelle screamed. "You didn't *catch* me doing anything. All we were doing was talking, like you just said. You talk to other women, and I don't act crazy when you do."

"All the while you were walking 'round here accusing me of this and that, what were *you* doing?"

Estelle felt like yelling at Roger for two reasons. One: she was innocent, and he was accusing her of wrongdoing. Two: perhaps he had every right to be upset, considering all the times she'd charged him with adultery. Tears welled up in her eyes.

She imagined how he must have felt whenever she'd accused him of the same thing. Nevertheless, she replied, "I'm not gon' dignify that with a response." Then she walked away.

When Roger made it to the bedroom, he found her snatching his clothes out of the closet and throwing them on the floor.

"What are you doing?"

"Helping you pack."

"For what? I'm not going anywhere."

"Well, one of us is leaving, and it sure ain't gonna be me."

"I'm not going anywhere," Roger repeated. "You're the one cheating. *You* leave."

Estelle stopped what she was doing to stare at him. "I'm sick of you saying that. You know what?" She stepped on his clothes as she made her way to her closet and started removing her own clothing. "You don't have to leave. I'm glad I saw your true colors before I stayed married to you for another second."

Roger hadn't expected her to really leave. He'd only been bluffing when he'd told her to. Walking toward her, he pleaded, "Stelle, you don't have to do this. Let's talk."

"One of us has to do it. You won't so I will. And I don't wanna talk to you about anything. All I want from you is a divorce. I can't believe I was crazy enough to plan a honeymoon cruise with you, you jerk." Closing her suitcase, Estelle grabbed it by the handle, swung it off the bed and said, "Get outta my way." As she brushed past Roger, she almost knocked him down.

Justine pleaded, "Mama, what happened?" as she followed her mother to the spare bedroom she would be sleeping in.

"Your daddy is a jerk is what happened."

"But everything was going so well with you and Daddy. What happened?" Justine repeated.

"He had the nerve to accuse me of cheating on him. I've been nothing but faithful to him since the day we met." Estelle quickly rattled off a short version of what had transpired in the store.

"Mama, you and Daddy both need to calm down and talk about this."

"The only time I'm gon' speak to him is when we go to divorce court."

"But Mama, what about what we talked about recently—about how you believe God moved you to go to church and hear the message about having a happy family life?"

"Justine, there's no such thing as a happy family life. If there was, people wouldn't be so miserable."

"I don't believe that, and you don't, either. If you did, you wouldn't have gotten back with Daddy."

"I was crazy to get back with him, and I was crazy to ever have married him. I wish I'd never met him."

Justine stared at her mother in disbelief. "Mama, don't say that."

Estelle looked at her daughter. "Why not? It's true. That's *exactly* how I feel, and nothing you can say or do will change that." She slammed her suitcase down on the bed, opened it and started removing her clothes and hanging them in the closet.

Justine's voice was shallow. "If you'd never met him—if you'd never married him—you wouldn't have had me and Justin. Is that what you want? For us never to have been born?"

Estelle cast a look at her daughter. Her expression changed and her voice dropped to a whisper. "Justine, that's not what I meant, and you know it."

"Mama, think twice about what you say before you say it 'cause you can say things that hurt people and that stay with them forever. Justin and I are a part of both you and Daddy. My baby is also a part of you. So is Justin's baby. Are you gonna destroy your marriage over some nonsense? No relationship is perfect 'cause they're made up of imperfect people. God didn't say we can just throw a marriage away when we have hardships. You know what the only scriptural ground for divorce is. You say you didn't cheat on Daddy, and I believe you.

"Deep down inside, I think he knows you didn't cheat, either. You mentioned some man he saw you talking to in the shop. I think Daddy just got scared because he loves you so much, and maybe he's a little jealous, too. After all, he thinks you're the most beautiful woman in the world. But more than that, Mama, he knows you're beautiful on the inside, too. I believe he feels any man would feel blessed to have you, and he just acted on impulse. Go talk to him. Try to work it out."

The next morning, Estelle was in a calmer mood. Off and on during the night she had contemplated what Justine had said. Roger had called several times before she'd gone to bed. When she kept refusing to talk with him, he'd come over. After she still would not speak to him, Justine and Evan had finally convinced him to go home, telling him to give her some time to cool off.

Now, as she and Roger sat in their living room, she shared her honest emotions with him.

"Roger, we're getting too old for this. We're in our fifties, and we've been married for almost thirty-eight years. I didn't appreciate how you started shooting questions at me yesterday as though I'd done something wrong. And I felt like no matter what I said, you'd take it the wrong way, and we'd get into an argument. And I'm tired of fussing. I guess you couldn't tell that from the way I acted last night, but you got me fired up.

"If you have something you wanna talk to me about, *talk* to me, but don't accuse me of doing anything. Now I realize how I must've made you feel all those times I accused you of being unfaithful. It hurt so bad because I know I haven't been with anybody else. Even when we were having serious problems, I was true to you. I guess that's all I really wanted to say."

Roger felt like the jerk Estelle had last night accused him of being. When he'd found out that guy was somebody she'd met at the company picnic, it had ignited a rage within him so fierce he'd thought he would erupt like a volcano. He supposed that was what he'd done, considering his behavior last night. And then when he'd seen the man—realized how good-looking he probably was in Estelle's eyes—he'd totally lost it.

"I'm sorry about the way I acted. When you told me you had talked to that guy at the picnic, I just went crazy. I got scared 'cause I know how unhappy you've been over the years, even though things had gotten better between us till yesterday. Sometimes I wonder what you see in me. How did I ever appeal to you in the first place? And then, when

I think about the things I put you through, I get more scared that you'll leave me again.

"The first time you took the kids and left me, it drove me crazy, but I didn't know how to express my feelings to you. So I just let you leave without even putting up a fight. When you left last year, I didn't want you to go, but I let you leave without telling you that."

Roger had no plans to make the same mistake a third time. "Please don't divorce me. I love you, and I need you. Please come back home. You mentioned something last night about a surprise honeymoon cruise. Well, I planned a surprise for you, too. But after the way I acted yesterday, you might not even want to go through with it."

Estelle asked, "What is it?"

"I planned a ceremony for us to renew our vows."

Estelle's eyes increased to twice their size. "You did?"

"Yeah. Things've been so good between us lately. We've been through so much. It's like our marriage died and was reborn. I just felt renewing our vows was a way to start fresh. Do you wanna go through with it? Will you marry me *again?* I mean, I know we've been through a lot. Not to mention the way I acted yester—"

Estelle finally got her husband's attention by covering his mouth with her hand. "I said yes. Are you gon' keep talking, or do I get a kiss?"

Roger took her in his arms. When their kiss finally came to a conclusion, Estelle let out a snicker and spoke. "We're pathetic."

Roger gave her a heartbroken look.

"Not the kiss!" she assured him. "That was good. I'm talking about our surprise anniversary gifts to each other. We spoiled our surprises last night when we were running off at the mouth."

Roger let out a hearty chuckle. "Yeah, we did, didn't we? Well, what d'you want to do? Forget renewing our vows and going on the cruise?"

Estelle snorted. "No way. Wild horses can't keep me from walking down that aisle and going on my cruise."

He grinned. "Me, either."

Chapter 40

Evan was coming up the hallway toward the master bedroom. "Justine, are you ready? We gotta be at the church in forty-five minutes." Stepping into the bedroom, he called again, "Justine?"

He spotted his wife in a heap, crumpled on the floor at the foot of the bed. Running to her, Evan got down on his knees, calling out her name several times, yet receiving no response. He raced to the telephone and dialed 911.

Medical personnel arrived in a matter of minutes and rushed Justine to the hospital, with Evan hovering at her side. She regained consciousness as they were en route. Evan called Justine's family and friends as soon as they got to the hospital. Estelle, Roger, Justin, Shayna and Catina were at her side in a flash.

Estelle whispered to Roger before they went into the exam room to see Justine. "Look at her, lying there so weak.

I knew something was wrong, but every time I asked her, she said she was fine. Now just look at her."

Roger rubbed his wife's back. "She'll be fine. She's under her doctor's care now. Come on."

When they entered the room, Justine smiled. "Hey, what're you two doing here? Aren't you supposed to be getting married?"

Estelle said, "We're not going anywhere. We're staying right here with you. How're you feeling?"

"I'm fine, Mama. Stop worrying."

Estelle protested, "If you were fine, you wouldn't be here in this hospital."

Roger said, "Hey, baby girl. You scared us. You hang tight, you hear?"

"I will, Daddy."

When Justine spotted Justin and Shayna, she smiled and said, "Hey, you two. Where's my nephew?"

The couple greeted her with hugs. "Chase is with Gloria and Donald," her brother replied.

Justine smiled. "That's good. Y'all better get going. You'll be late for the ceremony."

Estelle repeated, "I told you we're not going anywhere."

Justine looked around the room at her family. "Do y'all mind if I talk to Mama alone for a moment?"

Everyone left the room except Estelle.

"Mama, I'm gonna be fine. You and Evan were right. I should've listened to you. The doctor thinks it might be anemia. She's running some tests. Daddy worked very hard to put this ceremony together for you and him, but he did it mostly for you. Don't spoil it."

Justine slowly shook her head. "He loves you so much. It's not gonna make up for what you missed out on, but this is something he wants to do for you. Let him do it.

Go marry your husband, have your reception and go on your honeymoon."

"Justine, that's crazy. How can I do all those things and enjoy myself with you in the hospital?"

"Mama, you and Daddy put your own lives on hold for me and Justin. You made sacrifices for us. Yes, we had our share of problems just like everybody else, but you kept us together as a family. Now we're grown. Justin has Shayna and Chase, and I have Evan and our baby on the way.

"It's time for you and Daddy to start living your own lives again. Be happy and enjoy each other the way God meant. If you miss out on all the two of you have planned for each other, I'll feel guilty. Please don't put that burden on me."

Estelle was astounded at her daughter's maturity. Sometimes it seemed as though Justine was the mother and she was the daughter.

Estelle moved from the chair she was sitting on and sat down on the bed beside Justine. Taking hold of her daughter's hand, she murmured, "You've really grown a lot over the last several months. You got knocked down, but you got right back up and kept fighting. I've always admired that about you. You never give up, not even when all hope seems lost. I hope my grandchild has your strength and character."

Having said those words, Estelle leaned down, kissed her daughter's cheek and left the room.

"Baby," Evan said, "who was that on the phone? I told you to let the machine get it if I don't answer it. You know the doctor said you need to rest."

"I know," Justine replied. "That was almost a week ago. I'm feeling much better. Besides, when I saw the doctor today, she said I can start gradually getting back into my normal routine."

"Yeah, but that's no reason to overdo it."

"I know, sweetie. That was Justin on the phone. Guess what?"

"What?"

"He got his job back at the restaurant."

Evan grinned. "Really? How? What happened?"

"The owner discovered one of the other chefs sabotaging some of the dishes. He confessed to tampering with Evan's dessert and putting the peanuts in with the pecans. I can't wait for Mama and Daddy to get back from their cruise tomorrow so I can tell them."

Evan grinned. "Yeah, we've got a lot to tell them when they get back."

"Yeah. Catina and Darryl's engagement. I knew they'd get engaged sooner or later. And if I remember correctly, somebody didn't want me butting in." Justine grinned as she looked sideways at her husband.

Evan snickered. "I just wanted you to let them go at their own pace."

"Yeah. Uh-huh. Whatever you say."

As they lay on the bed, Evan placed his hand tenderly on Justine's stomach. "It's hard to believe we got two in there. I told you it was twins."

"Yeah, yeah. You're just not gon' let it rest, are you? You think you da man, don't cha?"

Evan cast Justine a warm smile. "I *am* da man. I was right about the twins. And *you* da woman. You were right about Darryl and Catina. Together, we make the perfect team."

"Yeah," Justine concurred.

They pecked each other quickly on the lips.

Evan said, "I wonder what Mom and Dad'll say. Did you tell Justin?"

"Yeah. He couldn't believe it. It took me a minute to get him to calm down. It seems like there's a lot of excitement going on around us, doesn't it?"

"Yeah. I have to tell you I've never been as happy as I am now. I love you so much. Thanks for making me feel whole again."

"I love you, too. Thank you for finding a place for me in your heart again and for not letting anything break us apart."

Roger put his arm around his wife's neck as she stood near the ship's railing and gazed out across the Atlantic. Shades of turquoise, aqua and yellow-green tinted the ocean, and up above, puffy white clouds dotted the clear blue sky. The combination took Estelle's breath away.

She faced Roger briefly so they could share a kiss. "Isn't this one of the most breathtaking sights you've ever seen?"

"Yeah," he agreed, inhaling the ocean air.

"Where have we been all our lives? All this beauty has been here for us to see, and we haven't seen it till now."

Roger removed his arm from around Estelle's neck. He took her hand in his and let their arms rest on the railing, their hands hanging over the edge, fingers entwined. "We were trying to live our lives. Raising our children. Somewhere along the way, we lost each other in the shuffle."

Estelle gave a slow nod of her head. "Yeah. I'm so glad we found each other again."

"Me, too."

Estelle allowed her mind to drift back six days ago, to when she and Roger had renewed their vows. She was disappointed that Justine hadn't been there, but the ceremony had been better than she could have ever imagined. At the reception afterward, when Roger held her in his arms and danced with her to Percy Sledge's "When a Man Loves a

Woman," she had felt as though she was floating on a cloud, just like the ones up in the sky now. She was Cinderella, and he was her Prince Charming.

It was clear to her that Roger's main concern was that she be happy and have the time of her life. He knew how much she loved to dance, and had kept her on the dance floor to almost every song thereafter. She'd finally had to tell him, "Baby, we gotta slow down. We're not as young as we used to be."

Her legs and hips were so sore after the reception that they'd had to stop at Wal-Mart on the way to the airport and get a bottle of Aspercreme to rub into her aching muscles. Within the next day or two, she was fine and ready to get out on the ship's dance floor. They'd gone dancing almost every night.

Their first night on the ship, Estelle had thought Roger's eyes were going to pop out of his head when he'd seen her in the nightie she'd bought when she and Justine went shopping. As soon as they got back to the States, she planned to make some more lingerie purchases.

The sun would soon be setting. Roger was having a good time with his wife. He missed their family and friends but wished this moment could last forever.

At the ceremony, Estelle had looked gorgeous. She was his beautiful bride, and he couldn't believe he'd almost let her slip through his fingers. Over the last few months, their love for one another had been rekindled. He had no intention of letting the flame flicker again. The love he felt for Estelle was so intense that he could hardly put it into words.

As they stood at the ship's rail watching the sun set, their hearts beating in tandem, neither had to say a word. They'd been through the best of times and the worst of times. They still had problems to overcome, but now that they were on the same wavelength, they could continue to conquer them together, in the united bonds of matrimony.

Dear Reader,

Since the release of my first novel, in April 2004, you have opened your hearts to me and shown me a great measure of support. Many of you have told others about my books, and I'm extremely grateful to you for helping to spread the word. I love hearing from you. Your letters help brighten my day. I would love to hear your thoughts about the characters in this book and the issues they faced.

Please include a self-addressed, stamped envelope with your letter and mail to: Maxine Billings, P.O. Box 307, Temple, GA 30179. Feel free to e-mail your comments to maxinebillings@yahoo.com. Please visit my Web site at www.maxinebillings.com.

Thanks again for your support and encouragement. I look forward to hearing from you.

From my heart to yours,

Maxine

A READING GROUP GUIDE

THE BREAKING POINT
by Maxine Billings

ABOUT THIS GUIDE

The questions and discussion topics that follow
are intended to enhance your group's reading of
The Breaking Point. We hope the book provided an
enjoyable read for all your members.

Discussion Questions

1. Did Estelle have valid reasons for believing Roger was having an affair? Explain.

2. Evan, Darryl, Ray and Jarrod enjoyed joking around with each other. Ray and Jarrod were always teasing Evan about his relationship with Justine. Evan and Darryl seemed to have more in common with one other. Should they have severed their relationships with Ray and Jarrod? Why or why not?

3. Why did Justin turn to alcohol when he lost his job?

4. Evan was a loyal and supportive husband to Justine. However, she betrayed his trust by taking birth control pills behind his back. Then she even went so far as to go with him to the fertility doctor and actually made an appointment for herself to see her own doctor, which she had no intention of keeping. How does what Justine did to Evan make you feel about her? Considering the wounds she still carried from the negative effects of her father's drinking, do you have any empathy for her?

5. Do you feel that Shayna was justified in her actions when she put Justin out of the house? If not, how do you think she should have handled the situation?

6. Estelle and Roger's marriage had been in trouble for fifteen years, yet they managed to stay together. However, the day finally came when Estelle told Roger that she wanted a divorce. If you had been them, would you have stayed with each other that long? Can you think of some things that they may have done differently, that could have lessened the tension in their marriage?

7. When Estelle and Roger got back together, their union was stronger than it had been in a long while. Justine and Evan had a good marriage except for her deceit, yet they didn't stay together long after their initial reconciliation. Why did the younger couple have such a hard time putting their marriage back together?

8. What do you think rekindled Roger's passion for his wife?

9. Do you think Evan should have gone back to Justine after what she did to him? Explain.

10. In the end, Roger finally confessed the feelings of resentment he had been harboring toward Estelle for fifteen years. How important is open, yet respectful, communication in a marriage?